REPLAY

Mandy Lawrence

This book is dedicated to my husband Shane. God blessed our broken roads and gave us a "replay." Our marriage both strengthens and challenges me, giving me many opportunities to grow into the woman I want to be.

A key character in Replay was inspired by my grandfather Carl Conrad, who passed away four days after the manuscript was submitted for publication. Therefore, this book is also in honor and memory of him. Papaw, I miss and love you so much, and I am looking forward to that glorious day when our family is reunited on Heaven's shore.

For the Mighty One has done great things for me—holy is his name. His mercy extends to those who fear him, from generation to generation. He has performed mighty deeds with his arm; he has scattered those who are proud in their inmost thoughts. He has brought down rulers from their thrones but has lifted up the humble.

Luke 1:49-52

CONTENTS

AUTHOR'S NOTE

Replay is a work of fiction. Names, characters, and incidents are all products of the author's imagination. Any character resemblances to actual football players is purely coincidental. Any mentioned brand or team names, places, and trademarks remain the property of their respective owners, bear no association with the author or the publisher, and are used solely for fictitious purposes.

Despite doing careful research of the NFL in attempt to create believable characters and situations, there may be inadvertent discrepancies between the reality surrounding this organization and the ways in which it is portrayed in this novel. Any such mistake is mine.

CHAPTER ONE

The honeymoon is over. The proverbial line echoed through Abby Holder's head as she approached the security line in Rome's Leonardo da Vinci International Airport. The phrase was literal in her case. The Italian honeymoon she and Derek had anticipated for so long was now officially over.

"Here's your passport." Derek's voice was scratchy, his eyes half-open.

"Okay, thanks." Abby yawned the words, taking the passport from her husband's hand. A double espresso was calling her name this morning. She and Derek were like zombies after waking up at 5:00 a.m.

After flipping through several pages, Abby found the foreign stamp which marked the beginning of their romantic honeymoon. How had two weeks already passed since their big day—the day she had dreamed of and waited for her entire life? The only things remaining now were cherished memories and the photos that captured them.

Remembering the image of herself in the bridal room's full-length mirror brought an instant smile to Abby's face. Her makeup was perfect, and her dark hair was loosely curled in an elegant updo. Vera Wang's satin and lace gown fell from her waist like a cascading waterfall, its ornate beads and jewels reflecting the sunlight, casting prisms of light across the floor. She felt like a genuine Disney princess. Would she ever look that pretty again?

If only she could relive the fairytale moment before her Daddy walked her down the aisle. He was smiling from ear to ear when she locked her arm around his. "You're absolutely breathtaking, sweetie," he had whispered, his face glowing with pride. Abby could still smell the lilacs and roses marking the pews of her childhood church…could still see the smiling faces of family and friends as she walked toward the altar where her handsome prince waited.

"Remove your shoes. Laptops go in separate bins. All liquids need to be visible in quart-sized, resealable bags." A man's stern voice, punctuated by a foreign accent, stole her away from the daydream. The dark-haired man wore a badge which read *Sicurezza aeroportuale*—the Italian equivalent of the TSA, she assumed.

Abby's pulse sped up, noticing an agent patting someone down in the line ahead. Why hadn't she changed the channel when a documentary about missing planes came on TV a few weeks ago? She was terrified of flying, and her fear had escalated to an entirely new level after watching the scary documentary.

The smell of Derek's sweaty tennis shoes in the plastic bin was actually a welcomed distraction, scattering her worries and bringing her back to the present task. Abby held her hands above her head in the x-ray machine, making sure her feet were on top of the indicated markings. A lady motioned her through, so she rushed to the end of the conveyer belt to gather her belongings. Perfect timing. Here came her blue Coach carry-on, emerging beneath the flaps at the end of the baggage scanner.

Abby slid her sandals on, letting out a measured breath of air.

"What do you want for breakfast?" Derek mumbled, nodding his head toward a McDonald's counter in the distance.

A buttery bacon, egg, and cheese biscuit—that's what she wanted. But what she needed? Unfortunately, that was a different story. Every fiber of her being dreaded the strict diet and exercise regimen looming on her horizon, but that's the price she would pay for pigging out on mounds of cheesy pasta and gelato. Even with all the walking they had done on various excursions in Rome, she had probably gained three pounds over the past two weeks. Maybe even five or six.

"Hmmm, I don't know," Abby said, straining to read the menu above the McDonald's counter. "Wow, they've got oatmeal. I think I'll get that and a Diet Coke. And a large cappuccino with an extra shot of espresso."

Derek scrunched his eyebrows and shook his head. Yes, it was an odd breakfast request.

"Order for me, please...I need to go to the bathroom," Abby said, pointing toward the restroom sign. "I'll hold us a table when I get back." She stood on her tiptoes to give Derek a quick kiss on the cheek, and a delightful whiff of his Polo Explorer carried her to another place and time. Less than a week ago, the two of them were stretched out in a hut on a beach in Sicily, her ear to Derek's chest. She was breathing in that same heavenly cologne, admiring a turquoise sea beneath a cloudless sky, not a care in the world.

Abby navigated through the crowd of people in the food court, wondering if every bride felt this down after her wedding and honeymoon were over. Seems like her sister, Sarah, had warned her about the post-wedding blues. But Abby wasn't your typical bride, so the typical rules shouldn't apply, right?

The wife of a gorgeous, soon-to-be-famous pro football player had no reason to feel down. Every woman on earth would love to be in her shoes. Derek was amazing, both on and off the field. Picked in the first round of the draft, everyone expected him to be a starting wide receiver for the Carolina Panthers next season. Abby's heart quickened, picturing him running out on the field of Charlotte's Bank of America Stadium in his tight-fitting, black and blue uniform.

Her smiling reflection in the bathroom mirror surprised her as she made her way to a stall, following the trail of her imagination. Abby could see it now: Derek leaping into the air to make an unbelievable catch, then sprinting down the field for a touchdown, the crowd roaring. The two of them celebrating his first win with a bottle of champagne and chocolate-covered strawberries in an upscale hotel room overlooking San Francisco Bay...The Niners weren't projected to be good this year, so Carolina should win that game—their first one of the season.

But now what? It was crazy how that one little question kept running through her head, draining the life out of her. What was even crazier, though, was she had no answers. Somehow, she had bypassed thinking about anything beyond the wedding and honeymoon since Derek's proposal. Her entire senior year of college, even her graduation day, was a complete blur. Had she thought the world would come to a sudden stop before they returned home from Italy?

The marriage was more important than the wedding, but Abby hadn't acted like she believed that. She didn't think her parents were right to push premarital counseling, because she and Derek had been together since their senior year of high school, but she would admit she hadn't given enough thought to what her new married life would entail. May 12th was just a 24-hour day which had come and gone faster than a shooting star, and now the only detail she knew about her future was that she wouldn't be getting a job.

Abby wanted to work—during football season, at least. She needed to find something to occupy her time. But what were the chances of her finding an enjoyable job which would accommodate her frequent travels for Derek's away games?

"I love your dress!" A lady's voice startled her as she washed her hands in the restroom. Lost in contemplation, Abby had to check herself out in the mirror to recall what dress she was wearing.

The sight of the colorful, dancing patterns on a favorite Lilly Pulitzer sundress instantly lifted her spirits. "Thanks," she said, looking the petite, gray-haired lady in the eyes. A genuine smile curled her lips as a memory surfaced, one involving her best friend and maid of honor, Carlee. The two of them had picked out the dress at SouthPark Mall while home over Christmas break. Gift money in tow, they were eager to buy some cute outfits for all the upcoming wedding festivities.

Abby's smile quickly faded. The past year of her life had been so exciting, so unlike the present moment. She and Carlee—along with Abby's mom and sister—had shared many unforgettable hours of fun as they shopped for just the right wedding dress, invitations, cake, and flowers...all the things needed to bring her dreams to life.

A thought flashed across Abby's mind, triggering a spark of hope: maybe a shopping trip with her best friend could pull her out of this slump. Walking into the bright, beach-themed Lilly Pulitzer store would surely put some pep back in her step. Seeing her sister, Sarah, and her four-year-old twin nieces was something else Abby had to look forward to. She couldn't wait to wrap her arms around Kayla and Lexi and kiss their chubby cheeks. She could finally give them the praises they were due for being the best little flower girls a bride could ask for.

A sea of people scurried through the food court. After coming close to getting trampled by a gothic-looking dude wearing headphones, Abby's positive thoughts were crowded out. If only she could continue reliving treasured memories or fantasizing about a larger-than-life future. But she couldn't. Not with such a nagging, unsettling feeling following her around. It was like a black cloud of confusion, a suffocating blanket of uncertainty.

Could she really be happy simply being a pretty, cheering wife in the stands of a football stadium?

CHAPTER TWO

Abby searched Derek's eyes while he finished his coffee in the airport food court. Desperate for an uplifting conversation, she hoped the caffeine had worked its magic.

"Can you believe we're actually husband and wife?" Abby knew the question was cliché, but it was hard to wrap her mind around the fact that they were married. Ten years ago, if someone had said she would be the wife of Derek Holder, she probably would've fainted.

"I know. Finally," Derek said, winking at her. His baby blues were full of desire. "I'm a lucky man."

Heat flushed across Abby's cheeks. The mesmerizing spell he cast over her was both a blessing and a curse as insecurities rose up against her control, memories of a different era of their lives flooding her soul. She was suddenly the pudgy, unpopular sixth-grader at Jay M. Robinson Middle School, her arm in a sling thanks to a clumsy fall at church camp. And Derek was the best-looking, most popular guy in their class...the genius star-athlete who only paid attention to Caroline Williams and Sierra Starns, the prettiest blondes on the cheerleading squad.

Thank goodness for the tenth-grade growth spurt that had thinned Abby out. If not for it—and her notorious green eyes—her husband probably wouldn't have crossed the friendship line between them.

Derek reached for her hands across the table, bridging a decade of time. A shock of electricity flowed through her as their fingers interlaced. Noticing the platinum band on his left ring finger, Abby's insecurities began to loosen their grip. That ring symbolized he was hers. Forever.

"I love you." The words fell far short of expressing what she felt for her dream man, but they would have to do for now...because she was practically speechless.

"I love you too, Mrs. Holder." Derek puckered his lips, sending her a kiss through the air.

Abby reciprocated, savoring the way his rough, manly fingers brushed over the back of her hand.

If only she could freeze time.

Because time may change things.

Derek would soon be a celebrity, and they would be on unequal playing fields like never before—much more so than when they were in middle school.

Abby swallowed, hoping to force down the lump in her throat. Ready or not, life was moving full steam ahead. She longed for answers to the questions bombarding her, but she wouldn't dare ask them out loud; that would be too humiliating. All she could do was stare into her husband's blue eyes and hope to find the reassurance she craved there, shining from his soul. *You love me now, but will you always? When you're America's new heartthrob? Will I still be enough?*

⚬⚬

Abby's stomach dropped as if she were riding the Intimidator Roller Coaster at Carowinds. The look on Derek's face was unmistakable; he was in pain. Severe pain. And his body language extinguished the small flicker of hope she clung to…that the pain wasn't coming from his bad knee. Derek grabbed it, falling into the seat behind him at the terminal gate where they waited to board the plane.

"No, this can't be happening now!" He hung his head down and massaged his right knee with both hands.

"Can I do anything?" Abby slid into the seat beside him and rubbed his back, hundreds of eyes glaring at them.

"Leave me alone a minute, okay?" Derek's harsh tone took her by surprise and hit her where it hurt, prompting a sigh of exasperation.

How was it possible for this day to have managed to get worse? Her nerves were already shot after their flight was delayed due to "unfavorable weather conditions." And now this?

Out of the corner of her eye, Abby noticed a kind-looking Asian man pick her purse up off the floor and place it on the seat beside of her. She had been so caught up in the moment that she didn't even realize she had dropped it. They had just stood up after the announcer called for first class passengers to board, and the next thing she knew, her husband was gasping out in pain.

"I'm sure it's nothing. It *has* to be nothing." Derek's voice was muffled, his face buried in his hands.

Abby ached for him. What could she do or say to alleviate the pain he was in, both physically and emotionally? Playing in the NFL meant everything to Derek. His knee couldn't give out on him now. She clenched her teeth, praying he hadn't somehow torn his ACL like he had during his junior year at UNC-Chapel Hill. That injury had cost him most of the season.

"We are now boarding Zone 2 for flight 429 to Charlotte. Zone 2, you may now board." A woman's monotone voice played over the intercom, triggering a wave of panic. What if they missed their flight?

She leaned in closer to Derek and massaged his back with an intensity that would will him to be okay. "Feeling any better?"

"Some," he answered, finally looking her in the eyes.

"Good." Abby forced a smile and brushed a stray blonde hair from his forehead. "What do you think's going on? Does it feel like a tear?"

If only she were half as calm as her voice let on, she might stand a chance of surviving this horrible day. Deciding she was too fearful of disappointing answers, she left no time for Derek to respond to her questions. Being the queen of denial was definitely the best approach.

"I'm sure it's nothing major, babe. We'll get you an appointment with Dr. H. tomorrow." Dr. Pete Hallenoirsky was Derek's orthopedic surgeon when he injured his knee. Although he never pronounced the doctor's name correctly, the man was his hero. There couldn't be a more skilled surgeon, nor a kinder one, in the entire nation. And he was a Christian. This fact hadn't impressed Derek any, but it was reassuring to the daughter of a church deacon.

Abby held her breath. Did Derek not expect to be home by tomorrow? Is that why he had yet to comment about seeing Dr. H.? She cleared her throat. "That is, we can go see Dr. H. tomorrow if you can make the flight." Her heart thudded harder against her chest, to the point where her neck was now pulsating.

"We are now boarding Zone 3 for Flight 429 to Charlotte. Zone 3, you may now board."

Abby searched her husband's eyes for a clue as to what their immediate future held. What would Derek want to do if he couldn't make the flight? She supposed they would have to go to the nearest hospital and hope he received adequate medical care.

The wheels in her mind stopped spinning when, much to her surprise, Derek began to stand up. Slowly. Tentatively. He suddenly lost his balance, causing Abby to suck in a breath—and hold it. Derek somehow managed not to fall. He limped and hobbled a few steps, then his gait returned to normal. Abby exhaled. Maybe this wasn't so serious after all.

"It's gonna be fine." Wincing in pain, Derek's words weren't entirely convincing, but the tide was certainly turning. "Sorry I snapped at you earlier," he said, walking toward her, wobbling only a little. His downcast expression pulled at her heartstrings.

"It's okay." Abby minimized the issue with a nonchalant wave of the hand. "I know you were in a lot of pain." He was probably *still* in a lot of pain. If not physically, then emotionally.

Derek had to be worried sick, wondering if his knee would keep him from his dream of playing pro ball. Although he would never admit it, Abby knew the real reason he was so determined to succeed: he had to prove himself to his father. A father who he wasn't even sure still existed, since he hadn't heard from the man since he was a four-year-old boy.

"I'm sure it's nothing. Probably just a little flare-up from all the steps we climbed in Rome," Derek said, unzipping the front compartment of his carry-on bag. He pulled out a small bottle of Advil, rattling it in the air. With all the aches and pains accompanying football life, ibuprofen was never far from reach. "My trusty friend here will probably fix it right up. Now come on, let's go home."

Let's go home. Abby replayed the simple statement in her head. It had just lifted a thousand-pound weight from her shoulders.

Derek grabbed his backpack and draped it over his right shoulder, his flexed bicep well-defined beneath his thin gray t-shirt.

"Yes, let's do this," Abby declared. The smile on her face was genuine. The bear hugs she would soon share with her family were great incentives to make the scary journey across the *big pond*, as her Granddaddy would say.

Mr. and Mrs. Derek Holder were heading home. Home sweet home. And if the clock had to strike midnight on her fairytale wedding and honeymoon, there was no other place she would rather be.

CHAPTER THREE

Derek stared out the airplane window until everything on the ground was blocked by fluffy clouds. Gigantic cotton balls stretched as far as he could see, a layer of Tar Heel blue above them.

Cold air shot full blast from the vents above, giving rise to goosebumps on Derek's arms. The warm aroma of coffee called his name, but caffeine was the last thing he needed right now. In a few minutes, he would be having a few airplane bottles of the finest vodka on hand. That was definitely one of the perks of flying first class.

"Can I get you something to drink?" A flight attendant stood in the aisle, her hazel eyes addressing him.

Before he had a chance to open his mouth, Abby put in her request for a rum and Diet Coke.

Thank goodness.

They typically weren't big drinkers, but with his wife's brutal flight anxiety, today would be an exception. Derek hoped she would settle down after the alcohol kicked in, and then he could get some sleep. "I'll take orange juice with two shots of vodka, please."

Face to face with the attendant, there was something familiar about her. What was it?

His mom's eyes—that was it. The woman had his mother's eyes. Although the color was a little darker, the expression was the same…joyful on the surface with sadness underneath.

Suddenly, his father's angry last words to him and his mom shouted through Derek's head, triggering a flush of heat which started in his chest and worked its way to his face. *"Y'all won't amount to nothin' no way!"* He heard the slamming door and felt the rush of relief and disappointment as if it were just yesterday.

"How's your knee?" Abby's voice rescued him from the past.

"It's okay. Don't worry about me. Just relax." Derek pulled her close, prompting her to rest her head on his shoulder. He couldn't let her see his face. It was probably beet red, thanks to his loser deadbeat dad.

Abby's quivering body redirected his thoughts. Her flight anxiety was still in high gear. He kissed her head and grabbed her hand. Truth be told, he needed Abby's touch to calm his own fears, maybe even more than she needed his. Derek swallowed, trying to push down the wave of nausea rising up as he rehashed the earlier incident with his knee.

It wasn't hurting much now, but something major had happened in the airport. The pain couldn't have been much worse if someone had stabbed him with a knife. It was a lot like when he tore his ACL in the horrible game against Maryland during his junior year. That injury made sense, though, because he had been plowed down by the Mack truck-linebacker Donny Staunton. Today, however, didn't make sense at all. Why would his knee hurt from simply standing up?

Derek leaned his head against the airplane window and closed his eyes, willing himself to believe he was too fit for the 551 steps he'd climbed at St. Peter's Basilica yesterday to have hurt him. Nothing major was wrong with his knee. There couldn't be. Not now, with mandatory minicamp with the Panthers less than two weeks away.

Fire suddenly returned to Derek's cheeks, along with more unsolicited memories of his dad. The man had no idea just how much his *good-for-nothing* son had accomplished... that he had been the salutatorian of his high school class and earned a full college scholarship to play football. It was highly probable his father had seen him play for UNC, but probable wasn't enough to satisfy his hunger for retribution.

David Holder *had* to know about him.

He had to eat every derogatory word that came from his big, fat mouth.

Derek would never lay eyes on the man again, but it wouldn't be long until Ole Dave had no choice but to see him. Exhilaration coursed through his veins when he pictured his father sitting on a couch somewhere—probably in some run-down apartment—watching Monday Night

Football, wide-eyed in disbelief after hearing the name of the MVP: Derek Holder. Yeah, that's right. That good-for-nothing son wasn't so good-for-nothing after all, now was he?

A firm squeeze to his thigh put a stop to the dark thoughts running through his mind. Abby was flipping out for no reason...just a little patch of turbulence. The fear in her emerald eyes was gut-wrenching.

"Don't worry, it's okay." Derek rubbed his hand along her forearm. Her skin was always so soft and smooth, just like velvet. "Everything is completely fine. Remember what we talked about earlier? There are thousands and thousands of flights around the world ev—"

"I know." Abby cut him off, nodding her head so hard it jolted the headrest. Then she pressed her head against it and let out a long, steady breath through pursed lips, bringing to mind a woman in childbirth. "I'll be okay. I said a prayer." She tilted her chin to the right, directing Derek's gaze toward a lady across the aisle who was reading a Bible. "And I'm sure she's said a prayer too."

"Okay, babe." He bit his tongue to refrain from commenting about his wife's religious ideations. He actually welcomed them right now if they would afford him some sleep.

Abby leaned her head on his shoulder. He ran his fingers through her long dark hair, catching an unfamiliar, yet pleasant whiff of citrus. She must have used the hotel's shampoo this morning instead of her usual kind.

Derek now had an unobstructed view of the woman reading her Bible, one which was so worn and tattered it was falling apart. He shook his head. How did people actually believe the things written in that ancient book? Life was way too short to spend it worrying about pleasing some unseen God. Pleasing people was hard enough. His poor Gram would've enjoyed life much more if she hadn't been so obsessed with "living by the Good Book." If only people would ditch religion—and all the fighting which came along with it—and simply follow the golden rule to treat others as they wanted to be treated, the world would be a much better place for everyone.

Abby believed in God, but thankfully, she wasn't a religious fanatic like the rest of her family. Their relationship got a little rocky during their sophomore year of college, back when he renounced the faith Gram had partially instilled in him, but they had learned to disagree peacefully about matters of faith. Unlike some religious people, Abby never let her beliefs interfere with living life to its fullest. As long as she knew how to cut loose and have a good time, he could handle a few remarks about God or prayer every now and then. He had even been a good sport about getting married in Abby's childhood church.

"When are Scott and Diana moving to Atlanta?" Abby's question regarding his uncle and aunt, Derek's adoptive parents, caught him by surprise. It also triggered more emotion than it should have. He took a long swig of his drink.

Abby's pat to his knee reminded him that he hadn't answered her. "Oh, I think Diana said they had to be out of the house by June 25th," he said, hoping his voice didn't reflect the grief he was wrestling. He let his feelings show every now and then, but this certainly wasn't the time or place.

"I wish they'd change their minds and stay," Abby said, making her sad puppy face.

You and me both. Derek loved his Uncle Scott and Aunt Diana, even though he had never bonded with them the way he had with Gram—the only mother he had ever really known. Derek respected the way they had stepped up to the plate to care for him after Gram died unexpectedly the summer before he started sixth grade, but he was hurt and disappointed by how seemingly easy it had been for his uncle to make the decision to take a job in Atlanta. Was Uncle Scott really okay with moving four hours away from him and his cousin Jeffrey—his only child?

"Well, you know Scott…couldn't turn down that money," Derek huffed. His uncle was known for being the best prosecutor in the state of North Carolina, but evidently he wasn't finished climbing the ladder of success.

Abby shifted in her seat. "Yeah, but poor Diana. How's she going to adjust?"

"She'll adjust." He thought about saying nothing more; this conversation needed to be over. "It didn't take her too long to get over moving from Tennessee to Charlotte. She handled it better than Jeffrey and I did." Derek was now thankful they had left his childhood home when he was 11 years old, but it had felt like the end of the world at the time. The move had led him to Abby and UNC-Chapel Hill, but Maryville, Tennessee was his only remaining tie to Gram. He had lived there with her in her cozy cabin since he was four years old…ever since his mom died of a drug overdose, not long after his father abandoned the two of them.

Derek picked up a magazine from the seat pocket in front of him, desperate for something to steal his attention away from wishes that would never come true. No matter how much he wanted another day with Gram—or even just one more moment of being wrapped in her arms—there was no going back.

Abby cleared her throat. "You know how you've always said Scott and Diana don't love you like their own?"

Derek offered a single nod, sighing inwardly. Where was this discussion going?

"Well, I definitely think you're wrong," she said. "Lately, I've been getting the vibe from Diana that she's going to miss you more than Jeffrey."

"Humph." He shrugged his shoulders as if there were a chance Abby was right. Which there wasn't. Whatever it took to bring a close to this drawn-out conversation. Derek exaggerated a yawn. "Like I've always said, I never expected them to love me like their own. I know they love me, and they've provided for me. And I love them. That's all that matters. Besides, we'll still see them some. Scott said they're coming to all my home games, plus the one in Atlanta, of course."

"Well, D.," Abby said, calling him by his nickname. "No matter what, you know I love you like *my* own." She giggled like a little girl and planted a kiss on his cheek.

The rum and Diet Coke had worked its magic quicker than Derek had anticipated. He pulled Abby close and kissed her forehead, relieved by her sudden lightheartedness. Under the influence or not, his bride meant those words from the bottom of her heart. And that was something he would never take for granted. Aside from Gram, Abby was the only person he had ever been able to fully trust, to count on through thick and thin.

"I know you do. I love you, too, baby." Their lips met for a second, then Derek reached down and grabbed his neck pillow from his backpack. "I think I'll take a little nap since you seem to be doing alright."

"K," Abby yawned.

Derek leaned his seat back and stretched his legs, testing out his knee. A sharp pain took his breath, but it didn't last long. And the dull ache which followed wasn't nearly as bad as it had been in the airport. Was that only because of the Advil and alcohol in his system, though?

He drained what was left of his drink. Positioning his head and neck just right, Derek closed his eyes, hoping they would be on North Carolina soil the next time he opened them. And maybe, just maybe, he would wake up to find this knee issue was nothing…nothing but a bad dream.

CHAPTER FOUR

The sound of the jet's roaring engines subsided as the plane slowed to a crawl. Abby released her fierce grip on Derek's hand and exhaled. "We made it!"

"Yeah, I just hope the feeling comes back in my hand before the season starts." Derek feigned pain, wiggling his fingers.

Abby nudged him with her elbow. "Sorry, babe! I just don't remember ever swaying so much on a landing."

She was definitely second-guessing her plans to attend most of Derek's away games. How could she handle all the flying, especially without him? If only they allowed spouses to go along with the team.

"Hello, everyone, and welcome to Charlotte." The pilot's voice over the intercom was deep and soothing amidst the crackling of static. "The current time is 4:04 p.m. The weather is clear and sunny with a current temperature of 79 degrees Fahrenheit." He cleared his voice before continuing his well-rehearsed, post-flight monologue. "We hope you've enjoyed your flight with us today. We appreciate you flying with us here on Lufthansa and hope to see you again soon on a future flight. Please keep your seat belts securely fastened until we've turned off the fasten seat belt sign at the gate. Thanks again, and welcome to Charlotte."

Clear and sunny. Abby let the pilot's words resonate within her, believing they were a forecast for her marriage. It was amazing how a little time for contemplation and self-reflection had improved her outlook. Over the course of the nine-hour flight, she had concluded that Abby *Holder* had no reason not to be happy. After all, she was now someone she had dreamed of being for so, so long.

Sure, she was still disappointed about the wedding and honeymoon being over. But her excitement about the future, with the exception of the strict diet and exercise regimen ahead, far outweighed her disappointment. In less than an hour, she would have a warm homecoming celebration with her parents, who were likely already at the airport waiting for them. And there would be plenty of time to spend with her sister and her adorable nieces. A smile tugged at her lips just thinking about Kayla and Lexi.

"Where do you want to go for dinner?" Abby was 99.9 percent sure she already knew the answer to her question, considering it had been over two weeks since Derek had eaten Chinese food—definitely a record for him.

"I guess P.F. Chang's, if it's completely up to me. But if your folks want to go somewhere else, it's fine. I could eat anything right now. I just couldn't bring myself to eat that *whatchamacallit*," Derek said, referencing their in-flight meal.

He made a face, and Abby laughed out loud. "I didn't think it was too bad," she said. "It's called beef bourguignon, by the way. And P.F. Chang's should be fine." That would actually be great because she could start her diet off right...with some steamed vegetables and rice. "Besides, I knew you would choose there"—she grinned at her predictable husband—"I didn't even need to ask."

⋟⊹ ⊹⋞

Abby took a sip of Stevia-sweetened green tea as Derek told her parents the story about the near-capsizing of their gondola in Venice. Her mom's dark brown eyes were wide, hanging on to every word; whereas she could barely keep hers open.

Jet lag was brutal.

It wasn't even 5:30 p.m., but it was past Abby's bedtime according to her body clock. And the dark, ambient atmosphere of the restaurant didn't help matters any. She yawned, resetting her watch six hours back.

"Well, let's just say if I hadn't finally leapt onto the dock, we would've been in the Adriatic," Derek laughed. "Whew, I couldn't believe how unsteady that thing was. Man, you should've seen the look on Ab's face!"

Her Daddy started laughing with his mouth wide open, never mind the fact that food was still in it. Abby blushed. If they didn't tone it down a notch, everyone in the place would soon be staring at them—not just the people at the next table.

"Oh, John, you're gonna love this one," Derek said, glancing at her before making eye contact with her dad. His eyes were so exaggerated.

Abby knew what was coming and how embarrassing it would be, but she wouldn't keep her husband from telling the story. It felt too good to see him joking around with her parents—something he usually didn't do. Eyeing his second empty glass of wine, she now knew the reason for his sudden lightheartedness. The issue with his knee must be worse than he was letting on...because Derek normally didn't drink around her parents either.

Abby forced the worrisome thought from her mind, determined to capture at least a little joy from this long, stressful day. "Babe, it's not funny!" Playfully slapping his shoulder, her smile contradicted her pouty words.

After hearing how she had walked into the men's bathroom in a restaurant in Lake Garda, Italy, her dad hooted out his infamous laugh, eliciting several stares from yet another table. Her mom's hands-to-her-mouth reaction expressed Abby's sentiments exactly. The look on that old man's face when she walked out of the bathroom stall still sent shivers down her spine.

"The signs over there were a little confusing"—Derek had to pause to catch his breath—"but you'd think she might've noticed the urinals on the way in!"

Heat rushed to Abby's cheeks as she hurried to swallow the bland bite of rice in her mouth. Even though the teasing was all in fun, she needed to vindicate herself. "Hey, my stomach hurt too bad to even think."

A serious expression suddenly replaced Derek's laughter. "Yeah, I'll have to say that lasagna was no joke. I was up half the night."

It was Abby's turn to laugh now. "Yeah, it was the best lasagna ever, and the atmosphere of that place...oh my gosh!" What she wouldn't give to be back in the quaint Italian restaurant built inside a real medieval castle. "We definitely paid the price, though. But it was the only bad experience we had the whole trip, wasn't it, D.?" Abby squeezed her husband's muscular thigh.

"Yeah, it was pretty awesome."

While Derek began rambling on about something else, a favorite memory from the honeymoon stole her away. In less than a second, she journeyed back across the Atlantic and landed in Tuscany. They had spent one day there just shooting the breeze, venturing wherever their whims took them in their white Fiat 124 Spider Lusso. Out of nowhere, Derek pulled the sporty car off the narrow road and halfway into a flat, open field. He rolled down the windows and cut the engine. For a moment, Abby was uncomfortable, scared they would get in trouble for trespassing. But the childlike expression on her husband's face quickly scattered her fears.

"Just look at this!" Derek's wide eyes darted all around, taking in the scenic landscape. "Man, imagine living here! I think I'll build us a house right over there on that hill, right above the vineyard." He pointed at a spot on the horizon. "And we'll live there during the offseason. Wouldn't that be awesome?"

The question didn't need an answer. Derek's smile was almost as big as when he saw her walking down the aisle toward him on their wedding day. Taking in the view of rolling hills, lush vineyards, cobblestone cottages, and cypress trees as far as the eye could see, Abby's heart leapt to her throat. "I'm all-in." She had meant it. Wherever he wanted to be, she wanted to be. "I guess you'll be making enough money to buy us a house almost anywhere you want. Isn't that crazy?"

When she turned to look at Derek, his eyes were no longer scanning their surroundings; they were fixed on her instead...more specifically, on her lips. Abby sucked in a breath of grape-saturated air and froze, completely mesmerized by his baby blues. She felt like a starlet in a movie scene when the sweet, delicate breeze began lifting strands of hair around her face. Derek caught hold of a dancing layer and tucked it behind her ear, all the while looking deep into her eyes, straight through to her soul. His eyes flickered with passion as he inched his chiseled face closer and closer. Until their lips meshed in warm, perfect union. Butterflies came to life in the pit of her stomach, their wings flapping faster at the feel of Derek's hand to the nape of her neck.

"Huh?" Her mom's voice abruptly ended her visit back to that quintessential moment in time.

Abby blinked her heavy eyelids. "I'm sorry, I didn't hear you. What'd you say?"

"I was just wondering if you've talked with Sarah? I know she's gonna be glad to have you back home."

Her mom's reference to Sarah, Abby's only sibling, helped her heart catch up to the present. "Yeah, I texted her when we landed. I'm going over there tomorrow. I can't wait to see the girls and give them the dolls we bought them in Venice."

"Oh, I'm sure they'll have a fit over those," her Mama said, grinning from ear to ear.

A young, violet-haired waitress approached their table. "More tea?"

"No, thanks." Abby placed her hand over her glass. A yawn sneaked up on her, and she was unable to keep from punctuating the end of it.

"Janny, are you about ready to head out?" Her Daddy glared at her mom with his *it's time to go-*look. Abby loved the way her dad referred to her mom by the name their granddaughters called her. Janny—derived from her real name, Janet—definitely suited her better than Granny. She was way too young-looking to be a Granny, or even a Nana.

"Yep, I'm ready. I'm sure y'all are bound to be tired," her Mama said in her thick Southern drawl.

Abby simply nodded, too lethargic to expend the energy to say something. It would be absolutely heavenly to lay her head on her pillow tonight. In her own bed.

"Alrighty then, we'll let these two lovebirds get to bed." Her mom reached for her purse—the Texas-sized pink one. Then she stared at her, a mischievous grin lighting up her face. "After all, Janny needs a little grandson."

With a smile tugging at her lips, Abby rolled her eyes. Now that she was married, a new grandchild was legitimately on Janet Gibbs's radar. She studied Derek, gauging his reaction. To her surprise, his face was glowing, and his wiggling eyebrows made her heart skip a beat. It would probably be a while before they started trying for a baby, but

Abby saw no need to burst her bubble of excitement...or her Mama's. After all, she was now a married woman. The wife of Derek Holder, the man of her dreams.

Which meant that sooner than ever before, she would be the mother of his children.

CHAPTER FIVE

Abby sat on the back deck, sipping her coffee while Derek took his morning run. With upheaval rising within, the ominous sky seemed only fitting. Derek better hurry home before a storm hit.

Abby sighed. Metaphorically, the storm had already hit.

Less than a year ago, she was so full of hope and dreams. How could things have nosedived so fast? The "c" word—that's how. Ever since the day it reared its ugly head, life had spiraled out of control.

One minute, she and Derek were practically living in a fantasy world; the next, everything was doom and gloom. Right before receiving the bad news, they—along with several of Derek's teammates and their ladies—had taken a trip to Barbados to celebrate a successful first season. The Panthers' 13-3 record was definitely something to be proud of. Once Derek's knee issue was resolved with a cortisone injection, he had become an overnight superstar, helping his team reach the semifinal game of the playoffs.

After celebrating and returning home from a tropical paradise, the devastating news was magnified.

Abby's stomach knotted, remembering the moment she first heard her mom's message...the dreadful message which had started it all. When her Mama practically insisted they come over for a family dinner, she knew something was wrong. She could still hear her mom's burdened voice as it played on the answering machine, echoing across the vaulted ceilings of their new home.

Abby blinked, allowing a few tears to escape.

How had a routine colonoscopy turned into her dad's death sentence? Why would God do that to him? To their family?

The flitting of several red birds fighting for a place at the bird feeder pulled her from the horrible memory of that evening. Abby gazed up at the dark clouds, entertaining even darker thoughts...thoughts which had crossed her mind a lot lately.

Maybe Derek was right; maybe God didn't exist.

Perhaps Darwin knew what he was talking about, after all. Perhaps the entire human race was merely the result of millions of years of evolution.

A robin suddenly startled her, darting from a nearby tree to the bird feeder to join in on all the commotion. Abby studied it for a while. "Maybe we're no more than a bunch of birds, fighting to survive in this cruel, chaotic world," she murmured under her breath.

It surely made no sense why a loving God would torture her Daddy, a man who had gone to church and helped people his whole life. All 57 short years of it.

The weight of her anger pressed the wrought iron rocker harder against the deck. Her dad shouldn't have cancer; there was absolutely no history of it in his family. Papaw and Nana Gibbs were in their late seventies and had no health issues whatsoever, aside from cataracts and arthritis.

If there were no apparent genetic links to the cancer, then the biology major in Abby said lifestyle would have to be the culprit. But that didn't make sense either. Her dad ate his fill of her Mama's Southern cooking, but he wasn't overweight...well, certainly by no more than 10 pounds. He had always been active, getting plenty of exercise from gardening and riding his bicycle. He didn't smoke, didn't drink alcohol. Nothing added up.

The way her dad took such good care of himself was probably the reason he was doing as well as he was, better than the doctors had anticipated with the chemo and radiation. Yes, her Daddy was proving the doctors wrong. And it would only continue. He was going to beat the cancer and make liars out of all of them.

Abby swallowed a sip of lukewarm coffee. Tears were prompted by a surfacing memory, but she gave it permission to play out. She traveled to the seventh grade, back to when her Daddy took her to the railroad tracks by their house in hopes of seeing a live president.

There was a rumor around town that the president would accompany the governor of North Carolina on a whistle-stop campaign tour of the state. So, her Daddy surprised her one Wednesday morning, keeping her out of school. "Instead of studying history, you're probably going to see it firsthand," he told her. And he was right.

Sarah was on a field trip, so it was just the two of them: Abby and her Daddy. Camped out by the train tracks, eating *KFC*. She couldn't resist a smile, remembering how wide her dad's eyes grew at the sight of a helicopter flying overhead. "It won't be long now, sweetie," he exclaimed. "They're scoping out the crowd to make sure it's safe."

Sure enough. Within minutes, they saw the President of the United States. He and the governor were standing at the rear of the caboose, smiling and waving at the small crowd of people gathered...the red, white, and blue flag dancing in the wind above them.

"We did it, Ab," her dad shouted as the train vanished in the trees, a forest of poplars and oaks standing proud in their array of October-colored splendor. "Not too many people can say they've seen a live president, but we just did!" He hopped up and down, holding his hand up for a high five.

Abby knew if it weren't for the other people there, her dad's excitement would've been even more exaggerated. Because there was a 10-year-old boy inside of him who had to come out and play from time to time. She was so privileged to know that boy, along with the kind and admirable man, husband, and father who equaled the whole of John Gibbs—her Daddy.

A tear tickled the side of her nose, stealing her from the past. It was back to reality, the reality that her Daddy was deathly ill. The reality that the little girl from the memories she cherished had grown up to be a defiant young woman…one who refused to speak to her dad because he stood by his moral convictions, refusing to pay her rent when she and Derek shacked up during their sophomore year of college.

Foolish pride was to blame for losing a year with her Daddy, a year of precious time she could never get back. The regret was strong enough to break down the floodgates which had been holding back a sea of tears. They now gushed out at full force. How was she supposed to stay afloat?

"Why, God, why?" Abby's body shook under violent waves of grief. Toxic emotions, like an angry riptide, threatened to pull her completely under as she realized she could simply be shouting to the wind…if God didn't exist. And if God didn't exist, then neither did Heaven. Which meant she may soon lose her Daddy and never, ever see him again.

Abby's lungs refused to cooperate. She was desperate for air, but she couldn't inhale with another wave of tears crashing upon her. Where were they all coming from? It's like they were springing up from hidden wells buried deep inside, like there were layers and layers of sadness in places she didn't even know existed within herself.

Hearing something, Abby stifled her sobs. What was it? Her phone? Yep, and she would have to rush inside to get to it in time.

A surge of wishful expectation propelled her to her feet and into the kitchen. *Please be Sarah.* If anyone could pull her out of this pit of doom, it was her big sister. Abby snatched up her Michael Kors handbag from the countertop and grappled with her phone—at the very bottom of her purse, of course.

"Sarah." The name lit up the screen of her iPhone, along with something inside of herself. Something resembling hope.

CHAPTER SIX

Perfect timing. Derek closed the back door, returning from his morning run just as Abby wrapped up the phone conversation with her sister. She placed her phone on the bathroom counter, giving herself a quick once-over in the mirror.

Her eyes were a little red, but at least they were dry. Big sis had come through once again, managing to coax out a remnant of optimism buried somewhere beneath the sadness. Thankfully, Sarah had insisted they spend some quality sister time together this afternoon.

Abby combed her chestnut hair into a ponytail before heading toward the kitchen. She opened the refrigerator, putting off eye contact with Derek as he rounded the corner.

"Man, it's muggy out there," he said, wiping beads of sweat from his brow. He breathed heavily, leaning forward with his hands on his knees.

"Is it raining yet?" She grabbed two glasses from the cabinet and began filling them with orange juice. Maybe if she postponed looking him in the eyes a little longer, he wouldn't notice she had been crying.

Derek practically stared a hole through the side of her face. "No, but it's gonna start any minute now. You've been crying again." It was a matter-of-fact statement. Without so much as a hint of questioning in his voice, there would be no pulling off a lie.

"I'm okay now," Abby said, forcing a slight smile as she set their glasses on the breakfast table.

Derek had to be reaching his limit with her fragile emotions; that was probably why he had been acting a bit distant lately. She needed to change the subject. Fast. "Sarah and I are going to do something this afternoon if it's okay with you." Abby didn't normally plan anything in the offseason without making sure he didn't have anything special he wanted them to do, but her sanity depended on some time with her sister today.

"That's fine. I was planning to go over to Colton's." Derek broke eye contact and chugged down half a bottle of water, his flexed bicep momentarily distracting her from the sting of his words.

Hadn't he spent enough time with Colton lately?

What about her?

"Okay." Abby fought her disappointment and jealousy. How could she blame Derek for wanting to hang out at the quarterback's new mansion? An indoor-outdoor pool, five-star gym, and private movie theater were certainly more appealing than her and her somber self lately.

"A few of us are going to start working out together again since minicamp is coming up." Derek yawned his infamous *nervous yawn*. He had obviously picked up on her discouragement and felt the need to explain why he planned to spend the day without her. "Plus, Colt is still down and out over Amanda, so I feel like I need to be there for him, you know?"

No, Abby didn't know. And she couldn't handle another conversation about Colton's marital woes. That's why she had to bite her tongue before giving her husband a nod of *approval*.

Resentment swelling in her chest, she headed toward the stove with two eggs, tempted to smash their gooey yolks in her bare hands. The story Derek told about the termination of Colton's marriage just didn't mesh, not to mention it contradicted the rumors she had heard. Besides, Amanda would've never left her millionaire Romeo without just cause. Abby tried to shove her insecurities aside, but they weighed too heavy on her soul. Who knew what temptations lurked out there for their men to fight—or not to fight—when they were away from home?

"You want an omelet, right?" Despite the inner turmoil, her voice was light and cheery.

"I guess. Thanks, babe. No, wait…When are you meeting Sarah? Cause I can just grab a bowl of cereal. I'm not all that hungry anyway."

Derek's gratitude and consideration of her plans smoothed the rough edges of her heart. He would tell her if he knew Colton had run around on Amanda, and he wouldn't be best buddies with the guy still.

"No worries. I'm not meeting her until one o'clock. Sit down. I'm going to make you the best omelet ever. I got some fresh gouda from the market yesterday."

"Yum." Derek's fake smile made her head spin. What could she say or do to elicit a genuine one?

An idea surfaced. "And after you finish eating, I'm going to give you a nice, long hot stone massage." Abby used to do this for him regularly, especially during football season. Back before he had professionals doing it for him.

"That'd be nice."

The lack of enthusiasm in Derek's voice prompted another wave of disappointment. Abby managed a giggle, though, determined to keep things positive and light-hearted. She was probably making too much of his unusual behavior lately. Derek was always a little uptight as the off-season dwindled down. And who could blame him? The demands on a pro football player were no joke. Much more work was involved than most people ever fathomed.

After eating breakfast—or in her case, fidgeting with food—in near silence, Abby placed their plates in the dishwasher. Derek got up and opened the refrigerator, pulling out a bottle of Aquafina. She closed the dishwasher and hit *start* just as he shut the refrigerator door, sending a cool draft of Cascade-smelling air past her cheeks. The refreshing breath prompted a burst of playful energy, so she crouched down behind Derek and swatted his firm tush with a dishtowel.

"Hey now!" He jerked in surprise, flashing a sideways glance. He laughed, but it seemed forced. Then he began guzzling down the bottle of water as if he hadn't had a sip to drink in days.

"I'm going upstairs to set things up for your massage." Abby rubbed Derek's flexed bicep, giving him a sultry look. "See you in a few."

"Sounds good," he said, taking only a momentary break from chugging his water. He crunched the plastic bottle, squeezing out every last drop.

Abby made her way up the stairs to their bedroom, wondering how weeds of distance had sprouted in their marriage. Fresh tears blurred her vision. Considering her humdrum behavior over the last six weeks, today's spontaneity and teasing banter were probably too little, too late. Had she allowed her dad's diagnosis to completely change who she was? To the point that her husband was falling out of love with her?

Another breakdown beat at the door, but Abby fought against it, determined not to be overtaken again. One way or another, she had to pull out of this slump and step things up a notch in her marriage.

She would start by lighting her favorite candle. With *Honeymoon Moonlight* aglow, scenting their bedroom with its notes of cashmere vanilla, peach, and jasmine, Abby walked into the closet to find the massage set. She had given it to Derek for Christmas during their sophomore year of college. Scanning the abundance of custom shelves in the huge walk-in closet, she followed the trail of her thoughts, reminiscing about days gone by. In college, she had had to pick up extra shifts as a waitress at Top of the Hill on Franklin Street just to make ends meet, Derek being too busy with football to hold down a job. Back then, they had dreamed and kidded about their future life of luxury. *One of these days...After he made it big...*

It was surreal to see how their dreams had materialized. Derek now had a professional massage as often as he wanted. Heck, he could afford to hire a masseuse to come to their house every single day.

Abby finally found the dust-covered box on the top shelf. Removing the sizable black crock and placing the accompanying stones inside, she considered how lucky she was that her husband hadn't allowed his newfound fame and fortune to go to his head. Sure, he basked in it to some degree and took advantage of being able to buy expensive things, but deep down he was still his humble self. Maybe even more humble than before. Her father's cancer diagnosis was the probable reason for that. Although Derek and her dad had never been extremely close—likely because of their vastly different beliefs—they had grown on each other over the years.

The creaking of stairs prompted Abby to hurry. Opening and getting through the bathroom door was a big challenge with the heavy load in tow, plus an electric cord to dodge tripping over. She quickly closed the door as Derek walked into the bedroom, hoping he hadn't seen the risqué outfit she was also carrying. She would surprise him by changing into it while the stones heated up.

"I'll be out in a minute," Abby said as she turned the water on to fill up the large crock. The peppiness in her voice sounded foreign. She spritzed some Daisy on her wrists and neck, admiring its sweet, uplifting fragrance. Derek would like it. After all, he was the one who picked out the perfume for a Christmas gift last year.

"Ab?"

"I'll be right out," she said, cracking the door.

"Okay."

Facing the opposite direction, Derek was in the process of removing his shirt, his shoulder and back muscles bulging. He was so good-looking. He still took her breath away... literally. More than that, he was a loving and supportive husband. A man whose shoulder she could cry on, and *had* cried on. Way too much here lately.

She certainly owed it to him to forget all about her worries—for now, at least—and to do her best to recapture all they had once been. And all they ever dreamed to be.

CHAPTER SEVEN

The ferocious bark of Sarah's dachshund, Oscar, announced her little sister's arrival. She smeared on her coral lipstick and gave herself a final glance in the mirror before rushing to the door.

"Girls, Aunt Abby's here," she yelled upstairs to her four-year-old twin daughters. Passing by the picture window in the living room, she saw Abby climbing out of her white Lexus. In the torrential downpour of rain, she would be making a mad dash for the door.

Sarah opened the front door for her sister as she ran up the steps. "Whew! It's raining cats and dogs! Be careful, don't slip."

"Ugh," Abby groaned, wiping her feet on the rug.

"I guess this makes for a good shopping day."

"Yep." Abby flashed a bogus smile.

Trying to recall the last time she had seen a genuine smile on her little sister's face, Sarah's stomach knotted up. She helped Abby out of her raincoat, noticing her bony arms and knees, which were highly exposed in the short purple dress she was wearing. The knot in her stomach tightened. How much more weight could Abby lose without blowing away?

"Oscar, no! Good gracious, get down!" Sarah scolded her stubborn four-legged child who never controlled himself when guests came over. Especially if the guest was Aunt Abby, who always spoiled him rotten. She pushed Oscar away. "You just had a nail trim, and Sissy doesn't need you scratching up her pretty little legs."

After Abby finished paying tribute to the beloved wiener dog, they embraced in a lingering hug. She felt Abby pinching the fabric of her blouse before pulling away, crinkling her eyebrows. "This is nice. Is it new?"

"This old thing?" Sarah chuckled, looking down at the blue and green paisley blouse which had hung in her closet for years. "No, I've had it forever…since before the girls were born. It's a wonder it still fits."

She pointed at Abby's dress, trying to pull off a believable smile despite her concern. "That's pretty, too, Miss Skinny Minnie."

Although her baby sister had always been obsessed with her weight, her recent weight loss was likely unintentional—the result of stress and fragile emotions. "You need to eat something. I'm going to fix us and the girls a snack before we leave. You want coffee or tea?"

"I'll take some of that peach tea you make if you have any," Abby said, her eyes suddenly lighting up.

Sarah turned to see her girls bouncing down the stairs.

"There they are!" Abby bent down, holding her arms out. The girls squealed, bombarding her, clutching their chubby arms around her legs.

Sarah tussled their hair, enjoying the loving exchange between her precious daughters and their favorite aunt. Now that Abby and Derek had finished college and moved back home, Abby and the girls were extremely close. Going out with Aunt Abby for ice cream or to the park was at the top of their list of fun things to do. It had been such a blessing, giving her some much-needed time to herself.

"Okay, girls, Mommy's going to fix us all a snack before we leave. What do you want?"

"I want goldfish." Kayla was quick to respond and began dancing around the room, expending a bit of her endless supply of energy. It was so good to see her acting like herself again since having strep throat last week.

"Me too," Lexi yelled. "And some apple *splices*."

She and Abby locked eyes, grinning about one of Lexi's frequent mispronunciations. After correcting her, Sarah walked into the kitchen to prepare their snacks while the girls insisted that Aunt Abby follow them to their room for a "surprise."

━◄╂ ╂►━

Abby's laughter floated downstairs into the kitchen, instantly lifting Sarah's burdened heart. She relished the melodic sound which had all but disappeared in recent months.

Apparently, her little sister was laughing so hard she could barely get her words out. "Poor baby...your little legs...are...are just too short, aren't they?"

Slicing an apple for the girls, Sarah couldn't help but giggle to herself, realizing what was taking place in her daughters' room. Kayla and Lexi must be showing Abby the new yellow raincoat they got for Oscar at Walmart yesterday.

She shook her head, imagining the poor little dog frozen in place, as motionless as a statue. She knew he would despise it, just like he had the hot dog costume they made him wear for Halloween last year. But Sarah had caved in to the girls' begging. Not without using it to her advantage, though, as it served as their reward for behaving and refraining from asking for anything else during the grocery run.

Her little sister's contagious laughter made the doggie raincoat worth every penny she shouldn't have spent.

It had been so heart-wrenching to see Abby slide further and further into a pit of depression lately. Sarah knew their dad's illness had been extremely difficult for her, just as it had been on the rest of the family. But she suspected something else was going on. Her intuition said Abby and Derek were having problems. They had definitely acted a little distant last week at Nana's birthday dinner. Sarah's mission for the day was to get to the bottom of whatever was going on. That's why she had asked her mother-in-law to watch the girls...to make sure she and Abby got some uninterrupted sister time.

Sarah's phone dinged, startling her from her thoughts. She wiped her hands with a dishtowel and grabbed her scuffed-up, needed-to-be-upgraded iPhone from the table. Her husband Zack had texted: "No New Year's Day to celebrate, no whatever the rest of the song says…I just TEXTED to say I love you from the bottom of my heart:)"

She smirked, appreciating her husband's goofy expression of love. She was so blessed to have him. Zack was a wonderful husband and a loving father to their girls. Most importantly, he was a godly man. Sarah responded to his message before returning to her task: "Thx! Luv u 2."

Joy began to dissipate like the setting sun when her thoughts returned to Abby and Derek. How she longed for her sister to experience the satisfaction of having a Christian marriage like she and Zack shared. But that was impossible. Sarah had to fight back her growing resentment toward her brother-in-law, the man who had distanced her Sissy from God. Her devotional reading this morning reminded her that poisonous emotions couldn't reside in her heart without weeding out the good, godly fruit she wanted to bear.

Regaining control over her thoughts and feelings didn't stop the tears from coming. Sarah blotted them with the back of her hand before they could leave telltale tracks in her makeup.

How had a young girl who practically lived within the church walls ended up where Abby was? Her sister's life would be so much richer—in the only sense of rich that mattered—if she had a solid relationship with Jesus. Sarah dabbed at another tear before sprinkling goldfish crackers on a paper plate of cheerful Disney princesses. If only real life could be like those fairytales.

She took in a shaky breath, her heart jumping wildly in her chest. No matter how much she dreaded it, she had to have a serious talk with Abby about her questionable faith. Sarah had avoided it long enough…ever since the family drama unfolded over her dad not paying Abby's room and board after she moved in with Derek during college. Anytime a conversation called for a deeper-than-surface-level discussion about God or faith, she had walked on eggshells, scared Abby may lash out or withdraw if she said something offensive. But now, considering how depressed Abby seemed, she had no choice but to have a weighty discussion with her. Because only Jesus could truly help her.

As far as Sarah knew, her Sissy believed in God, but that fact didn't ease her worries; the Bible said even demons *believe* in God, yet they're definitely not Heaven-bound. There was just no evidence of a personal relationship with Jesus in Abby's life. With the exception of the Christmas candlelight service, she didn't even attend church—not that church attendance could save someone.

Sarah had to take a moment to massage her temples. All of a sudden, her head ached. And the sound of the ice maker was only going to make it worse. "Lord, please help me," she murmured as she filled their cups with ice. She continued with a silent prayer while setting the table.

Sarah praised God for her many blessings, first and foremost, for the love and security she found in Him. She would be nothing without her Rock, the only sure Anchor in life's unpredictable seas. She thanked God for her family, for her Christian husband who worked hard to enable her to stay home with their girls. Then she asked Him to use her to reflect His light, love, and hope onto her baby sister today. She prayed for Abby to realize her need for a closer walk with Him.

"Okay, Moore's Cafe is now open," Sarah shouted, her soul surprisingly light and free. No doubt, because of her prayer. It never ceased to amaze her how quickly her anxiety could vanish and be replaced by an unexplainable peace after turning her burdens over to her Heavenly Father. Even her headache had disappeared.

When the girls bounced into the kitchen—Lexi tugging on Aunt Abby's right arm and Kayla holding her left hand—a *knowing* suddenly surfaced from somewhere deep inside. Without a shadow of a doubt, God had everything under control.

Sarah breathed easy, catching a whiff of something sweeter than the freshly sliced apples on the plate she carried to the table: the fragrance of an upcoming victory.

CHAPTER EIGHT

"Dang cat!" Derek swerved to miss the neighbor's tabby cat as he headed to Colton's house. The obese thing must really have nine lives; that made the third time he had almost hit it this week. The distraction was actually nice, though. It temporarily stopped the memories running through his mind, memories which still tormented him as much today as they had several months ago.

He was a despicable person, just like his dad.

Abby was his best friend, beautiful inside and out. She had been more than enough for him. Even in her sadness, she catered to his every want and need. He didn't deserve her, and a punch to his gut reminded him of this every time he relived that cursed night in Seattle.

The team had checked in to the Fairmont Olympic Hotel on a Sunday afternoon. With plenty of time to kill before their Monday night game against the Seahawks, most of the guys decided to hit the indoor pool. Derek tightened his grip on the red steering wheel of his black Maserati Ghibli, the nagging "if onlys" shouting through his head.

If only he had stayed in his room like he had first considered. If only she hadn't been passing by his door at the exact moment he walked out. If only she wasn't the most beautiful blonde he'd ever laid his eyes on.

Why couldn't she have been like all the other women who practically threw themselves at him? Someone he would've chalked up as shallow and uninteresting? Heat rushed to Derek's cheeks, just as it had when she introduced herself to him that afternoon.

Cassidy. The name sounded pretty and unique at the time, but now it was repulsive. It couldn't even cross his mind without generating nausea. He couldn't blame her for anything, though. All the blame was his. Cassidy was a respectable woman, friendly and professional, dressed in a modest black skirt and a white blouse—attire befitting a hotel manager. *"It's our pleasure to have you and your team with us. If you need anything, please let me know."* Her innocent greeting still haunted him.

The starstruck look in her eyes was flattering, but it was the genuine, businesslike way she carried herself that had him so intrigued. Her sky blue eyes and full, glossy lips had certainly factored into the equation.

Their first, 20-second encounter should have been all there was to it. With the unexplainable attraction drawing him to her, along with the twinge of guilt which plagued him when she walked away, "Danger Zone" should've been playing through his head at full volume. To his own defense, he never thought he was capable of taking things so far.

"Idiot!" Derek laid on the horn as a silver Toyota cut him off in traffic. He contemplated getting in front of the debonaire-looking dude and then slamming on his brakes. But his road rage was short-lived. He had no right to call anyone else an idiot. *He* was the real idiot.

He had badmouthed one of his teammates at the pool that day for doing the very thing he ended up doing that night. Thinking of Spencer's sweet wife and two adorable kids, he had been tempted to give the guy a black eye for bragging about his plans to get some "pregame action" with one of the groupies at the club. To think he had stooped anywhere remotely close to Spencer's level—or David Holder's—tortured him.

Derek shook his head, remembering how a few of the guys had teased him for being "whipped" because he had gracefully excused himself from their naughty conversations around the hot tub that day. If they only knew.

His heart skipped a beat. What if they did know? What if someone had found out? Thankfully, it wasn't likely. He and Cassidy had promised to never tell...to carry their dirty secret to their graves and never contact one another again. If she were going to tell, chances are she already would have, right? And no doubt, it would've been spread all over the tabloids by now.

Suddenly, Derek couldn't see straight. He felt like he had just stepped off of the Tilt-A-Whirl. He considered pulling off the road, but noticing no one behind him, he slowed down instead—both his driving and his breathing. *Slow and deep.*

He reestablished focus, but his eyes began to sting. If Abby found out what he had done, he would lose her...the only woman he had ever loved, the only woman he ever *could* love.

Derek could barely breathe. *Slow and deep, in and out.*

How had he gotten in this shape? Why couldn't he just forget the whole thing had ever happened? Other guys had no problem doing that. As long as Abby didn't find out, it didn't really matter, right? He loved her now more than ever and would never betray her again. It was all just one big, stupid mistake.

Derek may as well have thrown logic out the window; he wasn't buying it. His feelings were way beyond reason— simply irrational. Or were they? What goes around comes around. Wasn't that how karma worked?

His throat began to swell shut.

There was still no one behind him on the off-the-beaten-path road he was on, so he slowed down to a turtle's pace and leaned down to pick up an old bottle of Gatorade from the passenger floorboard. *Blue Cherry*—his favorite. It was warm, but he took a big gulp, appreciating how the flavorful liquid expanded his throat.

Pondering some of the major choices he had made in life, Derek concluded he had definitely reaped what he had sown. Trading his macho image and casual flings for a relationship with Abby was the smartest decision he had ever made. Unlike every other girl he had been with, she was the real deal. Her feelings for him went beyond infatuation. He had known she would always love him, always be there for him through thick and thin. The security he found in her arms was unlike anything he had known since before Gram died.

But his good days were probably behind him now. Consequences were sure to follow bad choices, that's what Gram always said.

Derek finished off the Gatorade with one swig, then crumpled the plastic bottle into a pancake. If he had learned one thing from his childhood, it was this: if something bad could happen, it would. One way or another, Abby was bound to find out what he had done, and he would have to endure the loss of yet another loved one. Only this time, it would be no one's fault but his own.

⊶⊷

"Five minutes away." Derek spoke into his phone, then glanced at the screen to check out the dictation before sending the message. Colton had texted him, inquiring about his whereabouts since it was nearly 45 minutes after the time he said he would be there.

Colt had been rather clingy lately.

Ever since his wife left him, the two of them had spent a lot of time together. If only they had been this tight back then—on that night in Seattle.

Needing some fresh air, Derek rolled the window down and leaned his head out. "Crap!" He grabbed his Tar Heels cap right in the nick of time and shoved it under his leg. The wind felt good sweeping across his face, making his inch-too-long sandy blonde hair go wild. He ran his fingers through it, trying to recall when his last haircut was. Abby's Aunt Rachel usually cut it.

Thinking of Rachel and the rest of Abby's family led to punches of guilt and shame. They would probably hate him forever if they found out what he'd done.

It was so twisted, and seemingly unfair, how his good intentions had been his downfall. If he hadn't left the club earlier than everyone else that night, nothing would've happened. The team had a midnight curfew, so he would've gotten a sufficient amount of sleep if he had waited to return to the hotel with all the others.

Derek's knuckles turned white as he took out his frustration on the steering wheel. He was a dang fool. He should've sprinted toward his room as fast as he did on the football field after seeing Cassidy behind the counter in the lobby, her long blonde hair—which had been pulled up in a bun earlier in the day—falling loosely around her shoulders. But no, he had opted to be a cheesy idiot instead.

Him and Jack Daniels.

Even now, heat rushed to his cheeks when he thought of how he had approached Cassidy that night. How ridiculous. The girl should've written him off as lame, teasing her with mock complaints about a broken coffee maker and low water pressure in the shower.

"Psht," Derek sputtered. What a Casanova.

He never should've underestimated the lure of fame.

He had so many chances to stop what had happened, and he had all intentions of doing just that. After coming to his senses, he planned to turn Cassidy away at his door if she showed up "to talk" when her shift ended, which was amply past curfew and bed checks. He was going to explain his situation—his love for his wife—and apologize for his flirtatious behavior. But he didn't.

Stupid. "Stupid, stupid, stupid!" Derek resisted the urge to slap himself across the face, punching the steering wheel instead. The horn sounded, bringing him back to the present. Craigmore Drive was only 20 yards ahead, so he had less than two minutes to get ahold of himself. And he *would* get ahold of himself. All this rehashing was pointless.

He had relived that night a thousand times and asked himself the same questions over and over again, and what good had it done?

No amount of regret or wishing could undo anything he had done. He just needed to suck it up and learn to live with it. Besides, everyone made mistakes. If Spencer's wife hadn't found out about his hundreds of affairs, it was possible Abby wouldn't find out about his one and only blunder. Just because he had no luck in dodging calamity in the past didn't mean his future was cursed. After all, he was living his dream, playing in the NFL.

After entering Colton's security code, a gothic wrought iron gate crept open. Driving through, he felt like a Hollywood movie star. How had his ordinary self ended up here, living this kind of life?

A man mowing the lawn tipped his hat, and Derek kindly returned the gesture. Poor guy. Being in charge of landscaping Colton's *estate* was no minor feat. It looked like he had planted a few more rows of trees and another flower garden since a mere two days ago.

Derek proceeded up the brick drive toward the house, which looked more like a modern Irish castle than a house.

Although he averaged only two million less per year than the Panthers star quarterback, he hadn't indulged in even half the luxury—yet, anyway. He was definitely going to pour some major cash into landscaping their backyard. And one of those waterfall ensembles like Colton had would be a nice addition to their pool. Abby would love that.

"Oh, great," Derek mumbled, noticing a red Ford truck parked in the driveway. He was pretty sure who it belonged to: Joe, Colton's obnoxious dad. Probably there to hit him up for some more money. Derek considered turning around, in no mood to listen to the two of them make jabs at each other all afternoon, bickering about everything from football to politics. But Colt needed him. And truth be told, he needed Colt too. It was twisted, but he always felt better after hearing about his friend's marital problems. He should probably tell Colt about his situation, just to get it off his chest, but he couldn't bring himself to do it.

Derek slammed his car door a little harder than usual, letting off some steam. That's when he noticed a twinge of pain in his chest. It was like a knot inside, being pulled tighter and tighter. And tighter. He held his breath and pressed a fist against his sternum. What did this make, like the third or fourth time over the past few days?

The knot gradually loosened, so he released the pent-up air from his lungs.

Voices were coming from the backyard. Derek walked slowly in that direction, keeping his fist snug against his chest, willing the pain not to return. As much as he hated to admit it, he needed to get checked out. Considering his age and fitness level, it was highly unlikely for something major to be wrong. But not impossible.

Chest pain was nothing to gamble with...especially when he was certain that, whether physical or not, there was something broken in his heart.

CHAPTER NINE

How in the world had her little sister ended up on the opposite side of the store? They had just entered Macy's a minute ago, and Abby was already in the formal department, grabbing a dress from the rack. Sarah figured she and Derek must have a fancy upcoming event to attend.

Sarah didn't; she couldn't remember the last time she had to dress to the nines. And it didn't hurt her feelings any.

She returned to browsing the clearance rack with *normal* clothes. There were some cute pants for dirt-cheap prices, but there was no size 12 in any of the colors she liked. There was a size 8 in one pair she loved…if only she could fit into them, her pre-kids size. Before Kayla and Lexi blew her stomach out like a hot air balloon—then deflated it—she had a pretty nice figure. She hoped she could get her figure back after doing *The Next 56 Days* program her sister-in-law raved about. Supposedly, it was a foolproof plan. And Sarah liked how it was geared toward overall health, not just weight loss.

"Come here." Abby mouthed the words, waving for her.

She hurriedly grabbed a shirt she wanted to try on, then headed in her sister's direction.

"Look at this dress," Abby said, running her fingers across the beaded neckline of a purple satin gown. "Doesn't it look like the one I wore to senior prom? You remember?"

Sarah nodded. Abby had looked stunning that evening. She and Zack, newlyweds at the time, had gone over to her parents' house to take pictures of the two lovebirds before they left for the prom. A framed photo of them standing in front of a white limo still hung on a wall in her house. "Wow, it does," she said, running her fingers along the silky fabric of the gown.

Abby suddenly let go of the dress and buried her face in her hands. Sarah's pulse quickened. Was she crying? "Sweetie, what's wrong?"

Abby sucked in a breath, dodging eye contact. She was crying so hard she could barely get her words out. "I don't know...I...feel like my...whole life's falling apart."

She placed her arm around her little sister's shoulders. "Come here. Let's go to that dressing room over there," she said, nodding to the right. She lifted Abby's chin and looked directly into her tear-filled eyes. "Hey. You need to talk to me, okay? I know something's going on—something besides Daddy." She brushed a stray hair from Abby's wet cheek, then kissed it.

Abby nodded her consent, so she grabbed her sister's hand and started walking. After passing a few ladies with clothes draped across their arms, Sarah was shocked to find no one in the fitting room. She breathed a sigh of relief, silently thanking God for the privacy. With her hand around Abby's tiny waist, she led the way to the very last room. Pushing aside a few clothes hangers and a leopard-patterned bikini, she made a place for them to sit down on the bench. *Of all places to have a serious heart to heart.*

Thankfully, Abby cut straight to the chase, oblivious of their awkward surroundings. She talked about her marriage, admitting there was some unidentifiable friction there. She feared Derek was tiring of her fragile emotions and felt like something had changed between them...like they were growing apart.

Sarah didn't say anything for a while. But she finally built up the nerve to ask a dreadful, yet necessary question. "You don't think he's been unfaithful, do you?" Derek loved Abby, no doubt. But since he had no established morals guiding his life and no God to be accountable to, it wouldn't be too surprising if he had strayed. Handsome, rich, and famous to boot, he was bound to have women throwing themselves at him every which way he turned.

"No," Abby shook her head adamantly, her green eyes aflame. "I know him. He's just not like that. Not since we've been together, at least." She paused for a brief moment, looking up at the ceiling. "Oh God"—her voice cracked— "I hope not."

Sarah fumbled through her purse, knowing there was a pack of Kleenex in there...somewhere. Somewhere amidst the sea of junk she intended to clean out—maybe one of these years when she had time.

Abby shook her head again. "No, it's probably just because I've been so down and withdrawn because of Daddy," she said, her lips quivering. "I've just got to…to start acting like myself again. I just don't know how," she shrugged in defeat. "I tried to this morning. I tried to be romantic, to act like nothing has changed. But it has. Something's definitely changed in me, ever since all this started with Daddy. It's almost like a part of me is withering away right along with him. I mean, what are we going to do if he…dies, Sare Bear?"

The intense despair in Abby's eyes when she called her by her special nickname cut her like a knife, leaving a gash for her own grief to seep through. Picturing life without her dad caused her stomach to cave in. But she couldn't give in to the tears pooling in her eyes. Not now, anyway, because her Sissy needed her to be strong.

"I know. Sweetie, if it weren't for my faith in God, I'd be a nervous wreck." Sarah took in a deep breath and massaged the back of her neck, which was growing tighter by the minute. How could she inquire about her sister's spiritual condition without coming across as confrontational? The last thing she wanted was to push her away. *Please, God, give me the words.*

As if an instant answer to prayer, she knew just what to do. She would bypass all the questions and still size up Abby's relationship with God by offering to take this matter straight to Him in prayer. That way, the door would be open for further discussion, yet she wouldn't feel threatened or as if she were being interrogated.

Sarah adjusted her position, sitting straight up on the bench in the Macy's fitting room. Not exactly church, but it didn't matter. With her brown eyes fixed upon her sister's emerald-green ones, she patted her knee. "So"—she cleared her throat—"I think we should take it all to God. Let's pray about everything, right here and now."

Pleasantly surprised by the calm assurance enveloping her, she grabbed Abby's hand. "Unfortunately, there's really nothing I can do about any of this. Oh, what I wouldn't give to be able to kiss all your boo boos away like I used to." She playfully nudged her sister's shoulder, unsuccessful in her attempt to elicit a grin.

"Ab?" Sarah wanted her full attention, so she waited until she had eye contact to proceed. "God knows just how to solve these problems…all of our problems. And He can work everything out for our good."

Abby looked away and shrugged her shoulders. "Go ahead and pray. I guess it wouldn't hurt."

I guess it wouldn't hurt. Did she really just say that? Sarah had to bite her tongue, frustration swelling in her chest. What an insult to slight God that way, to say she "guessed" the One who hung the moon and stars could help. Her heart sank to her feet. Fresh tears welled up, a wave of sadness replacing her irritation. Had her baby sister really strayed that far from God?

"I'm going to pretend you didn't just say that." She was careful not to season her voice with sarcasm, but she wanted Abby to know how her statement had crushed her. She lifted Abby's chin and looked her squarely in the eyes. "Ab, you *know* nothing is impossible for God."

Sarah quickly looked away, realizing her statement may not be true; Abby might not know—or believe—this truth anymore. What if Derek had rubbed off on her so much that she doubted God, even His very existence?

She shuddered at the thought. Her desire to have answers about her Sissy's faith, or lack thereof, was so intense she could barely stifle it. But she did. She had to. Sarah also had to resist her overwhelming urge to preach. God had clearly impressed it upon her to simply pray out loud for Abby—nothing more.

Surrendering her will to God's, she gently lifted her sister's hand. She interlaced their fingers and gave Abby's hand a gentle squeeze before bowing her head. "Let's pray."

"Father God, I want to thank You for this time together and for giving us the privacy to talk. We now come to You in the name of Your Son, Jesus, asking for help and guidance. Abby's broken, Lord—" Sarah stopped for a moment, hearing unsteadiness in her voice. *God, please keep me from breaking down.* "Father, I don't know what to do to help her. But, thankfully, *You* do. You know everything she's feeling, everything happening in her life. And You have the power to fix whatever's broken. However You see fit."

She took a deep breath, gathering her thoughts before continuing. "Lord, I ask You to plant seeds of hope and faith in her heart. Help her to be confident in You and Your ability to work everything out for her good. Also, Lord, please be with our Daddy. Please heal him. Perform a miracle if it's Your will."

Abby sniffled, so she put her arm around her shoulder, pulling her close. "Please comfort us. Be with Mama and the rest of our family, and help us feel Your peace, the peace that surpasses all understanding. God, nothing is impossible for You. I thank and praise You in advance for what You're going to do." Had she covered everything? There was so much more she wanted to ask God for concerning Abby—and Derek—but she decided those things were better left unsaid. Besides, God could hear and attend to the silent pleas of her heart.

The sudden influx of peace to her soul assured Sarah it was time to bring the prayer to a close. "Father, I claim today is a special day, a day of healing and restored hope. And it's in the precious name of Your Son, Jesus, I pray. Amen."

CHAPTER TEN

"Good morning, angel," Derek whispered into Abby's ear, slipping into bed beside of her. She was still sound asleep, but he couldn't wait any longer. It was their first wedding anniversary, and he was like a kid at Christmas, eager to see her expression when she opened the gifts he had for her. Especially the *big* one.

Abby mumbled something he couldn't understand. She was probably talking in her sleep, something she was known to do. He brushed a piece of her disheveled dark hair from her face and kissed her cheek, breathing in the delicate scent of her. The soft innocence of her sleeping face prompted an intense pang of guilt…guilt that had taken up permanent residence in his heart.

"Happy Anniversary, babe!"

How had they been married a year already? It felt like just yesterday when he had gotten down on one knee at the

65

Old Well in Chapel Hill, the moonlight reflecting in Abby's tear-filled eyes. What a special moment in time. Derek was glad he had decided to propose there, in front of her freshman year dorm: Old East, the first state university building in the nation.

He had almost asked her on the beach during their junior year Spring Break trip. But he knew it wouldn't have held nearly the sentimental value as asking her to be his wife at the spot he had pledged his forever-love at the end of their freshman year. He knew Abby would need evidence of his commitment before taking the leap of moving in together—since her parents were so opposed to it—so that's exactly what he gave her that night when he placed a promise ring on her finger. And it seemed only fitting for him to place the official engagement ring on her finger at the same spot. Plus, the Old Well was an iconic landmark in Chapel Hill, a town which would always hold a special place in their hearts.

The fluttering of Abby's long lashes brought him back to the moment. She tugged on the blue satin sheet and pulled it over her head, burying her face in the pillow.

Derek playfully swatted her hand and pulled the sheet away. "Nope! It's 10:00, lazy bones. You've got to get up." He leveraged his weight on his sore, post-workout arms, palms to the bed, gently bouncing her up and down.

"Noooo…please," Abby whined in a scratchy voice.

"Poor baby," he said in mock sympathy. "Get up! I promise you'll be glad. I've got some surprises for you, and I even made you breakfast."

Derek smiled, pride swelling in his chest. He realized he had been distancing himself from Abby, probably because he was subconsciously preparing himself for the worst—for her leaving. But he couldn't stand for her to keep blaming his weird behavior on herself. Pampering her, above and beyond normal, had been good for both of them.

Abby yawned and rubbed her eyes, then opened them ever so slightly. "Oh my gosh!" The gifts on the foot of their bed had captured her gaze. They were wrapped in purple, her favorite color, and topped with silver bows.

He laughed as Abby sprang to a sitting position, clapping her hands together like their little nieces did when they got excited about something.

"What in the world?"

"You've got to eat first, before you can open anything." He enjoyed taunting her and prolonging the excitement. Plus, he had to make sure Abby started eating better; if she lost another pound, she might blow away. "I've made scrambled eggs with cheese, biscuits—from a can, but biscuits nonetheless—sausage, and sausage gravy. So dig in. *Then* we'll get to the gifts."

Derek winked, holding up his hands in mock surrender. "I know, I know—I'm being cruel. But a little suspense never killed anyone."

"Yeah, yeah." Abby bumped her shoulder against his. "I know you just like torturing me. But, wow, this looks amazing, D."

"Good. Thanks," he said, setting the tray of food in front of her. It was embellished with a vase of red roses. Abby sniffed them and rubbed a petal between her fingers, her pink nail polish shimmering in the light.

"Awww, thank you, honey. I don't know what to say."

"Don't say anything. Just enjoy."

Abby caressed his cheek, her eyes full of concern. "You're making me feel bad. I didn't go all-out for your gift."

"I don't care." Derek pulled her head to his chest and kissed the top of it. With a whiff of her floral perfume, along with her silky red pajamas brushing his bare skin, she had taken captive his every sense. As she nuzzled closer, wrapping her arm around his waist, little did she know she had already given him the greatest gift he could ask for. "Besides, you're the only gift I need."

Abby pulled away and fixed him with her gaze, her innocent green eyes leaving him completely breathless. Her face, her neck, her shoulders—every part of her—radiated beauty. If there were a picture beside the word *gorgeous* in the dictionary, it would be of her.

Inching closer to her luscious lips, Derek's heart danced a few beats. But, all of a sudden, his chest tightened and he could barely breathe. He didn't deserve the admiration shining in his wife's angelic eyes. Unfortunately, the man she saw and the man he really was were two different people, and there was no way to fix it. Not even a million surprises or breakfasts in bed could erase what he had done.

——◆+◆——

So much for their anniversary. The tears Abby had been holding back began to spill out as she hung up the phone with her mom. She had called to share the good news that Derek had surprised her with a week-long trip to Cabo San Lucas for their anniversary, but her mom's news had completely shut down her excitement.

She flung off the new Michael Kors flip-flops Derek had given her for the trip and sat Indian-style on her bed. Her elbows dug into her knees as she hung her head in her hands. Only moments before, she was sporting the stylish sandals around her room—along with her new Panama hat and Lilly Pulitzer beach bag—as she began packing, imagining sun-drenched days on the beach.

"Why, God?" Abby cried the words, a tidal wave of worry engulfing her. Her dad had just been admitted to the hospital. Her head spun as she tried to process everything her mom had said…something about his oxygen level being low, which was likely due to a low blood count spurred by the chemotherapy. The doctors needed to run some tests to rule out a few other, more serious conditions. Meanwhile, her Daddy had to be on oxygen and receive a few units of blood.

Abby shook her head, staring at the animal print suitcase she had pulled out of her closet right before the dreadful phone call. What was she going to do now? She and Derek really needed this trip. And Cabo was somewhere she had dreamed of going ever since Sarah and Zack went there on their honeymoon. Nine years later, they still raved about its beauty.

Guilt rose up and nearly suffocated her. A trip was so insignificant in light of her Daddy's situation. He and his health were the main concerns. This may be something serious, possibly the *real* beginning of the end. That thought sucked away every remaining remnant of joy from her once-perfect day.

What am I supposed to do now, God? Ever since her sister prayed for her in the Macy's dressing room, Abby had been talking to God every now and then. But He had really let her down now. Big time. She longed for a romantic getaway more than her next breath, but how could they leave town with her Daddy in such an uncertain condition? Abby massaged her throbbing temples, fresh tears stinging her eyes.

No, she would *not* have a complete meltdown.

Not yet, anyway…not until she heard what Sarah had to say. She selected her sister's name from her list of *favorite contacts* and paced the floor, waiting for the call to connect. Abby clung desperately to a small sliver of optimism, hoping there was still a chance for her and Derek to be on a beach in Cabo this time tomorrow.

CHAPTER ELEVEN

"Hey sweetie, hope y'all are having fun! Good news: your dad is being discharged from the hospital:-) We'll be home soon!" After reading her mom's text, Abby had the notion to jump up and do a celebration dance on the beach. Since Derek was napping beside her, she settled for texting her mom a praise emoji.

Her Daddy's cancer remained, of course, but everything related to this acute situation had turned out okay...just as he had promised. Abby filled her lungs with a deep breath of salty air, thankful she had taken her family's advice to carry on with the trip to Cabo. Digging her toes into the warm sand, she took in the gorgeous scene in front of her: the brilliant, turquoise Sea of Cortez and Land's End—the monstrous rock formations, including the famous arch—which separates the bay from the Pacific Ocean.

A smile spread across her face as she recalled the day she and Derek spent snorkeling in the Sea of Cortez off of Lover's Beach, then basking in the sun on Divorce Beach, an adjoining beach on the Pacific about 50 yards away. Supposedly, Divorce Beach got its name from the turbulent waters which had fatally separated many couples. Thinking a more appropriate name would be Widow's Beach, Abby giggled out loud.

She could completely let go now, knowing her Daddy was going to be okay. Every ounce of tension in her body began to melt, evaporating in the midday sun. A mild breeze swept over her and flirted with the edge of her favorite beach towel, one with two dolphins facing each other, forming the shape of a heart. She leaned her head back and closed her eyes, tuning in to the relaxing sounds of crashing waves and squawking seabirds.

How was it possible not to believe in God? Why had she been doubting His existence lately? There was no way this vast beauty could've come together by chance...out of a Big Bang of objects which came from nothing. If only Derek could see that. She would like to have more of God in her life—to have faith like her sister's to help her cope during hard times—but the last thing Abby wanted right now was for her and Derek to start debating over beliefs again. Derek wouldn't keep her from going to church, but she knew it would stir up some disagreements. It just wasn't worth it, especially since she didn't get much out of church anyway.

Back when they first started dating, Derek believed in God. His aunt and uncle had taken him to church occasionally, at least for Christmas and Easter. And, although she and Derek didn't agree with everything the preacher said, the two of them used to go to her childhood church together. College changed things, though. All it took was one year at UNC, being taught by several skeptics, for Derek to adopt an *I'll have to see it to believe it*-philosophy.

"Let me get a rum and Diet Coke." Presuming him to be asleep, Abby jumped at the sound of Derek's voice.

"Okay, and for the lady?" A pair of dark brown eyes met hers. The poor guy had beads of sweat dripping from his forehead.

"I'll take a bottled water, please. Thank you."

The waiter grinned and raised his hand to his forehead, feigning a salute. "Coming right up," he said with a thick Spanish accent.

Abby turned to look at Derek, but he wasn't there...at least, not the husband she knew and loved. Swallowing her surprise, she studied the man glaring back at her. He had a glazed-over, vacant stare, his face lacking even the slightest trace of emotion. A fog of confusion and concern suddenly clouded her lighthearted, sunny disposition.

"What's going on? You've already had two mixed drinks and what"—Abby paused, counting in her head—"three beers?" She laser-focused her eyes on Derek's, hoping he could see her frustration through the new Prada sunglasses he had bought for her near the marina yesterday. This was absurd. It wasn't even lunchtime yet, and he was drunk.

Derek faced the ocean, obviously dodging her. "I don't know, I haven't been counting...Ain't that what vacation's all about?" He looked at her with a goofy smirk on his face.

Why was he acting this way? They had been on many vacations together, and he never drank this much, especially during the day.

She shook her head, refraining from saying something that may trigger an argument, her desire to keep this day happy and carefree overriding her frustration. Besides, there was probably nothing to make of the drinking. She would just keep an eye on it. "Whatever, babe." Abby shrugged her shoulders, managing a slight smile, but her voice was dripping with sarcasm.

━◁╂ ╂▷━

"Thanks, man." Derek took the rum and Diet Coke from the beachside waiter, then reached into Abby's beach bag, pulling out a wad of cash. Too dizzy to count out a $10 tip, he gave the guy the whole handful of bills and enjoyed watching his face light up.

"Thank you! Thank you so much!" The mix of sheer disbelief and joy in the waiter's eyes said it was probably more than his typical week's worth of wages.

Abby grinned and rubbed his arm, apparently approving of his generous act. Maybe he was back in her good graces. If not, he would be after implementing his plan to smooth things over.

"Here." Derek handed her his rum and Diet Coke, the drink heavy in his loose, limber hand. "You're right, I don't need this. Don't even know why I ordered it."

Abby took it from him reluctantly. "It's too early to start drinking, but I guess I'll take a sip," she said, lifting the glass to her mouth. "Ugh! You think they put enough liquor in it?" She coughed.

He patted her thigh, admiring her fresh tan. She was a bombshell in that new animal print bikini.

Abby placed the drink on the table inside their private tiki hut. He blew her a kiss in the air, and she reciprocated. Inwardly, he sighed in relief, knowing he was in *the clear.* He would be more cautious from now on. With football season right around the corner, he needed to lay off the booze, anyway. For the time being, though, he may as well enjoy what remained of his buzz.

Derek reclined his chair and took in the beauty surrounding him: His hot wife to the left. Bright blue water ahead. Above him, clear skies, sunshine, and palm trees swaying in the breeze. He was super-fortunate. Most people could never afford a trip like this. Just within the past four days, they had ridden camels and ATVs through the desert, taken a sunset dinner cruise, played with sea lions, and enjoyed a private beachside dinner and couples massage.

"Hey, aren't you Derek Holder?" His thoughts were interrupted by a middle-aged man in a straw hat, unashamedly approaching him with a cheesy smile. *Ugh!* He chided himself for not going back to the room for his baseball cap; people were much less likely to recognize him in it.

"That's me." Derek hoped he didn't seem rude, but he also hoped he didn't sound too friendly. He didn't want to come across as a jerk, yet he was in no mood to carry on a conversation with a complete stranger, especially while under the influence.

He talked football—as best he could—for a few minutes, signing autographs for the guy and his son. Then he adjusted his position and dug his toes in the sand, getting back to vacation.

Derek's growling stomach startled him.

"Hungry, babe?" Abby laughed.

"Evidently."

"Wanna grab some lunch? We haven't tried out that place yet," she said, pointing to a beachside cafe to their right.

"Maybe in a minute." Derek scanned the place and concluded there were too many people to contend with, even though he could probably count the total number on his hands.

But he couldn't get up now if he wanted to; he was too doggone lit.

Derek leaned his head against the chair and closed his eyes. Maybe they could order something to eat the next time the waiter came by and have lunch right here. A big, juicy cheeseburger would hit the spot. And he had earned it, working out an extra hour in the fitness room every morning to compensate for all he'd been eating—and drinking—this week.

Stretching his legs out in front of him, Derek realized, for all intents and purposes, he was living the dream. Anything from a cheeseburger in paradise to a Lamborghini was at his beck and call. No, he may not have a Super Bowl title under his belt yet, but that was well underway...and Dave Holder was bound to know it by now. Most importantly, he had an amazing wife, and the load of his guilt and regret had lightened significantly since he had been spoiling her so much lately.

Sinatra would say he had the world on a string. So, why was he so empty inside?

CHAPTER TWELVE

Derek took his position on the line of scrimmage, willing himself to concentrate. His body had simply been going through the motions of the game as his mind wandered here, there, and everywhere.

He knew why.

It had been almost a year since that fateful night in Seattle. And here he was playing the Seahawks again, only this time it was on his own turf. In Charlotte.

"Blue 20, Blue 20, Hut." Colton, his best friend and quarterback, cued for the ball to be hiked. After the snap, Derek ran down the field at full throttle, searching for an opening. But he couldn't find one.

The ball glided through the air toward the opposite side of the field. "Yes!" The pass to his teammate, Timothy, was complete.

The roar of the crowd was exhilarating. With the momentum in their favor and only 25 more yards to the goal line, Derek practically tasted a touchdown. *No, not a timeout!* He jerked his helmet off and jogged toward the sideline.

"Good catch." He gave Timothy a high five. "Stupid TV timeout…We would've already had the TD."

"Probably so." Timothy's eyes looked more serious than the moment called for. "You okay, man?"

Do I not look okay? Before he had a chance to answer, another teammate stole Timothy's attention with a high five, commending him for the catch. Derek was grateful for the distraction. Because, for some reason, he couldn't take in a full breath—even though the fall air was crisp and refreshing.

He glanced up at Abby in the family section. Maybe if she blew him a lucky kiss, he would feel better and finally score a touchdown. So much for that; her head was turned.

After a quick timeout, it was back to the line of scrimmage. He took his place and managed to draw in a few satisfying breaths of cool air. "Blue 20, Blue 20, Hut," Colton shouted.

Derek must have been running at record speed, the way the wind was sweeping past his face. There it was: an opening. He twisted around and positioned himself for the catch, his heart pounding as the ball spiraled straight toward him. Leaping into the air at just the right moment, he grabbed the ball and clutched it against his chest, anticipation and adrenaline coursing through his body. When his feet met the turf, there were only seven yards to cover before the goal line.

Two strides later, the unthinkable happened. Derek cursed and stretched out his arms, diving toward the loose ball which had somehow slipped through his hands. As if in slow motion, it bounced off the shoe of the opponent who had been covering him and landed perfectly into the hands of a Seahawks cornerback.

His heart sank. He reached out to grab the guy's legs, determined not to let this turn into an even worse scenario. "You ain't going anywhere, hotshot." Derek forced his opponent to the ground, the disappointing roar of the crowd nearly suffocating him.

"Fumble recovered by number 32, Demetry Jackson. It'll be Seattle's ball on the 6-yard line." The referee's words were like salt in a gaping wound.

What happened? How could he have fumbled? The pass was foolproof, his path clear all the way to the goal line. Flinging off his helmet, Derek looked at the scoreboard, even though he knew the score hadn't changed. They were ahead by two touchdowns—no credit to him—and there were only four and a half minutes left in the game. Thankfully, the pressure wasn't all that intense.

The bruise to his ego was, though.

"What's going on with you, man? You don't look so hot." Colton caught up with him as he made his way to the sidelines.

Derek cursed about his lousy playing, beating his chest in frustration.

"Hey, you said it—not me." Colton chuckled, slapping him on the back, concern flickering in his eyes. "Lighten up, we got this. Baldy won't even make it to field goal range, you wait and see. Seriously, D., you look pale. You alright?"

"I'm fine. Just can't get in the zone for some reason," Derek said, blowing him off. *Although I do know the reason.*

Coach stared him down with puzzled eyes, his dark brown eyebrows furrowed. Derek motioned him away. Being questioned and lectured surely wouldn't help him regain composure or redeem himself. He walked to the far end of the bench and took a seat, chugging down some water. "Come on guys!" He cheered as the defense ran out on the field, willing them to keep the Seahawks from scoring off of his stupid mistake.

He glanced up at Abby again, this time catching her eyes. She blew him a kiss in the air. Something inside him was sparked back to life, despite the fact that the Seahawks were sending in their kicker for an easy field goal attempt. Colton's prediction hadn't held true. Fortunately, it didn't matter; it was too little, too late for them to come back now.

Derek joined the team in a huddle, then headed for the field as "Eye of the Tiger" blasted through the stadium speakers. Electricity filled the air, everyone knowing the "W" was only a matter of minutes away. The cheerleaders had stepped it up, and the fans were loud and on their feet, helping him let go of his mistake. Approaching mid-field, his attention was drawn to the navy and gray pompoms shaking in the visitor's section, standing out among a sea of black and blue. That's when his eyes locked on her: a blonde in the second row.

Cassidy?

Derek's throat swelled shut as he studied the woman. Petite figure, long blonde hair. She was too far away to get a good look at her face.

There are millions of petite blondes in the world.

Unfortunately, his voice of logic did nothing to calm his erratic heart. It had crossed his mind that Cassidy might come tonight, but he figured it was highly unlikely. If she didn't have ties to someone on Seattle's team, it would be crazy for her to make the nearly 3000-mile trip. Unless—

Panic seized him, freezing him in his tracks. What if she had come to find him? Derek hadn't given her any contact information, so what if this was her way of tracking him down? Maybe she still had feelings for him. Or—

He could barely finish the thought, the blood draining from his face. *What if the two percent chance had been enough? What if he had gotten her pregnant?*

Something punched him in the chest, knocking the wind from his lungs. Steps away from his spot in the lineup, Derek stopped and grabbed his chest. It was still rising and falling, but he was suffocating. An intense wave of dizziness forced him to his knees, where all he could do was watch the entire stadium swirl around him. The pressure in his chest continued to escalate until he had no choice but to curl into a fetal position.

Abby! He had to see her, had to tell her he loved her one last time before he died from this massive heart attack. Why hadn't he gotten checked out after having those few episodes of chest pain a while back—before it was too late?

"What's going on? Where do you hurt?" Derek recognized the distressed voice of Dr. Nick, one of the team physicians. "Holder, are you with me? Talk to me!" Dr. Nick demanded a response, slapping him on the cheek. The sting was actually nice, temporarily distracting him from the elephant sitting on his chest.

Derek opened his mouth to respond, but he couldn't make a sound. Why were his lips tingling, almost numb? The only thing he could do was release the hold on his chest long enough to point at it with his index finger. Then he clutched it even tighter, scared his heart may rupture. He didn't have long now...because tiny specks of light were dancing around the darkening silhouette of Dr. Nick's face.

⇒╫⇐

"So I didn't have a heart attack?" Derek questioned the woman beside his hospital bed, his voice full of disbelief. Through slightly blurred vision, he strained to read the name tag hanging from her neck.

"Debra Norris, RN, Emergency Department." A nurse should know what she's talking about. But if he hadn't had a heart attack, why was his last memory the excruciating chest pain he felt before falling to the field? And why was he a patient at Carolinas Medical Center?

"No, sir." The nurse smiled and shook her head, her hazel eyes kind and reassuring. "Like I said, the doctor will be in to talk with you in a little while. Just relax."

She adjusted his pillow, glancing up at the beeping monitor above his head. "Here, push this button if you need anything. And leave this thing on," she said, pointing at the odd-looking device clasping his middle finger. "It's measuring your oxygen level."

"Whatever you say."

"And don't you get up without calling first, because you've had a lot of medicine that makes you drowsy."

"Ma'am?" Derek called out as the nurse slipped behind a blue and white-striped curtain.

"Yes?"

"Why is there nobody here with me? Is my wife out there somewhere?" He needed Abby. Right now.

"I'm sorry, I forgot to tell you that someone is out in the waiting room completing some paperwork. Not your wife, though. I believe it's someone from your team. I'll send him in if you'd like."

"Alright, thanks," Derek mumbled, looking around for his phone and wallet before remembering they were in his locker at the stadium.

Where was Abby? Surely they would have allowed her to be with him on the ambulance that had supposedly transported him here. He hung his head down, massaging his temples. It felt weird, like he had just stepped off of the Gravitron at the county fair. And the nurse was right; he was definitely drowsy. He had never been so baffled in all his life. It was crazy how he couldn't remember a thing about the ambulance ride.

Memories of the scenario which led up to the chest pain began to flood his mind. Being removed from the moment and under the influence of some type of oblivion-inducing medication, Derek was no longer concerned about the blonde in the stands; he was just worried about what was going on now. Something serious must be wrong for his chest to have hurt like that…enough to knock him unconscious.

Shivering, he pulled the blanket over his shoulders and slipped his hands beneath it. This place was way too cold. He was being held captive in a meat locker, dying for answers. And for his wife's warm embrace.

CHAPTER THIRTEEN

Abby couldn't take her eyes off Derek as he sat on the side of his hospital bed in the emergency room. Thankfully, he was alive…alive *and* well, from what she could tell anyway. The doctor needed to hurry it up and explain what was going on.

"So you're not hurting anywhere?" Abby rubbed her husband's calloused hand, sitting beside him on the bed.

"Nope." Derek smiled, but his eyes couldn't hide his fear.

She swiped a stray blonde hair from his forehead and caressed his cheek. A curtain suddenly swooshed back, startling her. Abby held her breath as a tall, gray-haired man wearing a white lab coat made his entrance. He had to be the doctor.

"Wow!" The man's eyes lit up as he scanned the roomful of people. "It looks like you're quite the celebrity, both on

and off the field. Hi, Mr. Holder, I'm Dr. Joseph Samuels."
The doctor smiled, but he seemed a little nervous as he extended his hand.

"Nice to meet you. Please, call me Derek."

Abby extended her hand and introduced herself when the doctor looked her way.

"I heard you guys had a big win today," Dr. Samuels said, looking at Colton—still in uniform, leaning against the wall of the cramped room. He and Dr. Nick, one of the team doctors, had rushed to the hospital right after the game ended, arriving just a few minutes before the doctor walked in.

"Congrats! Nice going!" The doctor shook hands with Colton and Dr. Nick. "Wish I could've been there. I've got season tickets, but as you can see"—he looked down at his lab coat—"I'm working today. So, I had to hand them over to my brother and nephew."

Blah, blah, blah. The man was out of his element; his blushing face said that much. But Abby couldn't take anymore small talk, especially football talk, at a time like this. They needed answers. Now.

From the moment she saw Derek grab his chest and fall to the field until the moment she saw him here, she had been a basket case. Thank God for Jerry, one of the team's water boys, who drove her to the emergency room after she made a spectacle of herself on the sidelines. By the time she made it from her seat, through the tunnel, and out onto the field, the ambulance had already left. Heat rose to Abby's cheeks as she imagined how crazy she had acted, demanding answers from everyone as she stormed the field like a protective mother bear.

"Okay," Dr. Samuels said, clasping his hands together. "I know you all are anxious about the current situation, so everyone except Mrs. Holder, please step out of the room for a moment while I go over everything." He politely nodded at Colton and Dr. Nick. Abby did the same, forcing a cordial smile as her heart raced out of control, anticipating the doctor's diagnosis.

⊷⊶

"Please, call me Derek." Hadn't the doctor heard him the first time? Fire spread from his neck to his cheeks as he thought of another Mr. Holder—one he hated sharing anything with, much less his very name.

Abby flashed him *the look*, the one that said his tone had been too harsh. Derek faked a half-smile, looking at the doctor again. The man was scooting toward him in a swivel chair, a stethoscope dangling from his neck and a clipboard in his hands.

"Alrighty then, I've got some good news. Everything with your heart has checked out okay. Although your pulse was elevated and the EKG in the ambulance indicated some questionable findings, you definitely haven't had a heart attack."

"Thank God," Abby said, squeezing his hand.

"Yes," the doctor nodded before continuing. "Your lab work was negative, as was your chest x-ray. There's no indication of heart enlargement, lung problems, and so forth."

"But the EKG showed something? In the ambulance?" Derek scratched his head. Something wasn't adding up here.

"Yes, it was likely what we call artifact," Dr. Samuels said, quickly chiming in as if he had been anticipating the question. *Artifact?* "Meaning, it was false...probably due to the jostling around on the ambulance. That happens someti—"

"Okay, so how do you explain the chest pain and high heart rate?" He interrupted the guy again mid-sentence. Abby's disapproving gaze practically stared a hole through his head. Derek feigned a laugh as he grabbed his chest. "I mean, I thought I was dying, man!" He should probably tell the doctor about the other times he had experienced chest pain and shortness of breath, but Abby would give him heck for not getting checked out.

"Yes, Mr. Holder"—the doctor cleared his throat—"I mean, Derek. I'm sure the pain was intense." The way the guy adjusted his glasses reminded him of his nerdy English professor at UNC. "But there are other conditions that can cause chest pain, which we'll discuss. And as for your heart rate, it wasn't all that elevated when you consider the fact that you were right in the middle of a football game. I can assure you most peoples' heart rates would've been much higher," Dr. Samuels chuckled.

The man had an obnoxious, goofy laugh. Derek made a point to keep his face expressionless as he released Abby's hand and slid himself up in bed. An awkward silence lingered a little too long before the doctor continued. "The symptoms you described—the chest pain, shortness of breath, dizziness, tingling in your lips, and so forth—are all classic symptoms of a panic attack."

⚊⚌⚊

A panic attack? Abby might have been less shocked if the doctor had said her husband had suffered a heart attack. What in the world would have caused Derek to have a panic attack? Judging by the expression on his face, he was just as shocked as she was. This Dr. Samuels had quite a bit of explaining to do. But he said nothing for several seconds, maybe to give them time to digest what he had said.

"We don't generally see a loss of consciousness with panic attacks, but I suspect you fainted due to a combination of factors," he finally continued. "Your electrolytes were a little off kilter, probably due to sweating and inadequate water intake. All the symptoms you described are definitely physical symptoms…you didn't imagine them. But they are physical manifestations of an inner anxiety of some sort."

Abby's feelings mirrored the look of sheer disbelief on Derek's face. The doctor kept talking, but she tuned him out as she tried to imagine what kind of *inner anxiety* had caused a problem of this magnitude.

"Are you under a lot of stress?" The questioning intonation in the doctor's voice brought her back to the present moment. Dr. Samuels looked at Derek with compassion. "I mean, I'm sure playing in the NFL is more stressful than most people realize. Or"—he scratched his head as if he were uneasy and searching for words—"are you depressed?"

Derek glanced at her. Why did he look so scared, like a deer caught in the headlights? He exhaled audibly before addressing the doctor. "No, I'm not. And, yeah, playing pro ball is more stressful than it seems. But I love it. It's my dream." He shot Abby another nervous glance before continuing. "My wife's dad has cancer. And, well, it's been hard on all of us."

"I'm sorry to hear that." The doctor's eyes shone with sympathy. He scooted his swivel chair closer to Derek and patted his shoulder. "Well, I believe the stress is certainly taking a toll on you, sir. You were in pretty bad shape when you got here. Hyperventilating, barely able to speak. But after the nurse gave you an anti-anxiety drug, you started coming around. That's another reason why I believe you were indeed having a panic attack."

Abby had never seen her husband's face change colors so fast. "Wow, I didn't know I was *that* stressed out." Derek shook his head, his eyes darting back and forth between her and the doctor. What was that look on his face? Worry? Shame, maybe? Hanging his head, he massaged his temples.

Abby's heart sank to her feet. All this was her fault. "I'm sure it hasn't been easy dealing with me lately—I've kept you on an emotional roller coaster."

"No, babe, it's not your fault," Derek interrupted, shaking his head. He wouldn't look her in the eye.

He turned toward the doctor. "So, what do you recommend, doc? Let me guess...you think I need some kind of *crazy pill*, right?" The sarcasm in Derek's voice made her want to crawl in a hole. Abby shifted her position and glared at her husband, begging him to be polite.

Dr. Samuels was seemingly unfazed by the snide remark. "Well, you need to follow up with your primary care doctor," he answered. "I feel sure he or she will believe, as I do, that an antidepressant would benefit you. Temporarily, at least. It'll help balance the chemicals in your brain which lead to anxiety and, ultimately, to panic attacks." He paused momentarily. "I'm sure you don't want to go through this ordeal again, am I right?"

"Of course I don't." At least Derek fake-smiled as he spouted out. Abby stared at the gray vinyl floor, eyebrows raised, heat rushing to her cheeks. "But it doesn't mean I want—or need—a mental pill."

An audible sigh should get her point across...that his childish behavior was embarrassingly rude. Why did Derek keep referring to a "mental" or "crazy" pill? A few of their friends and family members were on antidepressants, and he always seemed to share the same view as she did about them: that those people weren't crazy; they probably just had a chemical imbalance. As a biology major, Abby knew there was a real, physical science behind anxiety and depression, and it was a shame that some people—obviously, her husband included—still attached a certain stigma to those conditions.

"I understand your concern and hesitation," Dr. Samuels said, looking at Derek. "As I said, you need to follow up with your doctor...one of the team doctors, I'm assuming. We will fax all your records over, and you can discuss what route to take. In the meantime"—he pulled out a prescription pad from his lab coat—"I'm going to give you a medication to take if you feel another episode coming on. It's the exact same med you've had today. Xanax, a common anti-anxiety drug."

She caught Derek's eyes as the doctor started scribbling. He must have read her expression correctly because he shut his mouth. "Thank you, doctor." Abby stood up and took the prescription from his hand. "I'm sure we'll get everything worked out. I'm just thankful you don't think it's anything serious."

"Yep, I think everything will be fine." Dr. Samuels smiled, adjusting his glasses. "Well, take care now."

"Thank you so much," Abby said, shaking his hand.

"Best of luck," Dr. Samuels said, shaking Derek's hand. Making his way out of the room, a mischievous grin played on the man's lips. He adjusted the stethoscope around his neck, then pointed at Derek. "Next time I see you, you better be whooping up on those Falcons!"

After the doctor's jovial comment, Abby took her first satisfying breath of air since seeing her husband fall to the field.

CHAPTER FOURTEEN

"Ho, Ho, Ho! Merrrrry Christmas!" Abby's dad held the door and motioned for her and Derek to enter as they walked up the front steps, gifts in tow. Seeing her dad so bubbly, Abby's excitement escalated. It was going to be a magical Christmas morning.

"Merry Christmas, Daddy. You look great." She leaned into her dad's embrace, kissing him on the cheek.

"Thanks, shug. That's because Mrs. Claus over here is fixing up her famous cinnamon bun casserole, and I'm about to be a jolly old Saint Nicholas!" He laughed, rubbing his stomach. No matter how he tried, though, he couldn't produce a rounded belly—the cancer had made sure of that.

But today was no day to think about cancer. Or anything negative, for that matter. It was a day to celebrate and be happy.

"Merry Christmas, John." Derek greeted her dad with a hug, and they began chatting as she made her way into the kitchen. She was so thankful Derek didn't have to play a game today like he did last Christmas.

"Mmmm! It smells delicious, Mom." Even sweeter than the cinnamon and sugar lingering in the air was the love filling the room. Abby greeted her mom who stood by the stove wearing a candy cane apron, then she made her way to the living room to place the gifts under the tree.

"Merry *Kissmas*, Uncle *Dewek!*" Hearing Lexi's sweet voice in the next room, her smile grew even wider. "Guess what Santa *bwought* me?" Lexi proceeded to give a detailed account of everything from a tricycle to a new red dress for Carrie, her American girl doll.

After making a brief detour to the fireplace to warm her hands, Abby floated back into the kitchen where Derek was in the process of lifting her giggling niece to his shoulders, per her usual request. He winked at Abby, bringing goosebumps to her arms. He was going to be an amazing dad to their children one day, a day which might not be too far away if things kept progressing in their lives.

Thankfully, one of the team doctors had convinced Derek to give Zoloft a try...after a few more terrible episodes of chest pain. He had to deal with a few side effects from the medicine, but overall, he was doing better. He almost seemed like his usual self again.

"Aunt Abby?" Kayla squeezed her knees, startling her.

"Yes, sweetie?" She leaned down to hug her, her heart melting over the bashful grin on her niece's face.

"Did Santa leave us anything at your house?"

"As a matter of fact"— Abby said, widening her eyes in exaggeration—"I believe he did! And guess who else left one?"

"Who?" Kayla bounced up and down, squealing.

"Well, Uncle D. and I, for one thing. And"—she paused, feeding off the excitement and suspense building in Kayla's expressive brown eyes—"Rudolph!"

Lexi cackled from atop Derek's shoulders, and Kayla clapped her hands, spinning around in circles. Abby's heart swelled as memories of her own childhood Christmases with Sarah played through her mind. They, along with their multitude of cousins, had been every bit as excited as her precious nieces.

"Wow!" Sarah chimed in on the action. "Rudolph? Girls, you must be super-special if Rudolph the Red-Nosed Reindeer left you a gift!"

"Can we open *pweasants* now? *Pweeeeeeeease*, Aunt Abby!" Lexi looked like a sad puppy dog, her bottom lip turned out, obviously knowing the answer already.

Thankfully, the girls' Janny stepped in to deliver the disappointing news. "You know the rules: no opening presents until after breakfast and Papa's Bible reading."

"Janny, I know the real meaning of *Kissmas*. Do you?" Kayla stood tall, placing her hands on her hips. Abby and her mom exchanged glances, smiling.

"I sure do, darling. Jesus was born, and He's the best Christmas gi—"

"And Jesus loves me," Lexi announced, interrupting her Janny.

"That's right, Lex. Jesus loves everyone." Zack lifted his daughter to his hip, kissing the top of her head. He glanced at Derek. "The question is do *you* love *Him?*"

"Whoa, did you hear that?" Derek asked no one in particular, rubbing his stomach.

Yeah, right.

"Everything's just about ready," Abby's mom said, pulling a snowman casserole dish out of the oven.

Abby exhaled in relief, thankful that Derek's tactic to change the subject seemed to have worked.

"Janet, it looks and smells delicious." Zack walked up behind her mom, patting her back.

"Well, thanks. I hope it is. We'll see. I think the biscuits are a little overdone."

Abby shook her head, amused by how humble her mother was. She was easily one of the best cooks in the county, but she couldn't even accept a simple compliment from her son-in-law.

"Mom, everything will be perfect. As always," Sarah said, joining their mother by the stove. She opened a cabinet and began taking down glasses. "Okay, what do y'all want to drink? Coffee, orange juice…grape or apple juice?"

After everyone shouted their requests, Abby lifted Lexi to her hip and kissed her chubby cheek. She made her way into the living room as she nuzzled her little niece close, playing with her ponytail. The delightful sights, smells, and sounds of Christmas warmed her soul. Between the tree—decorated in blue, her mom's favorite color—the snow village, and the mistletoe, she was in the midst of a winter wonderland. Most importantly, she was surrounded by those she loved most. This was definitely the best day of the year.

John silently prayed Derek would ponder the words he had just read from the Old Testament. For the first time ever, he had decided to add some verses from Isaiah 7 and Micah 5 to his traditional Christmas reading. "Both of those Scriptures, which referenced Christ's birth, were written at least 650 years *before* He was born." He glanced at Derek, who seemed less-than-impressed by this fact. Thankfully, Abby seemed more attentive and engaged than usual.

John's heart quickened, wondering if his baby girl had a genuine relationship with Christ. His cancer diagnosis made the *not knowing* tougher to deal with. He just couldn't bear the thought of his daughter being one of the people Matthew 7:21 referenced—someone who falsely assumed they were going to Heaven. His and Abby's history of spiritual conflict made it hard to approach her, though. He surely didn't want to push her away...from him or the Lord.

"Now can we open our presents, Papa?" Kayla stole him away from his contemplations, raising and waving her little hand in the air.

John made sure his face didn't reveal his inward smile. Evidently, Sarah had taught his precious granddaughter to raise her hand when she wanted to say something, but she obviously didn't grasp the concept of waiting to be called upon. *Oh, to be a child at Christmas again...*

"No, not yet," he said, tilting his head down to get a direct look at Kayla above his glasses. "We're not finished reading about the *true* meaning of Christmas. It's not about those presents." He pointed at the array of gifts beneath the tree. "It's about receiving the gift of Jesus."

Disappointed by the cynical look in his son-in-law's eyes, John looked away. He couldn't allow Derek to see his frustration.

Gazing at his nativity scene—the one he carved by hand a few years ago—John was suddenly filled with a sense of peace. *Trust in My timing.* The voice echoed through his soul, lifting some weight off of his heavy heart. God was faithful, so he was certain He would somehow answer the prayer he prayed every single day: for Derek and Abby to surrender their lives to Jesus.

John exhaled, fully relaxed and confident, turning to an earmarked page in his Bible. A page more worn than most, having been handled an uncountable number of times over the years. He cleared his throat, then began reading Matthew 1:18-23, his favorite account of the Christmas story:

This is how the birth of Jesus the Messiah came about: His mother Mary was pledged to be married to Joseph, but before they came together, she was found to be pregnant through the Holy Spirit. Because Joseph her husband was faithful to the law, and yet did not want to expose her to public disgrace, he had in mind to divorce her quietly. But after he had considered this, an angel of the Lord appeared to him in a dream and said, "Joseph son of David, do not be afraid to take Mary home as your wife, because what is conceived in her is from the Holy Spirit. She will give birth to a son, and you are to give him the name Jesus, because he will save his people from their sins." All this took place to fulfill what the Lord had said through the prophet: "The virgin will conceive and give birth to a son, and they will call him Immanuel" (which means "God with us").

John barely finished the last sentence, his throat completely parched. He excused himself to get a drink of water from the kitchen.

The cold liquid felt wonderful going down…until some of it trickled into the wrong pipe. Coughing violently as he rounded the corner into the living room, he nearly lost his balance.

"Honey?" Janet was at his side in a flash, just as she always was when he needed her. Her arm around his waist helped to steady him, but unfortunately, it did nothing to help him catch his breath.

"Daddy, are you okay?" Abby's voice reflected the tension in the room.

John continued coughing in a hunched-over position. After a few more forceful ones, he nodded his head. Yes, he was going to survive. "Thanks, honey, I'll be fine." He smiled at his wife of 32 years, hoping to ease her concern. She was a tender-hearted worrywart, so he knew his effort was in vain. Letting go of her hand, he sat down on the couch beside Sarah. His oldest daughter rubbed his back while he took in several full, satisfying breaths.

He finally mustered the courage to drink some more water, hoping and praying he wouldn't choke again. No doubt, his swallowing problem was getting worse. And downright scary. The nurse at the cancer center told him it was a common side effect from the radiation he was receiving for the tumor in his right upper lung…a newly-discovered tumor which no one besides his wife knew about.

"Whew, I'm sorry for all the commotion." John looked around the room, feeling bad for causing the worried expressions on every face. He hated how raspy and strained his voice was. "I think I'm okay now. Zack, I believe you may need to finish the reading from Luke, though," he said, pointing at his Bible on the coffee table.

"Sure, no problem." His oldest son-in-law nodded, looking at him as if he had just seen a ghost.

Perhaps he did resemble a ghost, John thought. If he was even the slightest shade paler than he had been this morning when he looked in the mirror, he may as well change his name to Casper. Then again, after that coughing episode, his face was likely beet red.

No matter the reason for Zack's frightful expression, John didn't like him looking at him that way. Being pitied was one of the hardest hands his cancer diagnosis had dealt him. He hated to burden anybody, much less those he loved most. But what control did he have over how others viewed him or his condition? All he could do was trust in the Lord with all his heart and give up on trying to make sense of things…Proverbs 3:5-6 was his motto.

"Okay, Zack, whenever you're ready." John watched him thumb through his Bible, a wave of sadness crashing over him. This was the first time in more than 25 years that he hadn't read the Christmas story from Luke's Gospel. He looked around the room, glad to see everyone's attention had shifted to Zack. Maybe no one would notice the tears pooling in his eyes.

No matter how hard he tried, he couldn't focus on the Scripture reading. What if this were his last Christmas? He would be fine with that—better than ever, actually, as he celebrated his first Christmas with His Savior—but his family wouldn't be. He was blessed beyond measure to have the love and devotion of those gathered in this room, yet there was a flip side to the same shiny coin. Because the more they loved him, the harder it would be for them to carry on without him.

John wiped his eyes, having little time left to compose himself. Only a few verses remained, ones which would speak directly to him, though. He tuned in to his son-in-law's soothing voice as he read Luke 2:10-11:

> But the angel said to them, "Do not be afraid. I bring you good news that will cause great joy for all the people. Today in the town of David a Savior has been born to you; he is the Messiah, the Lord."

Do not be afraid. Do not be afraid. The words of the angel in the Christmas story resonated within his soul, urging him to *let go and let God.* John took in a deep breath, willing himself to cooperate with the Holy Spirit inside him…to allow the peace of God, the Christ Child they celebrated today, to fill and overtake his troubled heart.

CHAPTER FIFTEEN

The snow was coming down in huge, fluffy flakes. Derek sat in his leather recliner, gazing out at the winter wonderland through the floor-to-ceiling windows in his living room.

This was the biggest snowfall Charlotte had seen in over a decade. With six inches on the ground and four to five more forecasted before nightfall, this New Year's Day would go down in the record books.

The peaceful scene in his backyard took him back to a Christmas long ago, back when he was seven years old and living with Gram in Tennessee. It snowed more there than in Charlotte, but that was the first and only time he remembered having snow at Christmas. The snowfall began just as they headed to the Christmas Eve candlelight service at church, and by the time they walked out two hours later, the ground was completely covered. With a foot of snow expected by morning and Santa Claus coming that night, the excitement was too much for a boy to contain.

Reliving the special Christmas, Derek was suddenly overtaken by loneliness. Abby was upstairs asleep. And she probably would be for at least another hour or so, since they had partied it up late last night, ringing in the new year at Colton's house.

He grabbed his cup of coffee, appreciating the warmth of the mug in his hands. Heat would feel so good to his knee right now. But what he really needed to do was ice it. It had bothered him sporadically since the last home game when a former college teammate-turned-opponent tackled him. Derek's pulse accelerated, thinking of getting a cortisone shot before playoffs. The injection wasn't too painful and had brought him instant relief in the past, but the doctors had warned him that the more shots he had, the greater the chance of his tendons and ligaments weakening. Meaning, he was more likely to have another tear.

Suddenly, a sharp pain in his chest made his knee concerns seem trivial. Derek held his breath and pressed his hand against his chest. What was going on? Had he accidentally made regular coffee this morning?

He had decided to cut out caffeine when he started feeling a little anxious a few days ago. He was beyond anxious right now, though. Struggling to take in a breath, Derek was second-guessing his decision to stop taking Zoloft last week. Some of the medication's side effects were bad, but he would take them back in a heartbeat rather than feel this way. So what if he couldn't perform as well in the bedroom? At least he could breathe.

This just didn't make sense. He had been doing so much better lately. It couldn't have *only* been because of the medicine, could it?

Suddenly, he remembered something, something which gave him hope as beads of sweat emerged along his hairline: he should still have some of that medicine the emergency room doctor prescribed—the one he was supposed to take if he felt panicky. Derek rushed to the medicine cabinet and sifted through a few bottles, his hands trembling.

There it was. Xanax. "Take 1-2 pills by mouth every 6 hours as needed for anxiety," the label read. With the chest pressure getting worse, Derek crossed his fingers, hoping there were at least two pills left. *Yes.* Exactly two pills remained. Tilting his head back, he emptied the bottle into his mouth and took a swig of water. But right before he swallowed, he noticed something which made him uneasy about taking both pills. "No refills available."

His fear instantly subsided, remembering that Dr. Nick had also given him a prescription for Xanax—one he hadn't filled, since he already had a bottle from the emergency room episode. Derek swallowed the pills. He would go to the pharmacy and get more this afternoon…along with a refill of Zoloft, which he obviously shouldn't have stopped. What a good excuse to put his Dodge Ram 3500 to use. It hadn't left its space in his four-car garage but a time or two since he bought it on a whim six months ago. But he definitely needed a vehicle with four-wheel drive today.

Derek grabbed a bottled water out of the refrigerator and held it to his forehead. It cooled his broiling body down some, but not enough. *Deep breath in, deep breath out.* He headed toward the back deck. Standing out in a blizzard should do the trick.

Sheltered beneath the eaves, he pulled his cell phone from the pocket of his flannel lounge pants. They were billowing out due to the frigid wind. He savored the cold air—mixed with a few snowflakes—blowing over him while he dialed the mom-and-pop pharmacy he and his family had used since moving to Charlotte many years ago. He wondered if Phillip, the owner and a friend of his Uncle Scott, had returned to work since having open heart surgery. Evidently not; no one had picked up the phone after four rings. Derek glanced at his watch. Why wasn't anyone there at 10:00 a.m.?

By the fifth ring, he suspected he knew the answer, and it felt as if a rug had been pulled out from under his feet. Sure enough, the voice on a recording confirmed his suspicion, twisting his stomach in knots. "Stanley Drug is closed in observance of New Year's Day."

⇥⇤

Derek paced the floor of their master bathroom. What was he going to do? It was four o'clock in the afternoon, and the Xanax had definitely worn off. Probably because he had psyched himself out, worrying he would have a panic attack without anything to help him.

This was crazy. Despite the rough start to the morning, it had actually been a fun day. The Xanax had knocked out his anxiety, so he—along with a little help from Aunt Jemima—had made pancakes and served Abby breakfast in bed. Then she insisted they play in the snow, so they made snow angels and built a fine, yet noseless snowman. That wasn't so good for his knee, but all was well after warming up by the fire with hot cocoa. It had been nice and relaxing to just lay around and watch college bowl games all day. If only Carolina, his alma mater, could've made that last-minute field goal to beat Clemson.

"D., are you okay? You've been in there a while." Abby knocked on the door.

Derek stalled, not sure what to say. "Well, I've been better...I don't think the snow cream agreed with me. Or maybe it was something I ate at the party last night. My stomach just hasn't felt right today." It wasn't a complete lie; his stomach really was uneasy.

"Sorry, babe. You want some Pepto-Bismol?"

"I may take some in a little while if it's no better. Don't worry, I'll be out in a few minutes."

"Okay."

After Abby walked away, he started pacing the floor again. Why was he so anxious? He had no reason to be this worked-up. Unfortunately, his body couldn't be tamed by rational thought.

Maybe he should call Dray. His teammate probably had some kind of medicine to help him. Having issues with his nerves, Dray occasionally had to pop a pill before taking the field. But what would he tell Abby? With the worsening road conditions, he would have to come up with a legitimate excuse to leave the house. And telling her the truth was definitely out of the question. She would kill him for stopping the Zoloft, especially before consulting his doctor.

An idea finally came. Derek opened the bathroom door and walked swiftly through the bedroom, avoiding eye contact with Abby as she lay in bed watching TV. "I'm going downstairs to get something to drink. You need anything?"

"Hmmm. Yeah, bring me a Zevia cola."

"Sure." He darted down the stairs, triggering the familiar ache in his knee. Oddly enough, he was relieved to feel the pain. Because it helped legitimize the plan he was about to carry out.

After pouring a glass of orange juice, Derek swallowed the two pills he'd gotten from the medicine cabinet upstairs. The Vicodin may be over a year past its expiration date, but two of them, along with a few shots of vodka, should knock out his nerves. He grabbed a bottle of Grey Goose from the back of the cabinet and began pouring it in his juice.

"What pills did you just take? And why are you drinking vodka?"

Startled by Abby's voice, he jerked his hand. The cool splash of liquor to his shirtless stomach made him jump backward. His heart raced out of control, a moment of silence lingering for what felt like an eternity. How had he not heard her? She must have been right on his heels as he came down the stairs.

"Why did you come down here?" Derek asked before concluding it hadn't been wise to dodge a question—actually, two questions—by asking one. But it was too late now.

"I decided to make some more snow cream," Abby said, frustration saturating her voice. "But that's irrelevant. You still haven't answered me."

Derek's pulse throbbed in his neck, heat flaring in his chest. The wave of warmth rose to his face, surely leaving a telltale flush on his cheeks. He had promised Abby he wouldn't drink anymore unless it was a special occasion. His nose and eyes began to sting. A breakdown had suddenly become inevitable. It's as if someone had flipped a switch, and he couldn't keep back the tears any more than he could hold back the waters of Niagara Falls.

What's going on with me?

Derek's hand went limp, and he let go of the bottle of liquor. He leaned onto the kitchen counter, burying his face in his hands as sobs hijacked his body.

"D.?" Abby's voice was faint, yet full of concern. After a few seconds of silence, she came up behind him and leaned her head down next to his, rubbing his back. "Babe, what's wrong? What is it?" She rubbed his back harder, demanding an answer.

Derek could barely breathe, much less say anything. He hadn't broken down like this since he was an 11-year-old boy, back when his Uncle Scott had to pry him away from Gram's coffin in the cemetery. With thoughts of that horrible day playing through his mind, another body-shaking wave of grief pulled him under, leaving him even more hungry for air. And, suddenly, as desperately as he needed his next breath, he needed to tell Abby everything.

He had to confess it all.

He couldn't keep living like this. *Wouldn't* keep living like this. His life was on a steep downward spiral. He was doomed if he took the Zoloft, and even more doomed if he didn't. And it was all because of the guilt he carried from keeping his dirty secret. Not anymore. He wouldn't be held hostage a moment longer.

Derek opened his mouth, ready to spill it all.

No, don't you dare! You'll lose everything!

Obeying the internal shout, he closed his mouth and clenched his teeth. Hunching over, with his elbows against the granite counter, he gathered fistfuls of hair, pulling just enough to feel the pain. The internal wrestling match was too violent not to externalize.

"D., tell me. What's going on?" Abby's voice rose an octave, her patience wearing thin.

"I can't," Derek whispered, then surrendered to another round of tears. He cursed the night he'd ever laid his filthy hands on Cassidy.

"Why not?" His wife's voice was a mixture of anger and confusion. And appropriate fear. "Yes you can! Tell me," she yelled, pounding her fist on the kitchen island.

Derek shook his head in defeat, rising to a standing position. After rubbing his eyes, he covered them, leaving only a small peephole between his fingers to steal a glimpse of Abby. His beautiful, frazzled wife.

The battle raging within was unlike anything he had ever experienced. Two piercing voices played tug-of-war inside him, one from his head, the other from his heart. Logic said he couldn't keep living with this secret, that it was killing him. But how could he survive without Abby? If he confessed the truth, there was a 99 percent chance he would have to learn to, because she had said on more than one occasion that she couldn't stay in a relationship if she were cheated on.

Yeah, he might end up dead if he tried to keep up this masquerade, but at least he would die with a loving wife by his side. At least he would go down as a good and faithful husband in her eyes. Instead of a despicable, deceptive, pond scum-of-a-human being.

"Tell me!" Abby's shrieking command confirmed he had crossed the point of no return. She was far from stupid. No simple explanation would appease her after witnessing this dramatic meltdown.

"Ab, I love you so much." Derek looked his wife in the eyes, his voice cracking. "You know that, right?"

"Of course."

The fear in her emerald eyes jabbed his heart like a knife. But he could almost taste the sweet relief awaiting him on the other side of the lies. It was a new year, and there was no better time to come clean, to rid himself of the burden which was sucking the life out of him.

Derek opened his mouth, and the earth stopped spinning. Thousands of memories, in no particular order, flashed across his mind: Abby, his princess in white, walking toward him down the aisle, her glossy-lipped smile more radiant than ever. The two of them dancing in perfect sync on the high school gym floor to Bruno Mars' "Just the Way You Are" after being crowned prom king and queen. His biggest fan jumping up and down in the stands, wildly waving blue pompoms in one hand, blowing him kisses with the other. Abby belly-laughing during their Cabo vacation when Burt the camel refused to cooperate, kneeling down on all fours, nearly throwing him to the ground. His college girl, making jogging pants and a t-shirt look glamorous, serving him bowls of homemade soup topped with hugs and kisses of TLC when he was recovering from knee surgery.

Derek couldn't look at her, couldn't bear to see the pain and tears about to flood her beautiful, innocent eyes. He was about to rip their hearts right out of their chests, but there was no backing out now. "Okay, then there's something"—he swallowed—"there's something I need to tell you."

CHAPTER SIXTEEN

Abby fishtailed onto Sarah's snow-covered driveway. She had almost spun out a few times on her mad dash to her sister's house, the roads more treacherous than she had ever seen.

So what if she had a wreck, though? Nothing could make things any worse than they already were. Actually, the thought of being in the hospital, unconscious and unaware of her emotional misery didn't sound so bad...especially if Derek had to forever live with the fact that he'd been responsible for it. He had practically tackled her to keep her from getting in the car, begging her not to drive. But she had shown him. For the first time ever, Abby slapped him across the face. Then she shoved him away and slammed the car door, thinking if Derek had purposefully planned to spill his dirty secret when she was incapable of leaving, he had another thing coming.

Abby knew she was on the brink of insanity. She usually avoided driving in a rainstorm, much less a snowstorm. Something inside her had completely snapped.

The scene which had just played out at the Holder home rivaled one from a soap opera. Derek was crying uncontrollably, but she felt no sympathy for him and his cheating heart. Anger burned so deep that she shattered a vase of roses against the dining room wall, and her throat was sore from all the yelling.

A coughing spell hit out of nowhere as she parked the car...probably because her throat was so irritated. Abby searched the passenger seat and floorboard, praying she had left a bottled water laying around somewhere. There, she found one under the passenger seat. But she would be lucky to get a single drop from it because it was frozen solid. *Just like my heart*, she thought, realizing she hadn't shed the first tear.

After beating the Aquafina bottle against her steering wheel a few times, she managed to stifle her cough with a sip of water. Hands trembling, Abby opened the car door. The 28-degree, snowy weather didn't intimidate her one bit, even in the lightweight cotton pajamas and pink satin slippers she had been lounging around in all day. As long as her shaky legs could hold her up, nothing would stand in the way of her getting to Sarah.

Balancing herself against the car door, Abby took a few tentative steps. "Ah! Ow! Ah!" A series of incomprehensible syllables escaped her quivering lips as millions of tiny needles pricked her feet and ankles. Slamming the door gave her the momentum to take a few giant leaps toward the front porch.

The snow was practically up to her knees, and several flakes began to accumulate on her PJs and hair. A few of them got past her eyelashes and nearly froze her eyeballs, making it even more impossible to see through the blizzard. Heading toward the front door, Abby nearly ran into a snowman her nieces must have built.

Had it really only been a few hours ago that she and Derek built a snowman? They were like two big kids, the way they had played together in the snow. Derek, looking mighty fine in his bulky navy jacket and Panthers toboggan, had started a snowball fight. After they finished the snowman, they decided to make snow angels. Derek had rolled over on top of her and kissed her, his unshaven, scruffy face rubbing against hers. Then they warmed up by the fire with her homemade hot cocoa, wrapped up together in a fleece throw.

Suddenly, the stinging sensations in her cold feet paled in comparison to a stabbing pain in her chest.

Those fresh memories were the last happy ones she and Derek would ever share. The thought caused Abby's body to go limp. She fell to the snow-covered ground, something *popping* in her right ankle. "Ow!" A clump of snow entered her open mouth and went up her nose. She spat and wiped her face, then grabbed her throbbing ankle and forced herself to wiggle it, attempting to work the pain out.

"Ab?" Sarah's voice called out, frantic.

Abby sighed a mixture of pain and relief. Help was on the way. Sarah would definitely have to help her get up and walk to the house, but her bleeding heart was what needed immediate attention. Physical pain she could handle, but how would she ever get past the excruciating pain inside?

How could she ever be put back together again when every fiber of her being had been shredded into a thousand tiny pieces?

She just wasn't enough for Derek. Not pretty enough, intriguing enough, *anything* enough. She was naive enough, though, to believe she ever stood a chance of being the only one for him forever. Derek was her everything, her every dream come true. Why couldn't he have looked at her the same way?

Sarah was running toward her, plowing through the snow at an impressive speed. But Abby thought about telling her to just forget it…that it was no use trying to save her. She was going to die regardless, so why not get it over with now?

Suffering through a few hours of subfreezing temperatures would be rough, but it sure looked better than the alternative of living another day—much less a lifetime—with this gaping hole in her heart.

CHAPTER SEVENTEEN

Nearing the end of an exit ramp, Abby pressed the brake pedal. Immediately, a flash of pain shot through her right ankle...her post-fall-in-the-snow, sprained ankle. With some Advil, it was nothing she couldn't bear, though. Nothing that would keep her from doing what she needed to do.

A quick glance at the clock told her she had been on the road for three hours now. Abby couldn't wait to plant her feet on the ground. More specifically, on the shore of Holden Beach. The sooner she got to her Aunt Rachel's beach house, away from everyone, the better.

She was more grateful than ever for her friends and family—especially for her parents, who had taken her in after Derek's confession—but now she was desperate for some peace and quiet. Maybe she could sort through her feelings with some time alone. Time spent lounging around in her pajamas, rocking in the comfy glider on her aunt's screened-in porch, listening to the crashing waves.

Abby hit the *seek* button on the radio. Was there no station around here without static?

There. Just as the stop light turned green, she found one. But when she recognized the song playing, she wished it, too, was drowned out by static. Because the melody pierced her soul, allowing a flood of memories to seep out. Suddenly, she was back in the gymnasium of Jay M. Robinson High School, her head against Derek's chest as they swayed back and forth to this song. It was the night they were crowned homecoming king and queen.

A car horn sounded. Abby's knuckles turned white as she tightened her grip on the steering wheel. She tried to let up on the brake to move ahead, but her foot wouldn't cooperate. The words of the song held her captive to the past, eliciting memories that burned her chest with emotions too raw to simply pass through the recesses of her mind.

Several cars veered off the ramp to pass her, one driver giving her the finger as he sped by.

Finally, the sting of tears pulled her from the frozen stupor. She could press the gas pedal...and more importantly, turn the radio off.

A meltdown was imminent, though.

Abby studied her surroundings. Passing a familiar, fancy-looking bank, she was pretty sure a shopping center would be coming up on her left. A place she could pull over and have a good cry.

⊷⊶

Enough was enough. Abby's late great-grandmother, Granny Snider, would say it was time for her to put on her *big girl panties*. After sobbing in the Food Lion parking lot for 15 minutes, she had to get back on the road. Her goal was to get to the beach before dark.

Abby flipped her visor mirror open to straighten herself up. She dreaded being seen, but she needed to stop at the Chick-fil-A across the street for a bathroom break and some tea. She gasped, frightened by the horrid image in the mirror. With her red, puffy eyes and disheveled hair, she looked nothing like the homecoming queen who had danced with Derek that cool October night ages ago.

Her heart sank. Where had the time gone?

What she wouldn't give to be 17 again, oblivious to the ways of the real world. To be gullible enough to believe there was a chance for happily-ever-after. Heck, she would give almost anything to relive just one pre-affair day with Derek. Just one more kiss, even.

Abby did the best she could to look presentable, then made a quick visit to Chick-fil-A. As she walked back to her car, alone in a strange town, she considered returning home. The loneliness was overwhelming. In less than four hours, she could be wrapped in Derek's arms, breathing in the scent of him. She could lie with her ear against his chest, listening to the thumping of his heart as he stroked her hair and kissed her head.

Derek was sorry for what he had done. The pitiful state she found him in earlier this morning had confirmed that. Abby hadn't expected him to be home when she stopped by the house to get a few things for the beach trip. He was supposed to be at practice. But, much to her surprise, he'd called out sick. He had to be in terrible shape; calling out of practice was simply unheard of for him, especially with his first playoff game coming up next week. Aside from his ACL surgery rehab during his junior year of college, Abby could recall only two missed practices in Derek's entire college and NFL careers combined. And one of those was when he was at death's door with food poisoning, in the emergency room getting IV fluids.

This morning she had found him in bed asleep with a half-empty bottle of vodka on the nightstand. She had done her best not to wake him…The last thing she wanted was to rehash their situation for the hundredth time. But Derek woke up when a suitcase fell from the top closet shelf, hitting the floor with a loud clatter. And *Bam!*, just like that, another torturing fiasco began.

Abby punched a straw through the lid of her sweet tea and took a few big gulps. The sick feeling in her stomach had stolen her appetite over the past several days, but she was thirstier than ever. Probably because she was dehydrated from crying so much.

Pulling up to the stop sign, she debated which way to turn. Couldn't she turn around and go back home to her husband, accepting his apology and going on about their lives? Couldn't she pretend none of this had happened?

No, she couldn't.

Resisting the strong magnetic pull toward Derek, she made a left turn, driving the opposite direction from where her heart longed to be. There was no other choice. Nothing would ever be the same again—not after *Cassidy*. Just hearing that name in her head sent shivers down her spine. Abby fought the urge to punch the steering wheel.

Enough! Unless she wanted to swing right back into the Food Lion parking lot, she had to get her mind off of this impossible situation. She thumbed through her purse, pulling her phone out to call Sarah. She reconsidered, though. Sarah was bound to be tired of dealing with all of her drama by now. Abby selected Carlee's name from her list of *favorite contacts* instead. Best friends since sixth grade, they had been through thick and thin. Thankfully, Carlee meant it when she said she would be there for her anytime, night or day.

It seemed backwards for her to be calling Carlee about her problems, though. Lately, her friend had been the one leaning on her. The tragic death of Carlee's cousin a few months ago had nearly done her in. Now their roles were reversed.

The conversation with her best friend helped pass the miles, but it was time to bring the phone call to a close. A few landmarks were becoming familiar, so her full attention needed to be on driving. It had been a long while since she had traveled this road. Would she remember where to turn?

Abby decided not to rely on her horrible sense of direction; she programmed the address in her GPS. According to it, in approximately thirteen minutes she would be planting her feet in the sand, breathing in the salty air. She was smiling for the first time she could recall in days.

Was that the miniature golf course coming up? Yep. Although the sign looked a little different, the name was the same: Treasure Island Miniature Golf. Passing the colorful, jumbo octopus and sea horse statues on the green turf, she thought about the good times her family had shared there.

Taking in the familiar scenery was bittersweet. The cherished memories of carefree, childhood vacations collided head-on with the realities she now faced. Remembering lazy summer days on the beach with family, followed by delicious evenings of ice cream and mini-golf, only magnified the grief she now felt as two of the most important men in her life slipped away...one from infidelity, the other by cancer.

Abby hated thinking the worst about her Daddy's situation, but maybe she should. Maybe she needed to prepare herself for losing him too. After all, life was cruel.

Tears blurred her vision as she made her way onto the bridge which towered over the Intracoastal Waterway, the one connecting the mainland with the island. She blinked them away so she could see straight. One wrong turn of the wheel and she could be falling over the edge.

Considering her bleak future, that might not be such a bad thing, though.

For the first time, Abby understood how people could be desperate enough to end their lives. She wondered if anyone had ever jumped from this bridge, her toes curling at the thought of it. She would never do anything that drastic, but somehow she needed to escape.

How was she supposed to move on, still so in love with a man who had betrayed her? Where was God? Hadn't her dad's cancer diagnosis been enough for Him to dish out on her? Why did life have to be so hard? So unfair?

One week of contemplating by the beach would be nice, but Abby feared she wouldn't have answers to these questions if she had a thousand lonely years to ponder them.

CHAPTER EIGHTEEN

Derek held the phone at a distance to avoid losing a few decibels of hearing. Coach Ryan was definitely losing his cool. "Yeah, well, that's what you said yesterday," Coach yelled in response to Derek's promise to return to practice tomorrow.

He clenched his teeth. He shouldn't have called out of the last two practices, pretending to have the flu. Everyone knew he was lying; his refusal to be evaluated by a team doctor was a dead giveaway.

"If you don't show up tomorrow or check in with Dr. Nick or Saunders, there's gonna be some major consequences, ya hear? Lord knows, we need you next game, but we got rules, ya know?"

"Okay, okay. Just calm down. I said I'll be there. Whatever wrath you wanna dish out tomorrow is fine, but I gotta go because my head's killing me. Bye." Derek hung up the phone, his heart nearly pounding through his chest.

His life was falling apart. If he didn't get his act together soon, he may just lose his wife *and* his job...all in the same week. Derek laced up his tennis shoes. He was going for a run. A long one. Maybe it would burn off some of his anxiety. No matter what, he wasn't taking another Xanax.

Ever since he filled the prescription the day after Abby left, he had been taking it—along with a few shots of alcohol—to knock himself out of his misery. What choice did he have until the Zoloft got back in his system? The panic attacks were so bad he had to knock himself out in order to avoid going back to the emergency room. After his conversation with Coach, though, he knew he had to find another way to cope. If putting his feet to the pavement didn't stave off an anxiety attack, he would just have to call 911 or get a friend to drive him to the hospital. That way, he could get some relief without risking his job.

If only Aunt Diana still lived close by. Now that Abby was gone, she was his go-to person. But Derek hadn't even told her what was going on...partly because she lived four hours away and he didn't want to burden her, and partly because he just didn't want to face the truth. Telling someone would make it official: he had ruined his life.

He never should've told on himself. Coming clean was way overrated. His conscience may have always haunted him, even after the Zoloft kicked back in, but at least Abby would still love him. Derek swallowed the lump in his throat. Other than right after Gram died, he had never felt so alone in all of his life.

If he had another panic attack tonight, who would he call? His mother- and father-in-law probably hated his guts. And he sure didn't want to call Jeffrey, his cousin-slash-brother. They hadn't been close since his senior year of college. Derek wished they were still close. But, ever since he got drafted by the Panthers, his cousin had placed an impenetrable wall between them. Only one year apart in age, they had always been competitive. It was a shame, the way the two of them had grown apart. But what could he do about it? After many failed attempts to reach out and draw Jeffrey back in, he had all but given up hope. He called him about once a month, but their conversations never got past the superficial things.

Derek walked outside, locking the door behind him. At first, the cold air was a shock to his system—and his touchy knee—but everything was fine once he settled into a comfortable rhythm.

Was the weather ever going to warm up? This winter had been much more intense than usual, breaking all kinds of records. There was still a lot of snow lying around from the New Year's Day blizzard, since the daytime highs hadn't climbed much past freezing. Thank goodness the roads were clear.

Returning to his contemplations about this evening, he figured he would call Colton if he got into a bind. Derek would have a lot of explaining to do, though, beginning with why he had missed practice the last two days. His stomach suddenly twisted. Who was he kidding? He had no choice but to come clean about what was really going on. He couldn't fake a positive flu test; heck, he didn't even have a runny nose or cough.

What he wouldn't give to be able to confide in Colton and receive the support and understanding any typical best friend would offer. Having a teammate for a best friend wasn't exactly ideal. Yeah, Colton cared about him and his personal life, but he cared more about winning the game.

Worst-case scenario, Derek would call Timothy, an outspoken Christian teammate. He had tried to keep the guy at arm's length, but Timothy seemed to see straight through him, always making a point to say he was there for him if he ever needed to talk. If he thought the guy would give any advice which didn't involve God or prayer, he may have taken him up on his offer.

Derek built up speed, the weight of his anxiety lightening with each stride. With his heart pumping harder and a surge of adrenaline coursing through his veins, he felt capable of surviving for the first time since Abby left.

Yes, he was going to make it.

Because, no matter how bad things were in his personal life, his professional life held much promise...as long as he got back in the game.

The Panthers' 14-2 record was the best in the NFC. They had home-field advantage for the playoffs, plus a first round bye this coming weekend. So, if he and Colton— the best quarterback in the league—and several other key players on the team played their best for just three more games, there was no reason why they couldn't be Super Bowl champs come February.

Between the cold air tingling his lungs and the promising potential in his career, a refreshing boost of confidence swelled in his chest. There were still some things worth living and fighting for. Winning the Super Bowl was his biggest dream ever, a goal he had aimed for his entire life. And now it was actually within reach.

Just as Venus and Jupiter were now visible in the dusk sky, his dream was coming into focus.

With nightfall approaching, Derek slowed to a steady jog, rounding the corner which led to his house. At the thought of walking into an empty home, a hollowness in his chest threatened to suck him back into a black hole of despair. *No!* Even though the shout was audible only in his head, it was loud. It was time to man up and stop this pity party. He had to get back in the game. To push forward and succeed.

A good way to start would be by picking up some lettuce wraps and Sichuan Chili-Garlic Chicken from P.F. Chang's for dinner. Then he would melt away the tension in his muscles and the ache in his knee by soaking in the hot tub under a clear night sky. It should be a perfect night for stargazing, a favorite hobby since childhood. He and Jeffrey used to study the night sky with their telescope for hours.

By the looks of it, he would get a good view of the Winter Hexagon tonight: the big circle of stars including Betelgeuse, Capella, and Sirius. And Derek would unload all his wishes upon them. Wishes that were more likely than ever to come true. With the exception of one.

A big one.

But maybe, just maybe, if all his other dreams came true—if the Panthers won the Super Bowl and Derek was named MVP—then he would also receive his ultimate wish: the return of the dark-haired, green-eyed angel who had flown away with his heart.

CHAPTER NINETEEN

"How are you doing today, sweetie?" Wanda, her Aunt Rachel's neighbor at the beach, stood on her porch, waving at Abby as she walked along the shore. The woman gestured for Abby to come, her multicolored house-coat flapping around in the January wind.

"Better than yesterday, thanks." She forced a smile. Although the statement was true, she wasn't doing so well. An amazing dream last night left her sobbing in the reality of the morning light, desperately longing to fall back asleep and pick up where she and Derek had left off…kissing on the shore beneath a full moon. Now, here she stood on the beach, being assaulted by a frigid wind that chilled her to the bone. Abby blew on her frozen hands, wishing she had remembered to pack her gloves.

"Well, I guess that's better than being *worse* than yesterday." Wanda laughed the words, yet her eyes were full of concern. "Whew, it's too cold to be out here. I just brewed a pot of coffee, so come on in." Wanda held the screen door open with her left hand and pointed the half-empty mug of coffee in her right hand toward the kitchen table.

"Okay, thanks. It does smell good."

"It *is* good," Wanda exclaimed. "It's some kind of specialty roast from Colombia that Kelly sent. Please overlook my messy house. And my appearance"—Wanda patted the pink rollers on top of her head—"I know I'm a sight for sore eyes," she laughed.

"No worries," Abby said, chuckling as she gave the high-strung woman a head to toe once-over. She was a character, to say the least. Sort of like a younger version of the old lady she often saw on funny birthday cards. Studying the deep lines on Wanda's face, she concluded time hadn't been too good to her over the years…since those good old days when her daughter, Kelly, and Abby were summertime beach buddies.

"Thanks for inviting me in." She let go of the screen door and followed Wanda to the table, appreciating the warm air to her face. Two gray cats scurried out of the room as she pulled a chair out and sat down. A sneeze was coming. With the cats and the thick, musty air in the house, it was inevitable.

"Bless you, sweetie!"

"Thanks." She blew her nose, wishing Wanda didn't have cats. Abby enjoyed their talk the other day out on Wanda's porch, but her allergies wouldn't permit her to stay inside very long.

"Here you are, doll baby." Wanda handed her a Virginia Tech Hokies mug filled with coffee. "Cream and sugar's right there on the table."

"Thanks."

"So, did you write that verse down and post it on the mirror like I told you to?" Wanda asked, stirring her coffee. She was referring to a favorite Scripture she had shared a few days ago.

"Yeah." Abby had followed the woman's advice, but it hadn't helped. She didn't have much confidence in God. He had done nothing but let her down.

"And you memorized it?"

Abby nodded her head. "Romans 8:18 says, 'I consider that our present sufferings are not worth comparing with the glory that will be revealed in us.'"

"That's my girl!" Wanda patted her hand, her face beaming.

She forced a smile, bringing the steaming mug of delicious-smelling coffee to her lips. "Mmmm. This is excellent." Abby was hoping to change the subject, but the coffee really was some of the best she had ever tasted. It was rich and bold with a hint of sweetness.

"Isn't it, though? Kelly sent it in her box of Christmas goodies. Supposedly, it's straight from the coffee plantation right up the road from where they live."

Wanda's daughter and son-in-law were missionaries in Colombia. Abby stared at a picture of the two of them hanging on the paneled wall. They looked so happy and in love. She mentally took back the snide remark she made to her Aunt Rachel when she heard they had gotten married straight out of high school. Perhaps they weren't too young for marriage, after all.

"You know, sweetie, you can have what Kelly and Daniel share one day...if you pray and wait on God."

Abby squirmed under Wanda's lengthy stare, crossing her legs just to give herself something to do. How did the woman know exactly what she was thinking...wishing?

"God hates divorce," Wanda said, breaking the awkward silence. "But in your case, since your husband was unfaithful, He will look past it if you can't find it in yourself to stay. Especially since Derek isn't what the Bible calls, 'equally yoked'...or in other words, since he isn't a Christian."

Abby took in a deep breath as Wanda paused, scratching her head. Things were getting pretty deep.

"Marriage is hard enough for two Christians," the woman continued in her deep, raspy voice. "That's why Don stayed in D.C. this month. We just need little breaks from each other from time to time. We can get on each other's last nerve. Imagine that," Wanda laughed.

Abby vaguely remembered Don, Kelly's dad. He managed a company in D.C. where they permanently resided, so he was rarely able to vacation at the beach with Wanda and the kids during the summer.

Abby nodded her head, taking in Wanda's words. It would be nice to share her life with a Christian man, a man like her brother-in-law. A religious man would probably be less likely to cheat on her. "Well, I can't see myself with anyone else for a long time," she said, willing herself to push past her rising grief. "But when—or if—I move on, it will probably be with a religious man. If I can find one."

For some reason, tears were welling in Wanda's light brown eyes. "Yeah, there's fewer and fewer Christian men out there these days." She blotted her eyes. "I sure do wish Mark was still here"—her voice broke—"because y'all would be perfect for each other, I just know it."

Abby bit her lip, wondering how to respond. Mark, Wanda's oldest son, was killed on 9/11 while working in the Navy Command Center at the Pentagon. The fact that he would be a lot older than her, and likely married, if he were still alive was irrelevant and unnecessary to point out. Deciding there were no words to convey the sympathy in her heart, she simply rubbed the grieving woman's hand.

"I'm sorry," Wanda said, burying her face in her hands. "I haven't had a good cry in a while, so I guess it's overdue." Her unsteady voice was muffled behind her hands.

"It's okay." It clearly was okay, and she couldn't blame her for crying. But this emotional outburst put her in an awkward spot. Should she get up and hug the poor woman? Or let her cry it out?

Wanda finally looked up. Her eyes were full of unshed tears, but she was composed. "You know, God has brought good out of Mark's death, though. If it weren't for losing him, I don't think I would've completely surrendered my life to Christ." She paused to wipe her eyes and nose before continuing. "Before he died, I went to church most Sundays and knew *about* God, but I didn't really *know* Him."

Abby had to look away as she replayed that profound statement in her mind.

Wanda coughed and cleared her throat. "Sweetie, I'm going to ask you a personal question…How often do you read God's Word?"

Abby shifted in her seat, stalling. "Oh, every now and then." That was a lie; she hadn't opened her Bible in years. She swallowed and cleared her throat. "Not a whole, whole lot—I guess I prefer devotionals. They're easier to follow, and I get more out of them." That wasn't entirely false. Every now and then she really did read a devotional from a pretty book someone had given her as a graduation gift.

"No, honey, you can't get more out of any other book. That's God's love letter," Wanda said, tapping her index finger on a worn leather Bible at the center of the table. "My goodness, what woman doesn't want to read a love letter?" She chuckled, but her underlying tone was as serious as a heart attack. "You know, darling, God loves you more than you can imagine."

Heat rushed to Abby's cheeks. How could that be? How could God love her so much, yet dump so much on her?

Her stomach sank to the floor. She supposed she deserved to be punished for all the things she had done. For having sex before marriage. Partying too much. Cutting off her family when they didn't support her lifestyle. Never reading her Bible.

"I didn't mean to offend you, sweetie"—Wanda patted her hand—"or to come across as judgmental. It's just that Christianity is not a *religion*; it's a relationship. A relationship with Jesus." Wanda smiled from ear to ear as she spoke His name. "And how can we have a relationship with somebody if we don't get to know them? You see, this Book is the key to knowing Him. And boy, don't you want to get to know the One who loves you enough to die for you? The One who took the punishment for your sins so you can have a relationship with the holy, amazing God of the universe?" She practically shouted the words, raising a hand in the air.

Abby nodded her head, surprised by the stirring she felt within. Blinking back tears, she stared at the floor.

The touch of Wanda's hand against her back startled her. "Sweetie," the caring woman said softly, leaning toward her and placing her arm across Abby's shoulders. "Perhaps God has allowed this heartache in your life so you'll get to know Him better...so your relationship with Christ will be your utmost treasure."

There was no use in trying to stop the tears; something inside Abby *clicked*, and she came head-to-head with the reality that Derek had been her god. She had idolized and worshipped him instead of the One true God. Waves of regret washed over her.

"Excuse me a minute, I need to use the bathroom. I'll be right back," Wanda said, scooting past her. She must have sensed her need to be alone. Alone with God.

I'm so sorry, God. Please forgive me. More tears escaped Abby's eyes, even though they were closed. She rested her head in her hands, her elbows on the kitchen table.

God, I don't know where to start. I guess I've looked at You like some kind of genie, not Someone to have a relationship with. I sure haven't made it a priority to know You. I'm sorry for questioning Your existence and Your goodness. I guess I've just been selfish and bitter, thinking life should somehow be perfect. Please take over my life...take the wheel. Abby heard the chorus of Carrie Underwood's "Jesus, Take The Wheel" in her mind, and for the first time, she could truly relate with the words of the song.

I'm sorry for not putting You first. You're definitely worthy of being first...You're the One who gave me this life to begin with. Thank You for dying on the cross for all of my mistakes. Please help me, Lord. Please fix this mess I'm in and show me what You want me to do. I want a real relationship with You. I want to read Your "love letter." Please help me get to know You. Thank You, Lord. Amen.

An unexplainable calmness began to spread over her, from her head to her toes. Goosebumps pricked Abby's arms and legs. God was definitely here. His presence was practically tangible, more real than anything she had ever seen with her eyes or touched with her hands. Like a newborn baby, she was being swaddled in a Father's arms, the warmth of His love and grace rocking her regrets away, soothing her pain and fears.

Something captured Abby's attention while she scanned the room, soaking in all the details of this pivotal moment. It was a handwritten Bible verse on Wanda's refrigerator, posted right beside the verse from Romans which she had recited a few minutes ago. After reading it, happy tears flooded her eyes. The message was straight from God's heart to hers, meant for her to see at this exact moment. She read the verse again:

And the God of all grace, who called you to his eternal glory in Christ, after you have suffered a little while, will himself restore you and make you strong, firm and steadfast (1 Peter 5:10).

The "after you have suffered a little while" portion of the verse didn't appeal to her, of course, but the promise which followed completely cancelled out the negative part. Abby breathed out slow and steady, allowing the words to wash over her and penetrate deep inside her soul. Through her suffering, God was calling her to Him.

Joy swelled in her chest as she realized that, with God, she had an eternity of happiness to look forward to. Even without Derek in her life. The verse Wanda asked her to post on the mirror said that her heartaches weren't worth comparing to the glory awaiting her.

Tears streamed down Abby's cheeks.

Hearing footsteps down the hall, she sat up straight and wiped her eyes. Wanda shuffled around the corner, breathing heavily. She was carrying a yellow paperback book. "Here, I want you to have this," she said, handing the book to her. "I saw this on my nightstand and thought you may get something from it. My niece's friend wrote it, and she talks a little about her divorce in there."

Wisdom From Wilbur: How My Dog Has Brought Me Closer to God. The title and cover brought a smile to Abby's face, instantly lightening the moment. "Oh my gosh! Sarah has a dog that looks exactly like this," she said, referring to the cute black and tan dachshund on the front cover of the book. She laughed, and a few remaining tears spilled from her eyes. "We used to have a brown one when I was little. You may remember him...Toby?"

"Vaguely. I don't remember any of them specifically, but I know your family always had dogs. That's why I felt led to give the book to you when I noticed it in my room. Now, wait a minute," Wanda smirked, scratching her head. "I do remember one of your dogs: that yellow retriever. Sampson, right?"

"Yeah, Sampson. He was a mess." She laughed, remembering the goofy dog from her childhood.

"Yeah, he's the one who chewed up all my flip-flops out there," Wanda chuckled, pointing toward the porch. Abby scooted forward as she made her way back to her chair. Wanda sat down, then immediately stood back up. "Oh, I almost forgot"—she gasped—"I was gonna get some more coffee. You want more?"

"No, thank you." She smiled, thinking the last thing the woman needed was more caffeine. "But thanks for the book."

"Oh, you're welcome," Wanda said with a nonchalant wave of the hand, pouring coffee with the other. "But, first and foremost, read God's Word. I recommend—"

Abby interrupted her sentence with three consecutive sneezes.

"God bless you! You coming down with a cold?"

Abby shook her head, blowing her nose. "No, I don't think so. I'm just allergic to cats."

"Oh, I'm sorry, hon. Unfortunate for you, I'm the crazy cat lady," Wanda said, laughing. "Anyways…as I was saying, I recommend starting in the Gospel of John."

"My dad's name is John, you know, so I'm sure that's good advice," Abby said, wondering how her Daddy was doing. She hadn't talked to him or her mom today. "I think I'll go back and start reading it now," she said, wanting a legitimate excuse to head for the door.

She had enjoyed visiting with Wanda and was beyond grateful for the revelations the godly woman had inspired, but it was time to leave. Not only because of her sensitivity to cats, but because she had a date. And, with the possible exception of Ben and Jerry's, Abby's date wasn't with a man.

It was with *The Man*. The One and only Man who was loving and loyal enough to die for her...the One who had never been unfaithful to her, even though she had certainly been unfaithful to Him.

CHAPTER TWENTY

S arah couldn't wipe the smile from her face, crawling into bed beside her husband Zack. After the girls fell asleep, she had an amazing phone conversation with Abby. She couldn't wait another second to tell her husband the good news. What had started out as a typical, hectic day had ended like a fairytale.

"Well, I just got off the phone with Ab." She slid beneath the navy flannel sheet and goose down comforter, tapping Zack's arm for his full attention. He was reading his Bible, just as he did most nights before bed.

"And?" He rested the brown leather Bible on his lap and took off his reading glasses, looking at her through inquisitive, gray-blue eyes.

"She's all-in!" Sarah clapped her hands, needing to release some of the overwhelming excitement flooding her soul. "She gave her heart to Jesus. Today at the beach."

"Really?" Zack's face lit up like a Christmas tree.

Knowing he was just as excited as she was meant the world to her—to be blessed with a Christian husband who had consistently prayed hand-in-hand with her for this monumental breakthrough.

"Abby said that Wanda—you know, the lady who has the house beside Aunt Rachel's at the beach?" Zack nodded, so she continued. "Well, Wanda has reached out to her this week, and she said some things this morning which really made an impact on Ab...things that helped her see why her life's in shambles. Abby says it's because Derek has been the center of her world, not God."

"Whoa, that's big." Zack's eyes were wide, begging for more details.

"I know. She said she's realized that she's never had a real relationship with God...that she's been too caught up in herself and Derek to even want to know Him. She said she had even started doubting His existence because of Daddy's situation. Mostly, though, I think she was just angry and bitter toward God, especially since all this with Derek happened. Anyway, Ab claims to see things in a new light now. She regrets a lot of things, and she says she wants to start over with her life."

"Wow!" Zack repositioned himself, sitting up straighter against his pillow. "Praise God, the light switch has finally flipped on. Looks like Derek's cheating is the best thing that's ever happened to her."

"Yeah, it's a blessing in disguise," Sarah said, happy tears filling her eyes. "Abby says she wants to put God first in her life now, that she wants to really get to know Him through His Word. It's just incredible, almost too good to be true."

Zack nodded his head, staring at nothing in particular. "Yeah, it's amazing. Sounds like we can mark this prayer off as answered." He flashed his crooked smile, the one that had taken her breath a thousand times. "Now, if only Derek would come to his senses."

Sarah rubbed her husband's freckled arm, sorting through her feelings toward her celebrity brother-in-law. She decided she didn't want to spoil this wonderful moment by thinking of the man who had led her Sissy away from God...and then cheated on her. "Yeah, well, I'm just thankful Ab has finally seen the light. And now that she has, she doesn't need to get wrapped up with Derek again. He's committed adultery, so the Lord has set her free of that man. You know I love him, but that doesn't mean I have to like him."

"That may be true, hon, but we at least need to keep praying for him."

"I know, but let's not talk about him right now. I want to finish telling you about Abby. She wants to start coming to church with us, to get involved...the whole nine yards."

"Awesome." Zack's voice was chipper, but his eyes were getting heavy. "I can't wait to talk to her. This surely puts a positive spin on this crazy day, right?"

"No doubt. Thank You, Lord!" Sarah thought back over the stressful events of their day. A disgruntled customer accused one of Zack's lead mechanics at the shop of charging for work that wasn't done on his pickup truck. And she had had a hectic day getting Lexi to the doctor, resolving temper tantrums, and cleaning up spills and messes galore. But, somehow, God had wrapped this day up in a beautiful, sparkly package. In the midst of what seemed to be an ordinary, demanding day, her Heavenly Father had been working behind the scenes, answering the most desperate prayer of her heart.

Sarah leaned against her husband's chest, cherishing him and the way he held her, resting his chin on her forehead. Their lips came together in a butterfly kiss, both of them intuitively knowing it was nothing more than a simple goodnight kiss.

"Any issues, babe?" Sarah smirked, asking the question she and Zack asked one another every night before bed. Taking the advice of some seasoned couples and God's Word, they had agreed early on in their marriage to never go to bed angry. Next month they would celebrate their tenth wedding anniversary. Over the years, their ritual of asking that question had resulted in a few late nights of heated discussion, but she was 100 percent sure they were safe tonight.

"Nope. You?" Zack smiled, tapping her nose with his finger.

"No, thanks be to God. Good night, sweetie. Love you."

"Love you too. Good night."

Sarah kissed her husband once more before switching off her lamp. Yes, it was a good night. Actually, an unbelievably amazing night. She adjusted her pillow, getting situated comfortably on her right side. With all the excitement coursing through her veins, it was going to be next to impossible to fall asleep. For the first time in many years, she wasn't the least bit concerned about her Sissy's soul. Because she had confessed her sins, asked for God's forgiveness, and invited the risen Savior into the very center of her heart.

It was amazing how God worked, how He answered prayers and brought about His will using people like Wanda Patterson—a woman Sarah only remembered for being the coffee-crazed mom of their childhood beach friends. If God could orchestrate such as that for Abby, she knew He could work out everything weighing heavy on her mind: Their finances. Her parenting ability. Lexi's recurring strep throat. And even her dad's situation, which appeared to be getting worse by the day.

Thank You, Lord, for all You've done today…for Your miraculous intervention in Sissy's life. Also, for all You're doing in my life. I know You're at work behind the scenes, and You can bring forth Your good and perfect plans, even through the chaos. Jesus, I don't know what tomorrow will bring, but I know You hold all our tomorrows. And You are faithful, showing me more and more that I can trust You in all things. Thank You, Father. I love You. Amen.

CHAPTER TWENTY-ONE

Abby heard her name, but she didn't know who had said it, or why. She was a fish out of water, surrounded by a sea of unfamiliar faces at the Super Bowl party that her new church friend, Julie, was hosting. After noticing Julie's 16-year-old brother, Daren, wiping cheese dip from his chin and shirt collar, Abby figured it out: he had complimented her cheese dip.

"Oh, thanks." She smiled, trying to act normal…like your average sports fan getting ready to watch the Super Bowl with a group of friends. Like someone who simply knew the names and jersey numbers of the popular players, and perhaps a few stats.

She was sure most everyone there knew she was the cheated-on wife of Derek Holder, the star football player of the team they were pulling for. But, thankfully, they had been respectful—or more likely, uncomfortable—enough not to ask any questions.

Abby exhaled sharply, her skin prickling at every nerve ending. She needed to be at home in bed with her door locked. Maybe watching a movie or reading a book…with a small glass of wine. Actually, where she *really* should be is at MetLife Stadium, getting ready to watch her husband play in the Super Bowl.

Tears stung her eyes, but she blinked them back before anyone could see. What in the world was she doing here? This was definitely the last place she needed to be, getting ready to watch Derek's lifelong dream unfold and then spew like Old Faithful in front of a group of strangers.

Abby knew she shouldn't have given in to her mom and sister, who had practically insisted that she attend her Sunday School class's Super Bowl party in order to "cultivate" and "nurture" new friendships. Sometimes the wordy, former English teacher in Sarah thought she could persuade people to see things her way with just a few eloquent words. Abby smirked.

Where was Sarah, anyway? She and Zack were going to drop the girls off with his parents and come straight here.

"Hey, Caleb—" Daren yelled out in the direction of the kitchen. Sitting right beside him, Abby had to cover her ears to keep from losing her hearing. He continued yelling with a mouthful of food. "It's about to start. Star-Spangled Banner's on."

The angelic voice of Brooklyn Evans, the American Idol winner-turned celebrity, filled the room. After the fireworks exploded and the fighter jets zoomed over the American flag-covered football field, the camera operator captured an image which nearly paralyzed her: Derek.

Taking up the entire screen.

She knew seeing him tonight was going to be hard, but nothing could've prepared her for this. Abby melted into a puddle of wax as she stared at Derek in his blue and black uniform, his right hand over his chest. Breathing out the cold New Jersey air, plumes of smoke escaped his lips...lips that had touched hers every day for over six years. His lean, muscular physique, along with the impassioned look in his blue eyes, left her breathless. Completely helpless.

"Whoa! Derek doesn't usually look that intense, does he, Ab?" Hannah, the 18-year-old preacher's daughter, nudged her.

Abby cringed, annoyed enough by the girl's question, let alone the fact that she had called her *Ab*, a nickname reserved for Derek and close family and friends. She didn't respond, hoping Hannah would get the hint and leave her alone the rest of the evening. She had pegged the girl as nosy and obnoxious the very first time she met her. That was a few months ago when Hannah had tagged along with her father, Pastor Sam, on a visit to see her dad after a chemo treatment.

"I think I'm going to grab a bite to eat." Abby knew by the feeling in her stomach that she wouldn't be able to swallow a bite, but she had to get away from the television. And Hannah.

"Well, I'm going back for seconds. I want some more of your cheese dip," Julie said, smiling and rubbing her belly. Her compliment was genuine, but Abby knew the real reason she was following her to the kitchen. It was because she was worried about her.

She thanked God every single day for the blessing of her new friend. They had met at church only a few weeks ago, but it's like they had known each other for years. Being dumped two weeks prior to her wedding—because of another woman—Julie was someone who truly understood heartbreak.

Abby stopped short of the kitchen, drawing in a quick breath. Then holding it. She surely hadn't seen this one coming: a drop-dead gorgeous man standing by the counter. He was tall, and his hair and eyes were dark. And dreamy. He blushed when their eyes met. Where had she seen him before?

"Have you ever met Luke?" Julie asked.

"He looks familiar, but I don't think so." Abby looked the guy in the eyes again, but it didn't last long. Fire burning her cheeks, she turned toward Julie, hoping he wouldn't notice.

"Well, this is Luke. And Luke, this is Abby." Julie waved her hand in the air, supplementing the introduction with gestures. "Luke is my cousin. You've probably seen him at church. He's on the praise team, plays the sax."

Yes, that's where she had seen him. "Yeah. Nice to meet you."

Julie grinned at her with a knowing expression, making it obvious she was trying to play matchmaker. Then she turned toward Luke, casually placing her hand on his muscular arm. "Abby is my amazing new friend. She's Sarah's sister."

The guy's mesmerizing eyes flashed with recognition. "Oh yeah, I can see some resemblance there," he said, extending his hand. "Nice to meet you too." His nervous smile made her think he felt the same spark of electricity in their handshake as she did...an attraction which had taken her by surprise. A surprise that had conveniently taken her mind off of the man on the big screen in the next room.

⊶ ⊷

Abby felt awkward and a tad giddy as she and Luke sat down next to each other on Julie's beige leather sofa, bumping legs as they settled in. She slid to her left to make sure they didn't continue to touch. Catching a whiff of his woodsy cologne evoked more high school-like feelings she felt a bit guilty for having.

It was bizarre how she and Luke seemed to have known each other forever. After only a few minutes of easy conversation, Abby knew many impressive facts about him. He was a doctor who attended East Carolina University for undergrad, then medical school at Duke...a hard-to-swallow fact for a rival Carolina Tar Heel like herself. Luke was in his first year of residency at Charlotte's Levine Children's Hospital, on his way to becoming a pediatrician. He and his twin brother were born and raised in Newport Beach, California, and their dad's job brought them to North Carolina when they were 14 years old. Luke's favorite food is pizza. His favorite Bible verse is Philippians 4:13. And he hasn't dated anyone since the end of a long-term relationship two years ago.

Luke knew a lot about her as well, thanks to Julie's generous contribution of information.

A burst of laughter suddenly filled the room, interrupting Abby's thoughts. She looked up to catch the end of a

Budweiser commercial which featured a talking Clydesdale horse. She forced a smile to fit in, but a memory from last year's Super Bowl kicked her in the gut. It was about a week before her dad's cancer diagnosis, right before their trip to Barbados. She and Derek, along with several teammates and friends, were watching the big game at Colton's house. After seeing a Budweiser commercial with a Clydesdale and his cute puppy friend, she and Derek had talked about getting a puppy. But that had never panned out.

"AH-MAZE-ING!" The loud, obnoxious sound of Hannah's voice startled her. There was a sudden explosion of cheers and high fives across the room. Thanks to instant replay, Abby could see what all the commotion was about. Derek had caught a pass and run the football halfway down the field, dodging two opponents to score a touchdown.

Time stood still. Abby couldn't breathe, engulfed by a tidal wave of mixed emotions. Was she happy and proud, or bitter and resentful? If it weren't for Derek's amazing talent and athletic ability, he wouldn't have made it to the pros, and they would be living some sort of normal life. And he never would've met that home-wrecking tramp.

She was definitely more resentful than happy.

"Whoo-hoo!" Hannah continued to celebrate the touchdown. "Girl, you're crazy for not taking him back," she exclaimed, looking directly at her. "That man is F-I-N-E, fine!" She jerked her head back and forth rhythmically with each syllable.

Abby was dumbfounded. Speechless. Julie glanced at her, then at Hannah. "Hannah, please," Julie said, shaking her head.

"Well, it's true." The girl obviously didn't regret her tasteless comment before throwing another dagger right where it hurt. "I mean, why not forgive the poor guy? I mean, seriously, there's no way you can do better than *that!*" Hannah looked at her, then spun around dramatically, pointing at the television.

Unable to make a sound, Abby caught Luke's compassionate brown eyes. Actually, she captured every single eye in the room. Heat rushed to her face. She had to say something, but what? This was a church event, after all. She had to bite her tongue.

"Well—" Abby sprang to her feet, her frustration over what to say, or not to say, growing exponentially with each passing second. "Unfortunately, Hannah, it's not quite that simple." The anger and sarcasm in her voice were unmistakable. Everything in her wanted to punch the girl's smug face, but she settled for rolling her eyes instead. "Excuse me," she huffed, plowing past the drama queen.

Making her way past the crowd of glaring eyes, she heard Luke's voice. "Hannah, that was uncalled for!"

Abby wanted to hear more, to see what else the handsome doctor might do or say to defend her. But she slammed the bathroom door in fury, muffling out the voices down the hall.

"Are you okay? Need to talk?" Julie knocked on the bathroom door while Abby sat on a rug beneath the bathroom sink, fuming.

No, I'm not okay. "I'll be alright. Just give me a minute."

"Okay, can I come in? You want to talk?" Julie asked.

"No, not now. I just need to be alone for a minute." For the first time, it dawned on her that she may need to get out of the bathroom. What if someone needed to use it?

"Okay, text me if you need me." The kind nonchalantness in her friend's voice put Abby's mind at ease. She could take some more time to compose herself.

Thinking of Hannah's tasteless remarks, a surge of heat rushed through her veins. How was she ever going to show her face again? She figured Hannah would annoy her this evening, but she had no idea the brat would drag her and her marital issues into the center of everyone's attention. To be 18 years old, the girl was extremely immature. How could she be the offspring of docile Pastor Sam? *Lord, please forgive me for wanting to beat the living daylights out of that girl.*

Abby needed to control her anger before it controlled her. She reminded herself that people, especially people like Hannah, had no idea what it was like to be in her predicament. God alone could understand her feelings and the complexity of her dilemma.

She didn't want to live for just herself anymore; she loved Jesus, and the greatest desire of her heart was to serve Him. Seeing Derek on TV confirmed what her *fleshly self* wanted…her heart was practically bleeding, begging her to run back into his arms. But that's not what her spirit wanted. Because the minute she went back to Derek would be the minute her life would become both a fairytale and a suspense-filled horror movie. She would live in uncertainty and fear, knowing the clock could strike midnight at any second. How could she experience peace and freedom living that way? How could she focus on and serve God from that kind of prison cell? Hannah couldn't imagine having to count every single calorie and sweat her tail off at the gym every day to stay competitive with the millions of gorgeous women wanting to snatch her husband away.

Sarah, where are you? She and Zack should've been here a long time ago. What if they had been in an accident? Abby frantically searched through her purse for her phone. One glimpse at the screen and she could exhale. Sarah had texted: "Stuck on 77, appears to be a major wreck ahead."

Abby was simultaneously relieved and disappointed. She thanked God her sister and brother-in-law were okay, then cursed the traffic jam which held them up. She needed Sarah. ASAP.

Putting her phone back into her purse, it vibrated. Abby had a new message...from Derek. Her heart flip-flopped. "Hey Ab, just want you to know this night wouldn't be happening for me if it weren't for you. I'm so thankful for your love and support over the years we had. Miss and love you more than words can say."

"The years we had." She read that line again, the implication crashing on her like a tsunami. Trembling, Abby closed her eyes and pleaded for God to help her, for Him to stoop down and rescue her from this emotional roller coaster. To give her peace about not taking another chance on the love of her life. To convince her stubborn heart to agree with her mind.

Never again. Those words resonated through her while her body shook from the force of suffocating sobs. Never again would she put herself in such a vulnerable position. Because never again could she survive this. The only hope she had of living a God-honoring life, a life with any semblance of normalcy, was to gracefully bow out of Derek's world. She trusted God enough now to know He would fully restore her...somehow. And He would eventually bless her with a Christian man to share a meaningful, fulfilling life with.

Abby exhaled slowly, fixing her thoughts on the promises of God. His unexplainable peace began to flow from her head to her toes, right through the broken pieces of her heart. A heart which somehow managed to dance a few beats when a thought flashed across her mind: perhaps that Christian man was in the very next room.

Perhaps it was none other than Dr. Luke Jacobson.

CHAPTER TWENTY-TWO

Derek stood by a sideline heater, holding his hands as close as possible in hopes of feeling his fingers again. Those who made the decision for the Super Bowl to be held at MetLife Stadium in New Jersey were probably warm and cozy in their luxury box on the 50-yard line, while he and his teammates were freezing their butts off.

The weather was going to be a significant factor in this game, especially since it had started snowing. The Panthers were up by 10 points with less than four minutes left in the first half, but something told him they were headed for trouble. In these conditions, their opponents from New England had a huge advantage over a team of Southerners.

Derek stared into the glare of the stadium lights, the bitter wind assaulting his face. Thousands of tiny snowflakes were falling from the sky. Everything was surreal. Maybe he should pinch himself…maybe this was just a dream. Was he *really* playing in the Super Bowl?

Sure enough. He was no longer the lanky kid eating cheese doodles with his cousin Jeffrey, staring wide-eyed at the television from their spot on the floor, studying every move of their football idols.

Now he *was* the idol.

Butterflies fluttered around in Derek's stomach. Running onto the field at the beginning of the game was a moment he would remember for as long as he lived. Music blaring from the stadium speakers, the crowd roaring louder than thousands of hungry lions. Fireworks had boomed and crackled, lighting up the evening sky with every color of the rainbow. And the adrenaline high he experienced after scoring the first touchdown of the night was something else he would never forget.

A wave of nausea stole him away from his happy place when a nightmarish reality hit him head-on. Even if the Panthers won the Super Bowl tonight, his lifelong dream wouldn't technically come true. Because, in all the times he had pictured being a Super Bowl champion, never once had the love of his life not been with him to celebrate. Abby's absence was like a fist grinding into his gut.

The forceful blowing of whistles snapped him back to the present. What the—? A fight?

Derek couldn't see who was at the center of the testosterone-charged pileup, but the officials were going crazy, throwing flags left and right. His heart raced as he watched the instant replay on the jumbotron screen. One of their defensive ends had sacked Tyson Garcia, star quarterback for the Patriots. The ball was knocked loose and into the hands of his teammate, Tex, before someone on the opposing team threw a punch.

Unless he had missed something, it looked like a clean play from their end; the ball was theirs, fair and square. "Yes!" Derek searched for a teammate to high-five.

Colton jumped up and down behind him. "It's ours!" Colton's words fogged up the air where their hands met.

The white-capped referee's ruling made it official: the ball was theirs. He could finally release the pent-up air in his lungs. The ball had been fumbled on their 43-yard line, and the Panthers had recovered it. An added bonus was the penalty for unnecessary roughness called against the Patriots player who picked the fight.

"Let's do this, baby!" Evan, the team's kicker, swatted him with a towel. "Go show Ole Red who's boss."

"Let him grab my face mask again, and I'll show him, alright!" Derek laughed, joking about the arch-rival opponent who got called for a face mask penalty against him the last time their teams met, a game the Panthers had won by a last-minute field goal.

He ran onto the field, aching to have the ball in his hands with a clear path to the goal line. Or better yet, in the end zone.

Scanning the sea of people in the family section, he didn't see his Uncle Scott, Aunt Diana, or Jeffrey. But he knew they were there. And that meant more than ever. If only their presence could diminish the enormous vacancy in the stands…and in his heart.

Get it together, man. This game was way too important to give his emotions the upper edge. Not only would this game forever impact the careers of every player on the team, a Super Bowl win may help him get Abby back. She wasn't a superficial person, but being in the spotlight could only increase his chances of winning her back; the more times he crossed her mind, the better.

Two minutes later, the Panthers were on the Patriots' 14-yard line. It was first down, thanks to an amazing catch by his fellow wide receiver, Timothy. Derek's bad feeling had proved wrong. He practically tasted a touchdown as the crowd cheered louder and louder with each drive down the field.

The ball was snapped, and he ran full-blast into a wide-open space in the end zone while Colt danced around the pocket, dodging several defensive linemen. He reached out in anticipation of a throw, pretty sure Colt had just spotted him. Sure enough, the ball was launched and began traveling through the air like a missile toward its target: him.

Derek centered himself with the trajectory of the ball and leapt into the air. *Yes!* It was in his hands. But an opponent was fast approaching. He clutched the ball tighter, guarding it with his life, bracing for the hit.

"Ummph!" A helmet-to-leg hit forced Derek to the ground. The fact that he was able to hold onto the ball for a touchdown was of little consolation as dynamite exploded in his knee. His bad knee.

⇥ ⇤

Derek shouted a few choice words, crumpling his water bottle and throwing it to the ground. Due to his injury, he had sat out the entire third quarter. Now they were entering the fourth, ahead by only one point.

He had to get back in the game.

Colton had just thrown an interception, giving the Patriots a chance to take the lead for the first time if they scored on this run.

"This is ridiculous, man!" Spewing a few more choice words didn't ease Derek's rising tension. How on earth had they almost blown a 17-point lead?

The snow had definitely been a deterrent for the Panthers. But if he had been in the game, they wouldn't be in this predicament. They would've scored again, for one thing. And he would've caught that last pass. Yeah, it was a lousy throw by Colt, but he would have found a way to catch it...especially with Brandon Mabe, one of the most talented cornerbacks in the NFL, lurking nearby to pick up the interception.

If Derek had been in the game, they would be on the 30-yard line, where they could at least get a field goal. But no. Instead, their defense had to keep one of the best offenses in the league from scoring. Again.

He removed the ice pack from his knee and extended his leg. It definitely hurt, but not as bad as it had a few minutes ago. Not bad enough to keep him from wrapping his hands around that Lombardi trophy. Picturing his deadbeat dad and Abby watching the game on TV propelled him to his feet. Come hell or high water, he would be on the field for the next Panthers possession.

"You okay?" Juan, his favorite athletic trainer, wrapped his arm around his waist for support. The guy was biting his bottom lip, nervous anticipation written all over his face.

"So far," Derek said, knowing the real test was yet to come. The dismal expressions on the faces of his teammates gave him an extra dose of courage to take the dreadful first step on his bad knee. "Ow!" He held his breath as flames seared through it. After hobbling a few steps, he dropped to the ground to try a few stretches.

"Here," Juan said, extending his hand to help Derek to his feet.

Surprisingly, the pain was now bearable. He walked closer to a sideline heater and jogged in place, working out the ache even further. He could do this.

He *would* do this.

Contrary to what Dave Holder thought, he wasn't a loser. He was a winner, and whatever it took, the Panthers were going to win this game.

Dr. Saunders, the team's head orthopedic surgeon, walked toward Derek. His eyes toggled between him and Juan, who was still standing beside him.

"I'm going in," Derek declared with absolute resolution. "X-ray was negative...last game of the season...I'm playing."

CHAPTER TWENTY-THREE

It's over. Derek's chest caved in. The last attempt to win the Super Bowl had slipped right through his hands. Literally.

The world stopped spinning. How could he have blown it? He fell to the ground as mountains of regret, humiliation, and shame crashed upon him.

The Panthers had been on a roll, marching down the field, determined to retake the lead. Down by six points with three minutes in the game, they had called a fair catch on the 18-yard line. With two good gains from the running back and several complete passes, including a 14-yard catch he had made, Derek was sure they would come back to win the game. But they hit a brick wall on the Patriots' 26-yard line.

A field goal would've been useless, so they had to go for a touchdown on fourth down. Derek's gut feeling told him that the last play of the game would come down to him. And sure enough, it had.

And sure enough, he had failed.

Derek punched the ground. Colton had thrown him a perfect pass into the end zone. He wished he could blame his knee for missing the catch, but he couldn't. He just missed it, plain and simple. This was exactly like the upset against Clemson during his sophomore year at UNC—only this was on an entirely different scale. He had *really* lost it all this time.

The Super Bowl.

The biggest game of the year. Of his life.

The perfect ending to an awesome season, a lifelong dream come true...all this had been right at his fingertips. And in the blink of an eye, it was gone. All gone.

Derek's chest physically ached, thinking of all the people he had let down: Colt, his coaches, his team, the fans. Instead of ruining everything, he could've been a hero. A hero for not only his team, his coaches, the fans, and Abby—who was surely watching from somewhere— but also in front of someone else who was likely watching. Derek balled his hands into fists and groaned until all the air escaped his lungs. He could have sealed the deal, once and for all; could have proven he wasn't *good-for-nothing*. Dave Holder would've had no choice but to eat his words if he had made the game-winning catch of the Super Bowl.

Just as Derek willed the earth to swallow him up and hide him forever, something in his periphery captured his attention. And his breath.

A yellow flag!

He froze like a statue when it hit the ground several feet to his left. Still on the ground himself, he was eye level with a yellow slice of hope. Something jumped in his chest.

"Holding. Defense num—" The rest of the referee's words were drowned out by shouts of joy. Derek pumped his fists and kicked his legs in the air, hearing all he needed to hear. They had another chance. He sprang to his feet. His knee hurt, but he pushed past the pain, adrenaline coursing through his veins at an all-time high.

"Yeah baby, yeah! Whoo-hoo!" J.J., a running back, jumped all over him, nearly knocking him back down. Energy and life saturated the air. Everyone on the sidelines and in the stands jumped in excitement, shouting to the top of their lungs. The Panthers would advance five yards closer to the goal line, and with the automatic first down, they would get four more attempts to score a game-winning touchdown.

Elation turned to sheer panic when Derek glanced at the clock. There were only 38 seconds left in the game, no timeouts remaining. An avalanche of doom wiped his breath away when the play clock restarted.

Derek's lungs suddenly froze, making it impossible to draw in the tiniest bit of air. And it wasn't due to physical exertion. What he was experiencing was all-too familiar… the worst possible feeling in the world. He was on the verge of a panic attack. He hadn't had one in a few weeks, not since the Zoloft had kicked back in. But there was no doubt he was about to have one now. At absolutely the worst time imaginable.

Breathe. Just breathe. In…out…in…out. You've got a second chance. Don't screw it up!

Abby's face flashed before him, distracting him from his physical symptoms long enough for autopilot mode to take charge. He could finally draw in a complete breath. He made a mad dash to the line of scrimmage as chaotic shouting bombarded him from every direction. The pandemonium was practically tangible, the play clock dwindling down: 11, 10, 9…

Come on, Colt! What are you waiting on? Snap it!

"Black 7, Black 7," Colton hurriedly barked out a play, one which wouldn't involve him. "Blue 20, Blue 20, Hut." *What?!?* Colton had changed up the play at the last second. And Derek would be the go-to guy if Timothy wasn't open on the opposite side of the field.

The ball was finally snapped, and he sprinted down the field for an opening. He was lightheaded, his body and soul on the craziest roller coaster ride ever. There was no time to process anything. This was one of those play-or-bust moments, a moment he had trained years for. Gallons of sweat and thousands of hours of workouts and team meetings— everything in his life, really—had led up to this. This crucial window of time.

And he wasn't about to blow it.

Derek found an opening and whipped his body around. Two opponents were covering Timothy on the other side of the field. Which meant—

He hadn't even finished the thought before Colton's throwing arm was behind his head. *Would he really? Could he seriously trust him with the biggest game of their lives after that enormous mistake he had just made?*

Yes, evidently so, because the ball was launched, and here it came. Straight toward him. It was spiraling through the air on what appeared to be the perfect trajectory for him to catch. With most of his weight and momentum on his good knee, Derek sprang into the air, reaching his arms out as far as they could stretch. The ball was right at his fingertips.

Now he had it!

Surprised the slippery ball was secure in his half-numb hands, he hadn't even scoped out his nearest opponent or contemplated his next move. But he had to. The catch alone wasn't going to be enough.

When his feet finally touched the turf, he was 11 yards from the goal line. Derek's thoughts sharpened as he positioned the football with purposeful intent, gripping the point and covering the laces with his palm. He cradled it like a newborn, pressing it taut against his chest to protect it from any defenders.

All he had to do now was run. Like never before.

An opponent closed in from about five yards away. With outstretched arms, the guy dove at him, managing to get a loose hold of his right ankle. But Derek pulled it away. No one was going to stop him now, not even with pain spreading like wildfire through his right leg.

His eardrums vibrated with each beat of his heart. He was on his victory lap, mere yards away from scoring the winning touchdown of the Super Bowl.

His mind suddenly shut out everything. He had to stay focused on one thing, and one thing alone: running. With his eyes fixed on the goal line, an image of Forrest Gump flashed across his mind. Just like the character in the movie, he made the most of every single stride, each pump of his arms. He didn't think; he just ran.

The next thing he knew, teammates were bombarding him from every angle, their shouts deafening. Derek's legs buckled. He fell to the ground, stealing a glimpse of the replay on the jumbotron screen on his way down. Seeing the ref holding both arms in the air, confirming the touchdown, something exploded in his chest.

Colt and J.J. pulled him off the ground. Then into the air. He felt off-balance, but he wasn't worried. If they dropped him, there was a safety net of dozens below. His face toward the night sky, Derek shouted with all the breath in his lungs, sending a puff of smoke into the air. The snow had all but stopped, but a few stray flurries brushed past his lips and landed on his tongue. He tried to soak in the moment, to savor it as much as possible in the midst of all the chaos.

This was simply unfathomable. Surreal. He was living in a moment he had waited his entire life for...when one simple field goal kick was the only obstacle between him and a dream come true.

⚜

With a final score of 28-27, the Panthers were the champions of Super Bowl 52. After their kicker scored the extra point, making the win official, celebration had erupted on the field unlike anything Derek had ever seen.

Colton and J.J. dumped the traditional Gatorade bath on Coach Ryan. Photographers and reporters stormed the field as the team put on their Super Bowl Champion caps, streams of blue and black confetti raining down so hard it was virtually impossible to see five feet ahead.

Between the fireworks, screams and shouts, and Queen's "We Are the Champions" blasting from the stadium speakers, Derek would likely be deaf by morning.

He was bound to have looked like a deer caught in the headlights when reporters began approaching him. How was he supposed to describe a moment like this? It was all too exhilarating and overwhelming to take in, simply impossible to describe with words. But media interviews came along with the territory. Unfortunately.

He usually couldn't stand watching clips of himself on television. It was because of his thick Southern accent, the accent he couldn't ditch no matter how hard he'd tried. Considering how frazzled he had been a few minutes ago when Melinda Cameron interviewed him on the field, he was sure to have sounded like a full-blown redneck.

For once, though, he really didn't care. Let the local news stations make all the patronizing remarks they wanted about their hometown boy and his Southern drawl; it wouldn't phase him a bit.

Because he was a Super Bowl Champion now.

"Derek Holder." He jerked in surprise when the announcer called his name. Coach Ryan, standing beside him on the podium, smiled and offered him the Lombardi trophy. For the third time of the evening, Derek thought he was going to fall out. He was so lightheaded that he had to take hold of Colton's arm rather than the trophy.

Seriously? He was the MVP of the Super Bowl?

He steadied himself, but his heart nearly raced through his chest. Finally stable enough to take the trophy from Coach, he clasped his hands around the base of the shiny silver football. A layer of shock began to peel away, exposing him to the sheer magnitude of the moment. His eyes stung, and there was no point in trying to fight the tears back.

"So, what did it feel like to make the winning catch after it looked like all hope was gone?" The vertically-challenged announcer held the microphone up to Derek's mouth as he wiped a stream of tears from his cheek, shaking his head in disbelief. Never before had the spotlight shone brighter. Millions of people across the nation—probably all over the world—were watching him, waiting for his response. One person who was surely watching was Abby. And more than likely, David Holder.

He shivered, pretty sure it had nothing to do with the frigid temperature. "There's really no way to describe it, man. I couldn't believe it. It was like going from one extreme to the next. I'm just so thankful my awesome QB took another chance on me," he said, putting his arm around the back of Colt's neck.

Derek pulled his best buddy closer. Just moments ago, after fulfilling their obligations to the reporters on the field, the two of them had shared an otherworldly moment, unashamedly embracing one another. As Colton cried sentimental words of victory in his ear, Derek had nearly fainted in his arms. No one else in the world understood his feelings better than Colt. Only he could equally appreciate the glory of all this, rejoicing in the fact that all their hard work and dedication had finally paid off.

"Well, congrats on the big win," the exuberant announcer exclaimed. "It's amazing you scored three of your team's four touchdowns tonight, man! How does it feel to be named the MVP of Super Bowl 52?"

Derek looked into the video camera, blinding flashes of light striking his eyes from every angle. He sucked in a breath of cold air. What words could explain feelings like this? "Wow, I don't know where to even begin. This is definitely a dream come true." He lifted the trophy high in the air, his smile stretching from ear to ear.

"Hold-er! Hold-er! Hold-er!" The crowd went wild, the fans shouting his last name in their signature cadence.

"Thank you, thank you." He blushed, pausing until the chanting faded. "But I wouldn't be standing here without this great team of players and coaches," he said, scanning the beloved faces around him. "We've worked so hard and had a terrific season to be proud of. Thank you all—you're the best." Derek pointed the trophy toward his teammates.

"Also, we've got the best fans in the league. You all rock! Thank you *so* much!" He pointed toward the stands, triggering another round of heavy applause. "And my family, I certainly wouldn't be here without them."

He looked at his uncle, aunt, and cousin, but in his mind he pictured Abby and his late Gram. Abby and her family had been more of a family to him than his own flesh and blood. Back before he'd failed them. Derek shook his head abruptly, like a swimmer shaking water out of his ears. As if that could shake away his regrets.

"I'd especially like to thank my beautiful wife."

What? The habitual statement had slipped right through his lips. He cleared his throat. Abby was technically still his wife, so he should probably just continue on, acting as normal as possible. "She's always been my biggest fa—" Derek's voice cracked. Looking down, he forcefully blinked out the tears flooding his eyes. He quickly wiped his face before lifting his head, but a stray tear snuck by him. It trickled down the side of his nose and landed in his mouth, its salty taste lingering on the tip of his tongue.

An intense wave of sorrow suddenly rose up from that deep, wounded place inside, bringing an idea along with it: he could beg Abby back right now. He could break down and plead for forgiveness and another chance. Right here.

In front of the hundreds of cameras that were broadcasting him into millions of living rooms across the nation.

Wouldn't that prove his love? His regret?

If it would bring her back, he would do it. Derek Holder, Super Bowl MVP, would become a fool. Because, even as he basked in the glory of reaching the summit of his career, he didn't feel half the fulfillment as when he was in his wife's arms.

A harsh voice instantly snapped him back to his senses. Being a lovesick fool had gotten him nowhere. Maybe it was time to switch up his game plan. Maybe playing a little hard to get would work better, especially now that he was the reigning MVP of the Super Bowl.

Derek forced a big, cheesy smile—one big enough to make his jaws ache. "Wow! This is incredible," he shouted, a few more tears leaking out. He extended his arm as high as it would reach, pulsating the Lombardi trophy in the air. "Again, thank you all so much. I'm so honored to be a part of this amazing team! Here's to us, the Super Bowl champions. Whoo-hoo!"

He was finally able to catch a breath when the announcer moved the mic away from his mouth.

"Well congratulations again, young man. And on be-half of Chevrolet, we proudly present to you the keys to the all-new Chevy Colorado, Motor Trend's 2018 Truck of the Year. Chevrolet would like to officially congratulate Derek Holder for being named MVP of Super Bowl 52."

"Wow, thank you!" He laughed in disbelief, jingling the truck keys in the air. "Awww, man! Wow!" Continuing his happy charade, Derek curled his toes and squeezed hard, willing the announcer to be done with him.

It worked. The guy moved past him to interview Colt.

He let out the breath he'd been holding. Recapping the last few minutes, Derek was confident he had pulled it off: the biggest act ever. He had actually managed to surprise himself. Maybe he had missed his calling to Hollywood; he probably could've won an Oscar with a performance like that.

Because he was almost certain he had just fooled the world into believing his tears were the byproducts of overwhelming joy when, in reality, they were some of the saddest ones he had ever cried.

CHAPTER TWENTY-FOUR

Abby admired her new, post-salon look in the mirror of her parents' guest bathroom. The caramel streaks in her long dark hair, along with some side-swept bangs, gave her just the right amount of sass. The edge she had been seeking. She turned out the light, a boost of confidence propelling her lean body down the hall toward her room.

A six-pound weight loss was one good thing that had come from Derek's cheating heart. Before finding out about his one night-stand, when things seemed to be improving in their lives, she had put on a few too many pounds. Even though everyone said she was too thin, she felt more comfortable with sleeker thighs.

Abby closed the door to her room, drowning out the sound of her parents' voices down the hall. It was time for some serious searching and deliberation regarding her future. Sitting Indian-style on her bed, she opened her laptop. For the first time since moving in with her parents, the room felt like home. She admired the fresh paint on the walls: Sherwin-Williams Radiant Lilac. It made the light purple flowers on her comforter *pop* from among the other pastels.

Waiting for her computer to start up, Abby grabbed the new tube of lipstick from her nightstand. Applying some *Berry Bliss*, she imagined herself to look better with each velvety rub of her lips.

Daughter, you're beautiful just the way you are.

The voice wasn't audible, but it may as well have been. Needing to hear more, Abby tuned out of the here and now, tapping into her spirit. Suddenly, a Bible verse flashed across her mind, one she and her Bible study friends had discussed a few days ago. *"Charm is deceptive, and beauty is fleeting; but a woman who fears the Lord is to be praised."* Her soul instantly came into agreement with those words from Proverbs 31:30. Outward beauty was vain and temporary, so why put so much stock in it? The only beauty God cared about—therefore, the only beauty that really mattered—was on the inside.

Why had she taken several steps back lately? Deep down, she knew the reason, and it was time to fess up. After Derek won the Super Bowl several weeks ago, she had been defaulting to some of her old ways, putting too much emphasis on how she looked and what her surroundings were like... on material things that didn't really matter. The escalation of Derek's fame and success must have fueled the lingering embers of her insecurities, igniting a flame big enough to stunt her growth in Christ. She couldn't deny that she missed the glitz and glamour of being the *un-cheated on*-wife of a celebrity, the way it made her feel like she was some-body. But that was senseless. Being on the arm of a famous football player was nothing compared to being the cher-ished bride of Christ.

It may not be a sin to change up her appearance or de-cor every once in a while, but it was wrong to look to these things to fulfill her. Ultimately, happiness could only be found in God...in glorifying the One she loved by singing Him a beautiful song with the life He had given her. As "Lifesong" by Casting Crowns played in her mind, Abby typed "UNC-Chapel Hill physical therapy program" into the *Google* bar of her computer screen. Anticipation and ex-citement intensified with each spin of the browser's wheel. With her biology degree, she shouldn't lack much, aside from taking the GRE, to meet the requirements for admis-sion to the graduate program. Although she wasn't crazy about all the studying she needed to do in order to score well on that exam, she was up for the challenge. She was ready for a new chapter in her life.

Several links popped up on the screen. "Doctor of Physical Therapy program." She clicked on it, smiling at the thought of being Dr. Abby Holder. No, wait—the divorce would be final by then, so she would be Dr. Abby *Gibbs*. Her smile dis-sipated in an instant. The mere thought of erasing Derek's name from hers sent a dagger straight through her heart. Not only emotionally, but physically it seemed, because her chest actually ached.

A hopeful thought rushed through her mind, instantly reviving her heart: maybe Derek wouldn't sign the separa-tion papers. She had mailed them almost two weeks ago, and he hadn't sent them back yet. Maybe that meant he had ripped them to shreds, resolving to never let her go. What would happen if that were the case? Was it legally possible for him to remain her husband as long as he wanted?

Surely not. She wasn't that lucky…lucky enough to have no other option than to remain married to the man she still loved more than life itself.

Abby quickly chided herself, having no business entertaining thoughts such as that. She should be chomping at the bit to divorce Derek, to start the brand new life God had in store for her. The Lord had good plans for her future; that was a promise she had found in the Book of Jeremiah. Her Savior hadn't died for her in vain. He had given His life so that she could live…not only for eternity, but for here and now. Jesus died to give her a life of abundance, free of the bondages which had held her captive for way too long.

But why couldn't her heart know these facts, not just her head? Why didn't she have complete peace about moving forward, believing God had better things for her than a life with Derek could offer?

Abby exhaled in exasperation, massaging her tense neck. She reminded herself of the message found in Philippians 4:13—the favorite Bible verse of dreamy Dr. Luke Jacobson, who had been making an effort to speak with her every Sunday after church. "I can do all things through You, Jesus," she whispered in assurance, returning to her online search. The search that could lead to a rewarding, lucrative career.

As a physical therapist, she would easily be able to provide for her needs, as well as most of the luxuries she had grown accustomed to…especially now that she was determined not to depend on things money could buy to make her happy. And it would be so fulfilling to be able to help and encourage people, to shine the Light of Jesus in people's lives. Physical therapist or not, she wouldn't accept a large payout from Derek. No matter how tempting it was, the financial perks just weren't worth it. She wouldn't give him the satisfaction of thinking she needed him in order to make it.

She could—and would—make it on her own.

Abby nearly bounced off the bed when a knock at the door startled her. "Can I come in?" Her dad's somber voice accelerated her pulse. Something must be wrong; he never disturbed her when the door was closed.

"Sure." She swallowed hard, closing her laptop and sitting up straighter in bed.

The door creaked open. Seeing the look on her Daddy's face, Abby's stomach sank to the floor. His solemn brown eyes unraveled her, confirming her fears. Something was wrong, alright. Something major.

⥤⥢

John dreaded the upcoming discussion with his baby girl more than the plague. His soul pleaded the words of Jesus in Luke 22:42, the words His Savior said as He sweat blood in the Garden of Gethsemane the night before His crucifixion: *"Father, if you are willing, take this cup from me; yet not my will, but yours be done."*

Unfortunately, God didn't take his burden away, but He did send one of His most precious creatures to help lighten the mood. John couldn't help but laugh as his best four-legged friend shot into the room like a missile, jumping on Abby's bed and lunging at her like a lineman intent on sacking the quarterback.

"Scooter, you scared me to death!" She squirmed, unsuccessfully trying to dodge the beloved beagle's kisses to her mouth.

"Scoot, settle! Maybe I should put him out," John said as he silently prayed for Scooter to settle down. No doubt, the dog's wagging tail and clueless expression would help him get through this dramatic ordeal.

"No, he's fine. What's going on?" Abby's hands worked to calm Scooter, but her apprehensive eyes were intently fixed on his.

He had to look away for a moment to muster up some courage. He would start with the easier news first, although it would be far from easy to swallow. "I talked to Derek today." There, he had said it.

"Okay." The rising intonation in his daughter's voice commanded an explanation, along with her "if looks could kill" stare.

John cleared his throat. "I'd been feeling for some time that I should call to get some things settled between us, but God really impressed it on my heart yesterday."

Abby knew his stance on obeying God's voice, so he hoped she wouldn't question his decision. John thought about letting her respond, but he continued on instead; the sooner this night was behind him the better. "Anyway, I felt a prompting—what I knew was the Holy Spirit—telling me something was wrong and that I needed to check on him. So, I pretended to be calling to congratulate him on his big win, knowing it would help break the ice."

He reached over to pet Scooter, praying his next words would soften his baby girl's calloused heart. "Derek sounded terrible, Ab. Barely spoke a word. More or less, he just answered my questions with a word or two. And his voice kept cracking like he was about to lose it. I've never heard him like that before."

He held his breath as Abby opened her mouth to speak, her eyes aflame. "Why didn't you tell me you were going to call him?"

This wasn't the response John had hoped for, but it was the one he'd been expecting. He wiped the sweat from his forehead. The last thing he wanted was to make his daughter feel more betrayed than she already did. But he couldn't beat himself up for being obedient to God. No doubt, he had done the right thing in extending love and forgiveness to Derek.

"Well"—he stalled, certain he was treading on thin ice—"to be completely honest, I guess because I suspected you wouldn't want me to. And I knew I was going to have to, regardless of how you felt."

To his dismay, the spark of rage in Abby's eyes intensified.

John feigned a chuckle. "By your reaction, I'm assuming my hunch was correct. You probably would've tried to talk me out of it," he said as he tapped his daughter's knee, hoping the lighthearted gesture would stifle her fire.

"No, that's not necessarily true." Abby shook her head adamantly. Her lack of eye contact suggested she was having a hard time convincing herself of this, much less him.

"Truth be told, I didn't want to call him, Ab. Aside from you, we never had much in common. And now we don't really even have that. I knew telling you, getting you all worked up, would only make it that much harder. And God was clearly asking me to do this, hon."

Abby finally looked at him, calm resignation softening her face. He exhaled in relief, extending his hand to caress her cheek. She couldn't fathom how much he loved her. His precious baby girl.

"So, let's move past the reasoning and what-not, because that's not going to get us anywhere. Being upset with me isn't going to accomplish anything. And you know as well as I do that I'm completely on your side. You're my little girl, sweetie. Always have been, always will be."

The moisture in Abby's eyes made their green color even more vibrant. His daughter had been beautiful her whole life, but somehow she only grew in beauty. John smiled through his tears, taking her by the hand.

His heart leapt when she traced the back of his hand with her thumb. He wished she would say something. Anything. In the awkward silence, God spoke to his spirit, urging him to pray for his baby girl. So, John silently praised the Lord for the spiritual growth he had witnessed in her over the past two months. He was beyond grateful to see that she had a genuine relationship with Christ. But he knew she hadn't truly forgiven Derek. She said she had, but all the evidence pointed to the contrary. *Please break her chains, Lord.*

"It felt good to extend my forgiveness," John said, finally breaking the silence. "Maybe this will help chip away some of the pain and regret Derek is feeling. He doesn't know it, but what he really needs is Christ's forgiveness. And I haven't given up hope…I believe he will see the light one of these days." Abby shook her head with skepticism, but it didn't stop him. "Until then, he needs to see and experience Christ through others—through us." John pointed at himself, then at his daughter.

"I know you say you've forgiven him, but I fear you haven't, Ab. Not from in here," he said, gently placing his finger on her sternum.

Abby jerked back and looked away. Her mouth opened, but she abruptly closed it, apparently changing her mind about saying something. The tension in the room was thick, but he was determined to plow through it. There were too many important things to be said.

"I don't know what all is in your heart, sweetie, but I do know if there's bitterness, resentment—anything of that nature—it needs to go. There isn't room for it in a Christian's heart. Strife and peace cannot coexist. You can't experience God's complete peace and healing until you forgive Derek 100 percent, no holds barred." John didn't want to slow down; he was on a roll, feeling the Holy Spirit speaking through him. But his cancer-stricken lungs begged for air.

"Forgiveness doesn't necessarily mean you have to take Derek back, hon," John continued after taking a few quick breaths. "God hates divorce, but since this is a case of adultery, you're not in the wrong if you can't find it in yourself to continue the relationship. The two of you are certainly 'unequally yoked.' But, perhaps, forgiveness *does* mean being an occasional friend for him to—"

"You obviously don't understand, Dad," Abby said, interrupting him. "Derek does nothing but beg me to come back. That's why I refuse to talk to him. I've made my mind up to move on and live a godly life, but he can't accept that. And it's too hard for me to listen to the same old story over and over…and over again." She blew out an exasperated breath, lifting a few strands of the new bangs from her forehead.

"I know, sweetie. I don't know exactly how you should handle it." His little girl was certainly in a challenging situation, and John wasn't about to pretend he had all the answers. "But I do know if you've never truly forgiven him, you can't fully let go of the past and move forward. Just pray about it and remember the parable about the unmerciful servant: just as God has cancelled our debts, we must cancel the debts of those who have wronged us."

Abby stared blankly at Scooter who lay on her lap, dozing in and out of sleep. How he wished life could be that simple for him and his loved ones.

"I know," she mumbled, tears flooding her eyes.

John was thankful the message seemed to have hit home. But instead of relief, he felt like he'd just been kicked to the ground. Why was that?

The answer promptly surfaced. It was because after the issue regarding Derek had been addressed, it would be time to move on to the next subject. One which was far worse... the absolute worst he'd ever faced. But after the doctor's report yesterday, it was unavoidable. *God, how am I supposed to do this? Please help me.*

He rubbed Abby's back, allowing her to ponder all that had been said. He needed to muster up the courage to wrap up the forgiveness issue, but he was suddenly frozen in place. Unable to utter a word. It didn't take much self-persuasion to convince himself that Abby needed to know a few more things about Derek. "Did you know Derek has to have knee surgery?"

"Really?" Her jaw dropped, compassion washing over her face for the first time this evening. "Well, I guess I'm not too surprised."

"I'm really worried about him, Ab. Someone in his situation—hopeless and without God in their life—may consider ending it all to escape the pain. God forbid. As bad as he sounded, I wouldn't doubt that he's considered it." John's nose began to sting. He was truly worried about his son-in-law. Even though he had hurt one of his most treasured gifts, he wished only the best for Derek. All he could do, though, was to continue praying for the Lord's will to be done in both of their lives, whatever that may be.

Concern was written all over his sweet girl's face. She had always had such a tender heart.

"Well, I definitely think you should call and talk to him, maybe convince him to get some professional help. I don't know, maybe just be his friend…for now, at least. All I know is that you don't want to live with any regrets, sugar," John said, patting Abby's knee. "There's no time like the present to deal with any unresolved issues. Life's just too short."

Life's too short. That was ironic…a good bridge to the next subject. As good as it was going to get, anyway.

Forcing a smile, he looked into his daughter's green eyes—no question, the most stunning eyes he had ever seen. There was now a glimmer of optimism there, a peaceful look of understanding. It was encouraging to see God bringing good from this difficult conversation, but the complacent expression on Abby's face also made his heart hurt. Would this be the last time he ever saw peace in her eyes? What if the news he was about to deliver pushed her over the edge? What if it caused her to resent God again?

John paused to take a mental snapshot of his baby girl… to savor this brief moment of calm before the raging storm.

CHAPTER TWENTY-FIVE

The lights of the Queen City were alive and well, one constant in Derek's life of variables. He drove down Charlotte's Tryon Street with dinner from The Capital Grille in the passenger seat.

The gorgonzola-crusted ribeye smelled delicious only a minute ago, but now the scent prompted a wave of nausea. The happy couple he passed a few blocks back delivered the first punch to his gut, and this couple crossing the road with their kids twisted his stomach in knots. The man was carrying a little blonde-haired boy on his shoulders, and the smiling woman was pushing a pink stroller.

Derek swallowed the lump in his throat. Unless Abby had a 180-degree change of heart, he would miss out on one of the things he wanted most in life: to be a dad. A *real* dad, one on the opposite end of the spectrum from the man who'd done nothing more for him than contribute 23 chromosomes.

Images of dreams which would never come true bombarded him: Derek saw himself kissing a child's chubby cheek and then lifting them to his shoulders, just like he did with Kayla and Lexi. Playing catch with a little boy in the park. Coaching his teenager's football team. Reading fairytales to a miniature princess Abby.

A tear trickled down his cheek, and he didn't even bother wiping it. The irony of his situation was unbelievable. He had almost been trampled in the restaurant by a huge crowd of people wanting his autograph, and here he was going home to an empty house...where he would sit in a recliner and dream empty dreams. The only company he had waiting for him were some college basketball players on ESPN. Come to think of it, he didn't even have that; no team he cared to watch was playing tonight.

The black hole in his chest expanded—a deep, dark void sucking the life out of him. Was this really all there was for him? Even after accomplishing his highest goal? Winning the Super Bowl, the MVP, only to make more money, which was good for nothing but buying more useless things? Hearing thousands of strangers chanting his name like he's some super-human spectacle, then walking into a silent house and crawling into an empty bed?

Some of his teammates had normal lives with wives and kids to return to after coming off the high of a Super Bowl win. But he had nothing. His best friend didn't even have time for him anymore. Colton spent every waking minute with the new Hollywood bombshell, Mercedes Ammon.

And Derek's plan to take his uncle, aunt, and cousin on a Hawaiian vacation during the offseason had been shot down like a busted balloon after the doctor said the "s" word. Derek couldn't even think of the word *surgery* without shuddering.

The injury to his bad knee on the night of the Super Bowl was the final nail in the coffin—Dr. H.'s words verbatim. His ACL was supposedly hanging by thread. The operation had been scheduled quickly in order to give him more time to recover before the start of next season.

Derek's pulse sped up. Each passing day, he dreaded it more and more…the pain, the nausea, the physical therapy. And this go-round he wouldn't have Abby's TLC to nurse him back to health like he had in college. He hadn't known how good he'd had it back then. Things were so much simpler when he and Abby lived off of love and peanut butter and jelly sandwiches, back before fame and fortune replaced the normalcy of their lives.

There was still a little hope left, though. After speaking to John earlier in the day, Derek figured his chances of winning his wife back were increasing. Unfortunately, his father-in-law's news was bad. Really bad. It had crushed him, so he couldn't even imagine how devastated Abby would be once she found out, which was supposedly going to be soon. He felt so sorry for her, John, and the entire family, yet he couldn't help but see a bright side to this. Maybe Abby would come back to him now, needing his love and support more than ever before.

Blue lights began flashing in the rearview mirror, stealing him away from his contemplations. His breath hung in his chest, but after eyeballing the speedometer he let it escape, along with a few choice words.

"Less than two miles from home," he groaned, repeatedly banging his head against the headrest as a tall, rigid silhouette approached. Wait a minute, he hadn't been pulled over since making it to the pros; maybe he could charm his way out of this one.

Nope, no such luck. After getting a ticket for going 48 in a 35, he pulled his Super Bowl prize-truck into his four-car garage.

Grabbing the bag of takeout and his phone from the passenger seat, he noticed a text from Colton: "Don't guess you've seen it or u would've called, but there's a pic in NE of me, Mercedes, u and Brittany. Article says ur together. Sorry man! Can't talk now, just wanted to give u a heads up. Call u later."

Every muscle in Derek's body contracted, then went numb. "What? You've gotta be kidding me!" He slammed his truck door hard enough to dislocate a shoulder, then kicked his front tire. "What else, man?!?"

A wave of nausea suddenly rose up and chased him to the bathroom. There was nothing on his stomach to lose, but that didn't keep him from dry heaving over the toilet half a dozen times.

Once he was able, he pulled out his cell phone and looked up the article Colton had referenced. How could they print such trash? He had never laid a finger on that tramp! He clenched his teeth, debating whether or not to take out the bathroom wall. Figuring he would wind up needing another surgery, he refrained, tugging on a fistful of hair instead.

Derek should've followed his hunch to demand another seat at Colton's birthday bash after being seated next to the model-turned-actress Brittany Sterling. The event had been held in a private room at a discreet venue, but he was afraid something like this would happen. Someone attending the party—or one of the food servers—must have snapped a photo for some easy cash. And just when he thought things couldn't get worse, they had.

Abby was bound to see or hear about the scandalous article. And even though there was no incriminating evidence against him, she would probably believe he was sleeping with the girl…just because the photo showed him sitting beside of her.

He wiped the sweat from his brow, his hands shaking like a leaf. His head was throbbing. No doubt, it was partly due to this new dilemma, but his blood sugar was probably low as well. He recognized the symptoms of what Dr. Nick called hypoglycemia. Derek had experienced this on the field a few times when his body had expended every last bit of energy—or sugar—he had. If Dr. Nick were here, he would give him a squirt of dextrose gel. But he was going to have to fix it by drinking some juice.

The thought of consuming anything sent him to his knees again, hovering over the toilet.

Finally able to get up, he buried his face in a cold washcloth and draped it across the back of his neck. Then he made his way to the kitchen, steadying himself along the mahogany, granite-covered countertops until he reached the refrigerator. The cool draft felt so refreshing that he rested his forehead against one of the refrigerator shelves for a few seconds before searching for the orange juice.

It was no wonder his blood sugar was low. He hadn't eaten anything in six hours. And even then, he had only had a protein bar. He was literally a lovesick fool, barely able to eat or sleep.

Derek's shaky hand nearly knocked over a half-empty can of soda water. Where on earth was the juice? He had looked in every nook and cranny of the refrigerator, moving around half a dozen containers of leftovers that should've been thrown out days ago. And there was no OJ to be found. He must've forgotten to put it on the grocery list for Marlene, the woman he recently hired to clean and run errands for him three times per week.

He chugged some milk from the carton, trying to shove his frustrations down with each forced gulp of the too thick, white liquid. Maybe there would be enough sugar in it to keep him from hitting the floor.

Milk in tow, he made his way to the kitchen table. Catching a whiff of his takeout from the bag in front of him, he was reminded of his dreadful upcoming task: eating dinner. Alone. *Oh look, it gets even better,* he sarcastically thought to himself as he eyed the separation papers from Abby, also on the table. They had harassed him for over a week now, shouting "You're a good-for-nothing loser" every time he walked by.

He just needed to get it over with and sign them. It's not like Abby couldn't contest if he refused to. And a piece of paper wouldn't really change things anyway. She wouldn't be here whether his signature was on the dotted line or not.

Derek couldn't keep living like this. He *had* to get Abby back, she being the only cure for this deadly disease. He had to see her...to assure her with his "truth eyes" that there was nothing going on between him and the superficial movie star. Yes, there *could've* been something between them—Brittany had made that very clear the night of the party—but nothing had happened. He didn't even give a second thought to her offer. He did find her physically attractive, as did every other man on the face of the planet, but his heart belonged to only one woman. Somehow, he just had to convince her of that. How could he, though, when she refused to talk to him, much less *see* him?

A spark of hope suddenly flickered, an idea coming to mind. Derek reached across the table for the separation papers, his hands no longer shaky. He stood up and walked to the junk drawer, shoving the papers to the very back, then slamming the drawer closed with forceful resolve.

He had never been one to go down without a fight, and he wouldn't start now. He would sign the papers for Abby if that's what she wanted, but only under one condition.

She would first have to meet with him in person...to come face to face with his bleeding heart.

CHAPTER TWENTY-SIX

W hy did he have to look so good? And smell so good? Abby inhaled the intoxicating scent of Derek's Polo Explorer, which mingled with the new-car-smell of his truck. The truck he won for being named MVP of the Super Bowl.

Abby's heart fluttered as she replayed the image of him on the big screen TV at Julie's house, his blue eyes sparkling, a sexy smile on his stubbly face as he jingled the keys in the air. Before that, he had mentioned her name, nearly breaking down in front of the entire nation. It was simultaneously one of the worst and best moments of her life.

Abby's chest was caving in, making it hard to breathe. Why in the world had she consented to this torture? If Derek refused to sign the separation papers until she met with him in person, she should've insisted they meet in a crowded restaurant. Or somewhere she would be less likely to fall under this spell he was casting over her.

She searched for a Christian station on the radio. Derek told her to listen to whatever she wanted, and that was definitely what she wanted—no, *needed*—to hear right now. Abby turned up the volume when she recognized Chris Tomlin's "Waterfall," hoping and praying the comforting words of the song would flood over her and wash away her pain.

The music did help, filling the awkward silence between them. Derek had tried to strike up conversation several times, but she kept shutting him down with simple, one-word answers to the questions he asked. She had no choice if she wanted to maintain her composure, especially since most of his questions regarded her dad, who was currently sicker than she had ever seen him.

Somehow, she had to come to terms with reality, with the fact that her Daddy was projected to live only three more months. At most.

The chirping of her phone brought her back to the current situation. She had a text message from her mom. "Where are you? How's it going?"

Janet Gibbs was probably a basket case by now. Although she didn't fret as much as she had when Abby was younger, she had a bad habit of worrying. She responded to her mom's message, assuring her that she was fine. She couldn't possibly tell her how uncomfortable and fragile she felt right now, knowing her mom had too much to deal with already. Abby knew she was drowning in a sea of sadness over her dad's condition, yet feeling obligated to stay strong for him and the rest of the family. The whole situation was terrible for all of them.

Abby grabbed a bottled water from her purse and took a few sips, attempting to push down the growing lump in her throat. How did she have any tears left? All she had done was cry since hearing the devastating news from her dad.

Between the drama with Derek and her dad's grim prognosis, she would have lost her sanity by now if it weren't for God and His peace. The peace which truly surpassed all understanding.

Her heart quickened when Derek turned into the entrance of Freedom Park. It wouldn't be long now until he cut to the chase; they would soon be rehashing everything they had already been through a hundred times. And her partially-healed wounds would be wide open and bleeding again.

Heat flushed across her face as Derek's forearm muscles flexed to push the gear into *park*. For the first time since hearing about her dad's death sentence, something sprang to life inside her. Abby savored the feeling, allowing herself to pretend for a moment they were still together...that infidelity had never tainted their love story.

Derek opened the center console and pulled out his Atlanta Braves ball cap, his trusty ticket to incognito. It was highly unlikely he would need it, though, because she hadn't spotted a single soul after scanning the perimeter of the park. Thinking of being alone with him in such a picturesque setting caused her stomach to do somersaults.

Abby opened the door, and Derek, being a Southern gentleman, rushed around the truck and extended his hand. "Here, let me help you. This thing is a little higher up than the Maserati," he chuckled.

It certainly was. And that's why it was perfectly justifiable for her to take his hand.

"Thanks," she whispered, the electricity of his touch stealing her voice. Then her breath. For the first time in way too long, her world was right-side-up. It required every ounce of willpower she could muster to peel her hand away from his.

Who was she kidding? Abby would be lying to herself if she didn't acknowledge the fact that she was happy Derek had imposed this stipulation on her: to meet with him before he would sign the papers. Because it had left her no option *not* to see him. Even her lawyer encouraged her to comply.

She distanced herself a few feet as they began walking, determined to get ahold of herself. The picture of Derek sitting beside the gorgeous Brittany Sterling flashed across her mind, jabbing her heart. He had texted a mile-long explanation as to how he wound up in the photo with Hollywood's latest "it-girl," adamantly denying the two of them had any romantic involvement. But, whether he had hooked up with her or not, the photo served to say Derek had plenty of options to choose from in a prime buffet of women. And with no moral compass to guide him, he would eventually cave in to the temptation.

If she took him back, she would find herself back at ground zero in just a matter of time. She needed to move on with her life while she was still young enough to find a good Christian man to share it with…to start a family with.

Abby took a deep, steadying breath. With God's help, she could do this. She could follow the rationale of her mind instead of the desperate longing of her heart. But she had to be prepared and predetermined to reject Derek when he became super-convincing. Because he would definitely sound convincing.

No doubt, she was about to be up against the strongest temptation she had ever faced. *Lord, lead me not into temptation.* Her silent plea to God would help, but ultimately, she was the one who was responsible for doing the resisting. Therefore, one rule would absolutely have to be followed: there could be no more physical contact. Zilch. None. Nada.

Because what her Nana always said was surely true: she couldn't play with fire without getting burned.

"I can't believe how cool it is today," Derek said, interrupting her silent pep talk. He gritted his teeth and zipped up his gray NorthFace hoodie, the one she gave him last Christmas.

It really was a cold day for mid-March, but his statement was obviously a continuation of their small talk-charade.

"I know. I'm sure this weather isn't good for your knee. It's hurting pretty bad, isn't it?" Abby was surprised by how much he was limping as they made their way into the park.

"Oh, it's not too bad." Derek brushed her off, but she wasn't fooled. A few months apart couldn't erase what six and a half years had taught her.

"Your surgery is when?" Her question was merely for the sake of filling in the gap of awkward silence. He had told her the date a few days ago, back when she finally broke down and followed her dad's advice to call him. Thinking of her dad, Abby felt for the sunglasses on top of her head and slipped them on.

"Twelve days." Derek's short-and-sweet answer left her fishing for what to say next, but she became distracted by what he was doing...unzipping the side pocket of his jacket and reaching inside.

She held her breath, remembering he had said something about having a gift for her when they talked on the phone. How was she going to respond to that?

"Wanna feed the ducks?" Derek pulled out a wadded-up, plastic bag filled with smushed bread. His enthusiastic smile contradicted the sad look in his eyes.

Abby looked away, his kind gesture putting a dent in her plan to remain detached. Why did he have to love her so much? Whoa. Never in a million years would she have thought she'd be asking such a question. Wasn't that her deepest desire, to be the idol of his affection? The air he breathed?

She forced herself to swallow as a growing lump threatened to cut off her airway. Yes, she would love to feed the ducks, and he already knew that. He knew her well, better than anyone else did.

A nod of her head would have to suffice for an answer. Because, as sure as the world, her voice would crack if she tried to say something, and that would be the start of an emotional avalanche which wouldn't stop until it completely buried her. There were just too many memories here.

By the way she was acting, Derek probably thought she was still angry and bitter toward him. But she wasn't.

Her dad had been right about her withholding true forgiveness. She prayed and did a lot of soul searching before calling Derek a few nights ago. It felt amazing to finally rid herself of all the resentment she had been harboring...to leave vengeance in God's hands, where it belonged, and to extend sincere forgiveness. But, even though she had completely let go of her hostility and ill-will toward Derek, she couldn't act the way she used to around him. If she did, she may mislead him into believing there was a chance of them getting back together.

Abby balled her hands into fists and squeezed so hard she nearly cut her palms with her fingernails. Now she knew why she had chosen to live behind a cloak of anger and bitterness for so long. Although the toxic emotions had been corroding her soul like battery acid, they were much easier to withstand than feeling the way she did right now. They had effectively served as protective mechanisms, shielding her from more pain—the kind of pain that may totally wipe out her resolve.

⇥⇤

If this was forgiveness, Derek must've had the wrong idea of the word. If Abby had forgiven him, as she sincerely declared on the phone a few nights ago, then why was she stone cold?

It had been stupid to get his hopes up. The magnitude of this letdown was more likely to send him to his knees than the actual pain in his knee, which jabbed him like an icepick every time he took a step.

Nearing the pond in the center of Freedom Park, Derek spotted two ducks. *What?* Where were all the other ducks? There was supposed to be a huge flock of them waddling around and quacking in every direction. He scratched his head. Obviously, he had watched *The Notebook's* swan-scene a few too many times.

He always pretended to be in agony when Abby stumbled across the movie—her favorite—but he secretly enjoyed Allie and Noah's love story.

Derek pulled out a handful of bread for the two measly ducks, supposing he should be thankful there were two versus none. "So—" He took a deep breath, readying himself to play the pathetic, lovesick fool. He had nothing to lose. He may be the reigning MVP of the Super Bowl, but he might as well have been a pooper-scooper at the circus. That's how much pride he had left. And he was willing to swallow the last ounce he had in order to have his Abby back.

"So, the reason I insisted on seeing you is because I found something I want you to have." He was telling the truth, but not the whole truth. He did want her to have Gram's angel pendant, even if it meant parting with the special piece of her he had discovered in a box of his old things; mostly, though, it had given him a good excuse to insist on seeing her.

It had been way too long since he had gotten lost in the heaven of her eyes, in those rare emeralds which now held him captive.

Derek forced himself to breathe. "Here," he said, placing a tiny, purple-wrapped box in Abby's hand. In his periphery, he saw something fall from her other hand, making a soft landing on the freshly mowed grass below. It was a piece of bread.

Oops, they were supposed to be feeding the ducks; he was getting ahead of himself. What a goofball. "Oh, my bad!" Derek chuckled as he snatched the gift out of Abby's hands.

Another mistake. What kind of idiot stole a woman's gift away? Too late now. He had already stuffed the box into his pocket and was fumbling around for another piece of bread, heat rushing to his cheeks. "Sorry, we haven't even fed—"

"It's fine," Abby said, cutting him off. Her touch to his forearm took his breath. So did her genuine laugh. "This is so si—" She couldn't even finish her sentence, overtaken by laughter.

Derek didn't know how to respond, not quite sure what was funny enough to warrant such an outburst.

Abby sucked in a gulp of air, holding her hand over her chest. "This is so silly...us being so uptight around each other. Over ducks, for crying out loud!" She started laughing again. Hysterically.

A smile stretched the skin on his face for the first time since the Super Bowl. It's like he had just been released from prison, hearing Abby's laughter. A sound he hadn't heard since the playful snow day which had led to the worst night of his life.

His *real* wife was finally within reach. He had missed her even more than he'd realized.

The laughter was contagious. Cool, crisp air now filled his lungs as he gasped for breath. The sound coming from him had become so unfamiliar that he felt like a stranger in his own skin.

Abby's smile gradually dissipated as she repeatedly ran her fingers through her long hair. A telltale sign she was nervous. "I've got to stop this charade, D." Her words continued, but as soon as she said "D.," he checked out. She hadn't called him that in forever.

"I'm sorry, what'd you say?"

"I said that from now on, I'm just going to be real with you. You know, like I said the other night, I've finally reached the point where I've completely forgiven you." Abby broke eye contact, looking down. "And I still love you."

Those words were like magic, the way they made something spring to live inside of him.

"Wow, I actually said it. It feels so good to admit that," Abby said, her lips curling into a smile.

Man, she was gorgeous…so gorgeous it hurt. If only he could run his fingers through her hair, through the highlights she had recently added that glistened in the sunlight. He had to be the stupidest man on the planet. Why had he gone and slept with another woman when he already had the most beautiful one in the world?

Abby's expression began to harden. Her sharp exhale brought Derek's world to a standstill; a *but* was definitely coming.

"But that doesn't mean we should be together."

"Yes it does, Ab!" He whined the words like a bratty child. Determined to regain his composure after being deflated like a busted balloon, he took a slow, deep breath. "If you still love me, we can make it work. I know we can."

"No." Abby's firm assertion tied his stomach in knots. She started talking again, but with tightness migrating from his gut to his chest, he couldn't focus. The vice grip finally loosened a bit—enough that he could tune back in to her voice.

Hearing the word "God," Derek's hope instantly resurfaced. Because he had made a decision that would change everything. One which would prove to Abby how much he loved her and how committed he was to making their marriage work.

"I'll stand behind you in your faith, Ab. I won't say a word if you want to go to church…I'll even go with you during the offseason if you want me to." Derek could barely believe his own ears. "And we can go to marriage counseling if you want. Whatever it takes, I'll do it."

He stopped and stared at the long-lost treasure in front of him, willing her to read the sincerity in his eyes. "I'm begging you, please give me another chance. I love you more than anything in this world. I'll even quit football if you want me to."

Had he really just said that? The thought had never even crossed his mind. Derek scratched his head, wondering if he truly meant those words. Looking at Abby, the answer was perfectly clear: yes, he did. He would even quit football, the second love of his life, to have her back again. "It all means nothing without you, babe."

Derek didn't try to stop or wipe the tears escaping his eyes. They could help him plead his case. "I actually have a legit way out…I can just pretend my knee is still too painful to play, even after the surgery. Money won't be a big deal if we downsize. We can always sell off a few vehicles if we need to. But we'll have money coming in from endorsements and stuff. And I've always got my business degree to fall back on. So I can quit all this crap, and we'll have somewhat of a normal life again. How's that sound, baby?"

Breath hung in his chest, his entire life swinging in the balance. The monstrous sunglasses covering Abby's eyes made it impossible to read her. A few tears began to stream down her cheeks, but she smiled. Derek's heart was pounding so hard that she probably heard it from four feet away. A smile meant her tears were happy ones, right?

But why wasn't she saying anything?

Abby inched closer to him, and the answer suddenly came, illuminating his mind with an understanding which sent surges of electricity through his veins. Some moments were just too powerful for words: that must be the reason for her silence. He had finally convinced her to come back, hadn't he?

Derek's knees nearly gave way, a sense of urgency overtaking him as Abby reached out her arms. He couldn't get his arms around her fast enough. But once he did, he was never letting go.

CHAPTER TWENTY-SEVEN

The feel of Derek's hand along the small of her back sent more shivers down Abby's spine than the frigid ocean water rushing over her feet. She drew nearer to him, savoring the warmth of his body and the rays of sunlight warming her face. God was definitely smiling down on her.

In her periphery, she noticed Wanda making her way toward the shore in front of Aunt Rachel's beach house. Abby threw up her hand and waved, hoping Wanda could see the genuine smile on her face from this distance. She couldn't wait to catch her up on the things God had done in her life since their last meeting.

Abby glanced up at her husband, admiring his chiseled, scruffy face and cute dimples as he squinted in the afternoon sun.

It was definitely a bright, bright sunshiny day.

"Come on," she insisted, grabbing Derek's hand and laughing. She hopped a few steps ahead, tugging on his arm. They should take a playful skip along the shore. Like two big kids.

Derek joined her, and the sound of their laughter was louder than the crashing waves beside them. They skipped hand in hand, swinging their arms in the air. A splash of cold water to Abby's stomach caused her to squeal out, and Derek came to an abrupt stop. Supposing his knee had given out, she held her breath...only for a second, though, because the smile on his face contradicted that frightening thought.

Derek suddenly pulled her close, whisking her into his arms. As her feet left the ground, she felt no bigger than a toy doll, the way he was able to manhandle her in his strong, muscular arms. Abby wrapped her arms around his neck and her legs around his waist, pulling him in for a kiss.

Finally. Finally she was happy again. Complete. Pain was a thing of the past. There was absolutely no doubt in her mind that Derek was hers, and only hers. Forever. She totally trusted him with her heart, knowing he would never break it again.

Derek pulled his face back and removed his sunglasses, resting them on top of his head. His sandy-blonde hair glowed in the sunlight. Lifting Abby with only one arm, he adjusted her position around his waist. Her hair and sundress were swept up in the sea breeze, dancing across her skin as a whiff of Polo Explorer sent her to the clouds, soaring. With his sunglasses off, she could now see the passion in Derek's eyes. Eyes bluer than the Atlantic behind him. They were windows to his soul, radiating the light of his love—love coming from the deepest parts of him, the intensity of it scorching a pathway to her soul, bringing butterflies to life in her stomach.

"I love y—" Before Derek could finish his declaration of love, a wave came up out of nowhere and crashed upon them. It separated them and pulled them out to sea.

Abby tried to scream, but she couldn't. The ice-cold water stole her breath, even before it sucked her under. She kicked and flailed, but there was no use trying to fight the raging current. Someone or some*thing* was now grabbing her ankles, pulling her even further down.

Everything was pitch dark. Cold. Hopeless.

Her lungs were burning for air.

A glare of light suddenly appeared. Above her, to the right. The light grew brighter and illuminated the surface. Even though it was way, way above her, there was a ray of hope...until the grip around her ankles latched on tighter.

God! For the first time since going under, Abby thought of God. He was with her. All she had to do was call out His name, and He would rescue her. *Jesus, help me!*

A split second after her heart's cry, the grip around her ankle vanished, leaving her free to swim toward the surface. Toward the light. Adrenaline and hope propelled her. She would soon be able to put out the blazing fire in her lungs.

Something was wrong, though. Why was the light getting farther away? Abby felt like she was moving through the water at the speed of an Olympic athlete, but she was still losing ground. The light was now far, far away.

Too far away.

It would be impossible to hold her breath long enough to cover that distance. But what choice did she have other than to keep trying?

After an eternity of strenuous swimming, Abby was no closer to the surface. It was no use. She was about to make a huge mistake, one which would take her life. But she was helpless to stop it. There was simply no way to fight it any longer...the most basic and primitive instinct of man: to breathe.

⟞⟞ ⟝⟝

Abby awakened in a state of panic, coughing and drenched in cold sweat. Realizing the near-death experience was only a dream, she savored the air rushing into her lungs. Her heart wouldn't settle down, though. It was like a drum about to explode through her chest.

She sat up and switched on her nightstand lamp, hoping to shed some light on this crazy situation. The nightmare was so real.

And so was the part before the nightmare.

If only she could fall back to sleep and pick up where she and Derek had left off, right before the scary part. What a cruel reality to finally have what her heart had longed for, then to awaken to an even bigger void—a more intense yearning after being teased by a delicious taste. Suddenly, more than her next breath, she needed to be in Derek's arms. How could she go on living without ever feeling that way again?

Abby grabbed her pillow, hugging it to her chest as if it could somehow fill in the black hole-sized vacuum left there in the wake of her dream. A cool draft from the ceiling fan swept over her clammy body, bringing goosebumps to her bare arms. She scooted beneath the covers and rolled over, coming face to face with a favorite photo on her nightstand. One of her and Sarah when they were kids. She grabbed the multi-colored jeweled frame to take a closer look at the snapshot, even though the image was practically seared into her mind from all the times she'd studied it before.

How she longed to relive the day that moment was captured on film. To see the world through that four-year-old's sparkling eyes again...the little girl whose biggest disappointment was that Daddy wouldn't buy more tickets for her to ride the Ferris wheel "just one more time."

Abby returned the photo to its place and grabbed a box of Kleenex. "Why, God?" She wanted to shout the words, but she mumbled them softly before being swept away in a flood of tears. It wouldn't be long until she had *two* gigantic holes in her heart. How did God expect her to live without Derek *and* her Daddy?

Just as she was climbing out of the valley after that emotional day at the park—the day she had to pry herself away from Derek and reject a sincere offer she desperately wanted to take—everything toppled over again like a tower of toy blocks. The few steps she had taken forward were negated by a hundred steps back when a hospice nurse showed up at the front door.

Abby stiffened, startled by some unknown sound. There it was again. Scooter, pawing at the door. He whimpered a few times. Had he heard her crying from her parents' bedroom down the hall?

Opening the door to a wagging tail and precious puppy-dog eyes, Abby's heart was instantly lighter. But that changed after one glance at herself in the dresser mirror as she carried the smelly pooch to bed. Her eyes were so puffy she would have to hold ice cubes on them all morning in order to look presentable for the wedding this afternoon. A couple from her Sunday School class was getting married today at three o'clock, and she couldn't miss it.

Her pulse accelerated at the thought of Luke, who had mentioned something about them sitting together during the ceremony. Abby hadn't thought much about it during their casual conversation at church last week, but the more she pondered it, the more she read into it. Would it be considered a date if they sat beside each other?

Her feelings for Luke were so complicated, just like the rest of her life. There was definitely an attraction there, but she wasn't ready to date yet. Or was she? Maybe that was her only hope of getting past her feelings for Derek.

If only she could put a *hold* sign on the tall, dark, and handsome doctor—who seemed to be just as good on the inside as the outside—because he wouldn't stay single very long.

A hot flash suddenly worked its way over her, proving she was more anxious about sitting next to Luke than she had realized. Thankfully, her mom and dad were planning to attend the wedding too; it shouldn't feel much like a date if they sat next to them. Then again, recalling her dad's coughing spell at dinner, she wondered if her parents would even be able to go.

Scooter tilted his head and perked his ears, looking at her with a confused expression on his face, almost as if he sensed her worries regarding her dad…his dad. Abby laid down and nuzzled him, utilizing his soft, floppy ear to soak up a tear which slid down her cheek. Was God really going to call her Daddy home within the next six weeks? How were they all going to survive without him?

Suddenly, Abby understood the meaning of her horrific nightmare: she really was drowning. And unless God came to the rescue ASAP, she wasn't going to make it.

Lord, help me, please. I don't want to be angry at You. I know You have Your reasons, but I just don't understand why You won't heal my Daddy. He's such a good and faithful servant, and I need him. Please, God! Please perform a miracle.

Abby wiped her eyes and opened her Bible.

CHAPTER TWENTY-EIGHT

John couldn't catch his breath. What was going on? Where was he? He forced his eyes to open, and the fog of confusion began to clear. A little. He was in the hospital... with pneumonia? No, that wasn't right. He *had* been in the hospital, but they moved him to the hospice house...maybe two or three days ago now? He had lost track of time.

Fatigue beckoned him back to sleep—or Heaven's gates, perhaps, since he had seen Grandma Ava—but the shortness of breath kept him awake. He was expending every ounce of energy he had just to make his lungs rise and fall. Was there anyone here to help him? He tried to turn his head, but it was too heavy.

"Daddy?"

Ah, the precious sound of Abby's voice. Or was that Sarah?

"Mom, he's awake!" The voice got closer and someone clasped his hand. Sarah appeared in his periphery. He found the strength to turn his head a notch, needing to see her sweet face. "Hey Daddy. How are you feeling?"

A mixture of joy and grief flowed through him as he beheld his firstborn daughter's smile—one which was likely forced, considering her red-rimmed eyes. How he longed to wrap his arms around her and pull her close, to assure her that everything was going to be okay. But all he could do was lift the corners of his lips.

"Hey, sweetie." His wife's voice was like a breath of fresh air. There she was: Janet, the love of his life. Tears were streaming down her cheeks.

John had to get up—and get better—to console her. He somehow managed to pull himself up to a sitting position using the side rail of his bed.

"No! You can't get up. Lay back down, honey." Janet meant business, so he gave up the useless fight, letting go of the bedrail and sinking into his pillow. Now he was even more short of breath.

"Daddy, are you hurting?"

He didn't want to burden them with the truth, but his chest did ache. The pain wasn't as bad as the shortness of breath, though. Overall, he hadn't experienced a tremendous amount of pain, especially when considering he was walking through the valley of the shadow of death. The Good Shepherd was definitely with him. Never once had He left his side during this difficult, uncertain journey.

John tried to nod his head to indicate he was hurting, but it wouldn't budge. And the only result of his attempt to speak was one incomprehensible syllable of raspiness, followed by a rattling in his chest.

"Okay, sweetie, I'm going to get the nurse." His wife squeezed his hand and walked away.

The inability to communicate was the worst part of all this. How he longed to express his love to his family and tell them about seeing Grandma Ava...and what he just now remembered her telling him: "Johnny, I can't wait for you to see the glory of the Lord and the place He's prepared for you! It's beyond anything you can imagine."

Lord, I'm thankful I'll be seeing Your face soon, and I'm excited to see the place You've prepared for me, but please let me tell my family how much I love them one more time. Please comfort them and give them Your peace in the days ahead. Most importantly, Lord, please see to it that Derek and everyone in my family—those I know and those who are yet to be—invite You into their hearts before they leave this earth, so that we can all have a glorious reunion in the sky. In Jesus' name, Amen.

"Hey, Papaw...and Nana," Sarah said, looking toward the door. "Daddy, look who's here."

John's mom leaned down and kissed his cheek. His dad stood beside him, grabbing his hand.

"He seems to be a little uncomfortable, so Mama just went to find the nurse," Sarah said.

"Yeah, we passed her on the way in." His dad's voice cracked. He let go of John's hand and wiped his face, then hobbled to the couch beside of the bed.

"Hang in there, darling. The nurse is bringing you some medicine. You'll feel better soon." His mom's soothing voice, accompanied by her gentle strokes to his forehead, transmitted the timeless, unconditional love only a mother could give. He did his best to clasp her fragile, arthritic hand when she reached for his.

A tear trickled down John's cheek. He was one blessed man. He had loved and been loved by so many special people. Even though he would be outlived by both parents, he couldn't have asked for a fuller, more meaningful life.

And his mom had just declared a sweet truth, one which brought him hope and joy that far outweighed the discomfort he was experiencing. Yes, he was going to feel better soon. *Much* better. But it wouldn't be on account of any medicine.

⊱⊰

Rays of moonlight crept through the blinds and shone onto the floor of her dad's hospice room as Abby lay on the pull-out couch beside him. She must have drifted off to sleep. But now she was wide-awake, analyzing her dad's breathing pattern: Inhale, exhale. Inhale, exhale. Inhale…exhale. Another pause, or maybe—

No, she wouldn't go there. Couldn't go there. All this had happened way too fast. Abby willed her Daddy to breathe again, counting the seconds since his last breath. Sixteen, seventeen…Was this it? The end?

She jumped to her feet, rushing to her Daddy's bedside. Where was her mom? She had been laying right next to her. Noticing a sliver of light beneath the closed door of the room's private bathroom, she assumed her mom was in there. Abby was about to call for her, but the sweet sound of another breath stopped her.

Thank You, God! Her Daddy was still here. Well, not really, because he had been unresponsive since this afternoon. But at least he was still alive. She cradled his face in her hand, pressing her cheek to his. "I love you, Daddy."

Abby kissed his forehead, then stood to her feet and began pacing the floor with balled fists. Swallowing hard, she tried to shove down the rising resentment in her chest. Why had her mom given up on him so quickly? The social worker had explained that her dad's "hospice benefit" could easily be revoked, and then he could be admitted to the hospital where they would do all they could to treat the pneumonia. Here at hospice, they wouldn't even give him IV fluids... which he desperately needed, being that he hadn't been able to eat or drink anything in over two days.

Her Daddy was a fighter. If they treated him with antibiotics, she was 99 percent sure he would recover from the pneumonia. She understood her dad's wishes to avoid drastic measures, but IV fluids and antibiotics didn't seem drastic at all.

An opposing inner voice suddenly convicted her. Abby shouldn't be angry with her mom. She was his wife and appointed healthcare power of attorney, so the decision was hers to make. And there was no doubt she was doing what she believed was best for her dad, trying to make decisions based upon his wishes. Whom was she kidding, anyway? Treating the pneumonia would only be prolonging the inevitable. Her Daddy may live a few more weeks, but the extra amount of time wouldn't be worth all the torture he would have to endure. He had been through enough already.

Guilt gnawed at her. Her poor mom needed all the love and support she could get, but Abby had been short with her for days now. Why hadn't she realized how selfish she was being? If she were in her dad's shoes, there's no way she would opt to be poked and prodded by needles to simply survive a few more pain-filled weeks...especially when the alternative was to take the hand of Jesus and go to a place more beautiful than the human mind can imagine. This was definitely the most difficult situation she had ever faced. Longing for inner peace, Abby did something she had trained herself to do over the last few weeks: she implemented Philippians 4:6-8, one of her new favorite Scriptures. No matter how troubled her soul was, every time she followed Paul's words of advice, a peace beyond understanding enveloped her. Just as God promised.

Exhaling slowly, she gave God thanks for the blessings He had given her. She had a lot to praise Him for, even in this storm. She thanked God for giving her the chance to interact with her Daddy one more time. While at the dentist's office this past afternoon, God had prompted her to postpone having a cavity filled in order to be at her dad's side. If He had not impressed this upon her spirit, she would have been too late; her dad would've been unresponsive the next time she saw him. And she would have missed out on the special conversation the family had shared...probably the last one they would all share.

The clicking of the bathroom door suddenly scattered her thoughts. Abby caught her mom's eyes as the door creaked open. "Hey, why don't you leave that door cracked with the light on," she said softly. "He had another pause, close to twenty seconds."

Her mom nodded. "I counted twenty-eight a little while a—" She was unable to finish the sentence, coming to a complete standstill at the foot of the bed. Her hands flew to her face, and her body started shaking.

Abby rushed to her side. They came together in a tight embrace, crying on one another's shoulders. There were simply no words for a moment like this, so she said nothing. But a loud wail suddenly escaped against her control.

"Shhh! He can probably hear us," her mom said in a forceful whisper. "You need to step outside?"

Abby shook her head, not wanting to leave the room. Her mom was right, though; the nurse told them hearing was the last sense to go. She had to get ahold of herself. She wanted to take advantage of every second she had left with her Daddy, and he sure didn't need to be burdened by her crying.

She hugged her mom for a few more seconds, then pulled away and looked at her dad. With light from the bathroom shining into the room, Abby could make out a peaceful expression on his face. His calmness affirmed there was a place of refuge for all of them...that God's comfort and peace could be experienced even in moments like these.

"The nurse said this could go on for days." Her mom's voice was now collected. "She said the pauses between his breaths could last almost a minute at a time. I don't know, I just pray he's not suffering. I don't think he is. And I don't think he has much longer," she said, making her way to the chair next to her dad's bed.

"Only God knows," Abby said, taking her dad's hand—a limber block of ice. A knowing deep within concurred with her mom's grim prediction. Promising Sarah she would call if there were any major changes, she grabbed her phone from the tray table beside her dad's bed.

Studying her Daddy's face again, her heart was completely torn. It was like a knife had been jabbed through part of it, while another part danced for joy, imagining her Daddy skipping down the streets of gold without an ounce of pain. More than likely, that's what he would be doing before the morning light.

His color had definitely changed. But the main reason Abby knew it wouldn't be long before her Daddy reached those pearly gates was because of the expression on his face.

His eyes were closed, but he was smiling from ear to ear.

CHAPTER TWENTY-NINE

"Derek, are you okay in there?"

Where am I? Derek awoke to the sound of a man's muffled voice in an unfamiliar bathroom, face down on a gray rug.

"Huh?" It was the only response he could muster. Who was he even talking to?

"Can I come in?"

"I guess," Derek said as he rose to a sitting position, feeling like he was on a merry-go-round. He wasn't crazy about allowing a guy to join him in the bathroom, but he needed some answers.

"You feeling any better?" His teammate, Timothy, stood at the door holding a glass. "Here's some aspirin and Coke. Hopefully you can keep it down."

Taking the glass from Timothy, a few fragmented memories began piecing together in his mind. The team had been celebrating Coach Ryan's birthday in a private room at a restaurant uptown. He remembered sitting next to Colton, downing a few beers, but that was about it.

"What's going on? What am I doing here?" His speech was slurred, and a wave of nausea rose up, confirming his suspicion. He was stinking-drunk.

"Man, you kept ordering more and more shots until you finally lost it all in the parking lot. You were as sick as a dog, so I just brought you home with me since I live only five—"

Before Timothy could finish the explanation, Derek's stomach revolted against the few sips of Coke he had hesitantly swallowed. He crawled to the toilet as fast as he could, clutching the cold porcelain for dear life. He retched time after time after time, his body evidently unwilling to accept the fact that there was nothing left to come up.

"Here." The cold, wet cloth Timothy draped over his neck caught him unaware, pulling him from the grip of death.

"Thanks." Derek wiped the cool cloth across his face. Surprisingly, the nausea subsided.

"I'm sorry for all this." The words fell drastically short of excusing his pathetic, humiliating behavior. He hoped with everything in him that he hadn't awakened Timothy's wife and kids. "If you call me a limo, I'll get out of your way."

"No, you're staying here tonight." His teammate's voice was stern, yet full of compassion. "The guest room is right through this door," he pointed. "Let me help you to bed. I'll put the trash can right beside you."

Even though his vision was blurry, Derek could see the kindness which always shone from Timothy's dark eyes. He felt a little guilty for considering the guy a nuisance at the end of last season. Obviously, he genuinely did care about him. Timothy had always asked him how he was *really* doing, even though he had repeatedly brushed him off.

"Okay." Derek reluctantly conceded to stay.

Why was Colton not looking out for him instead of Timothy? He was sure it had something to do with Mercedes; that conniving, controlling bimbo had practically stolen his best friend.

He grabbed Timothy's outstretched hand. How humiliating. But, considering the heaviness in his legs, it was either that or lay back down on the bathroom floor.

After practically dragging him to bed and tucking him in, Timothy sat down on the edge beside him. His dark brown eyes were focused like a laser, zeroing in on his, somehow conjuring up tears. Derek quickly looked away, blinking. Already on the verge of losing his *man card*, he wasn't about to cry.

"I know I've told you a hundred times, but I'll say it again: I'm here for you. You are—" Timothy abruptly closed his mouth and bit his bottom lip. Were those tears in his eyes? "I'll be right down the hall, three doors down to your left. And my phone will be on the nightstand beside me, so give me a shout if you need anything." He stood to his feet, patting Derek on the shoulder.

Relieved, he allowed his lungs to deflate. Being that Timothy was so concerned about him and held his undivided attention, Derek had been sure a lecture—or worse yet, a sermon—was coming.

"I'm praying for you, my friend."

Derek offered a quick nod, unsure what to say. If only things were that simple. "Thanks for looking out for me, man," he said as Timothy approached the door.

"Anytime, bro. Anytime."

As soon as Timothy closed the door, Derek rolled over in bed, allowing a few tears to spill onto the yellow satin pillowcase. If only he could be that naive, believing prayer could magically fix everything...like a fairy godmother.

If there was really a God to pray to, then there would be no need for prayer. Because if there was a good and all-powerful God—the way Christians believed—things wouldn't be so messed up to begin with. Derek would've been born to functional, loving parents instead of a deadbeat, alcoholic father and a mother who didn't love him enough to hold it together after the fool walked out. Gram wouldn't have died either. And if she had not died, he would have never moved to Charlotte with Uncle Scott and Aunt Diana. Therefore, he wouldn't have met Abby. And wouldn't he be better off if he had never met her?

The ache in his chest confirmed that he would be.

Whoever said "it's better to have loved and lost than to have never loved at all" was wrong. With his unlucky past, he should've known better than to fall in love with anyone, not even a good girl like Abby. Because if she didn't love him enough to give him another chance after all he'd promised her that day at the park, she would've eventually fallen out of love with him whether he had cheated or not.

Derek scooted to the edge of the bed in a hurry, feeling for the trash can as another wave of nausea hit.

"Ow!" A stabbing pain in his bad knee stole his breath. All it took was one wrong move lately. Grabbing the ice-cold glass of Coke from the nightstand, he was unsure whether to press it against his forehead or hold it against his throbbing knee. Derek did the latter until he no longer felt pain with every pulsation of his heart. Then he rubbed the cold glass along his cheeks and forehead, hoping to freeze the nausea too.

How on earth was he going to deal with feeling this way for a whole week after his knee surgery? He dreaded it worse than anything he had ever faced. When he had surgery on his knee in college, the recovery was horrific. Even with Abby's outstanding care. He hadn't been able to survive without one of the strongest narcotic pain meds, but almost every time he took it, he had another beast to battle: nausea.

Thankfully, the current wave of queasiness had let up. Derek took a small sip of Coke and placed the glass back on the nightstand. That's when he noticed a remote control— the only thing that had excited him all night. After one touch of the blinking power button, the TV came to life with the promise of a much-needed distraction. Anything would be better than just lying here, wallowing in physical and emotional agony.

Anything besides listening to the preacher man coming into focus on the screen.

CHAPTER THIRTY

Timothy peeked in on his youngest son, Josiah, hoping he hadn't been awakened by the commotion with Derek down the hall. His heart felt lighter than it had all night when the light from the Noah's ark nightlight confirmed that his 14-month-old was sleeping as a baby should.

Next up on his rounds was Jewelia Faith, his three-year-old. Timothy couldn't help but stare at her for a while, her face in sweet slumber with Simba the lion clutched in her chubby arms. *Thank you, Father.* Happy tears pricked his eyes as he praised God for his only daughter. She had just recently recovered from the rare, mysterious Kawasaki syndrome. Thankfully, the diagnosis was made early enough to manage it, significantly reducing the chances of any long-term complications. Their prayers had been answered thus far, and he claimed victory in Jesus' name over the precautionary heart screening she had coming up next week.

"Daddy!" Timothy jumped, startled by his oldest son's voice. Jude was running down the hall toward him.

"Shhh." He pressed his finger to his lips, begging his little chatterbox not to wake up the rest of the household. Timothy picked up the five-year-old kid who appeared to have grown two inches since the previous day. He chuckled to himself, pulling Jude's pajama top down to cover his exposed belly; even though he had clearly outgrown them, he insisted on wearing his favorite pair of Carolina Panthers pajamas. The boy was stubborn…just like his Daddy. "What are you doing awake, buddy?"

"I had a bad dream," Jude said, his bottom lip protruding. He locked his little arms around Timothy's neck and snuggled against his chest. One of the best feelings in the world. "There was a monster in my closet, and it chased me down the hall, and when I got to yours and Mommy's room, the monster was in y'alls bed, and—"

"Shhh!" He cut the boy's panicked recollection short, squeezing him tighter and kissing the top of his head. "It's okay now. Daddy's right here. It was just a bad dream."

The kid had always had an exaggerated imagination, so his subconscious had probably gotten carried away after hearing the ruckus with Derek across the hall. "Let's go lay back down. You've got school tomorrow. I'll stay with you till you fall back to sleep."

After crawling into bed with his son, struggling to scrunch his 6'2"-205-pound frame into a full size bed, he began to read Jude's favorite Bible story about David and Goliath. Thankfully, Jude fell asleep about halfway through it. Timothy crept quietly out of the airplane-themed room and headed toward the master suite down the hall.

Jazmin, his lovely wife, was sound asleep. She was snoring softly, as she often did after a hard day's work of being the best wife and mom in the world. He was careful not to make much noise as he stripped down to his boxer shorts and laid his jewelry on the dresser: a watch, his wedding ring, and two Super Bowl rings.

It was hard to believe just how far he had come—or rather, how far God had brought him. Timothy made millions of dollars a year playing the game he loved, and the Lord had entrusted him with such an amazing family. Why had God blessed him so abundantly? It was humbling, especially considering all the ways he had failed Him in the past. In some ways, Derek reminded him of the *B.C. version* of himself. That's probably why his heart had been so burdened for the guy.

Timothy's stomach knotted, remembering the man he had been up until his junior year at Ohio State, until the November night he gave his life to Christ at a Campus Crusade meeting. There were simply no excuses for the things he had done. He had known better, being raised in a Christian home. Basically, he had been the modern-day prodigal son.

He swallowed the lump of regret rising in his throat. How could he have treated his parents the way he had? Or cheated on such a special woman...multiple times? Thank God, Kendra, his high school sweetheart, ended up leaving him; if she hadn't, Timothy wouldn't have found his soulmate. But he was ashamed of how he had treated her, and he hated they had ended on such bad terms. According to his sister, even though he had apologized and asked Kendra to forgive him, she still hated his guts.

Jesus had forgiven him, though. Thank God for His saving grace…and for the shoulder injury his junior year which led him to rock bottom where he found that grace. He had definitely been on the road to nowhere. Nowhere but Hell.

Timothy thought of Derek down the hall. Maybe he should go check on him. *Pray for him.* The familiar prompting came straight from his spirit.

He had been praying for Derek ever since he joined the team nearly two years ago, but over the last few months, he had stepped up his game. Here lately, the guy seemed so down and withdrawn. Timothy assumed the rumors about him were true, that his wife had left him because he'd cheated on her in Seattle last year. But he had never heard Derek say a word about it to anyone.

Father, please help him. Help him realize his need for You. Show him that all his fortune and fame are worth nothing without You. Please heal and restore him. His marriage too. Please change Derek's life like You did mine. In Jesus' name, Amen.

Timothy was hopeful. No matter how closed off Derek seemed, he knew he was reachable. Because there had always been a *searching look* in his eyes, a look crying out for there to be something more to life. A look which gave him hope that the lost sheep would somehow come to know the Savior.

And this was all part of God's plan: Derek being at his house tonight. Suddenly, he knew it in the depths of his soul. It all made sense now, why the enemy had been hard after him over the last 12 hours. There was the family drama regarding his deadbeat brother-in-law this morning, an upset stomach this afternoon, and a flat tire en route to the restaurant this evening. For these reasons, Timothy almost backed out of Coach's birthday party.

God must be up to something major. Because the thief—who came only to steal, kill, and destroy—had definitely been trying to wear him down all day. "Devil, get out of my way. You're a defeated foe. God's plan will prevail." He whispered the words, sensing he was in the middle of some serious spiritual warfare.

Another prompting began to gnaw at his spirit. He tried to dismiss it, but the Holy Spirit was persistent. Timothy had learned he couldn't ignore that voice, no matter how irrational it seemed.

He gently nudged Jazmin's shoulder and whispered in her ear. "Babe, wake up." He hated to interrupt his wife's much-needed sleep, but God was definitely directing him. And she would understand once he explained the situation to her. Being a courageous prayer warrior and the leader of their church's prayer team, she was always willing to step up to the front lines of battle.

Jazmin moaned, pulling the sheet over her head. He pulled it back and kissed her soft, mocha cheek. "Babe, wake up a minute, okay?"

She rubbed her eyes and rolled over to look at the clock on her nightstand. "Timmy, it's two o'clock in the morning! What is it?"

He felt a little guilty, but knowing he was doing the right thing, he flipped on his reading light. "Honey, you know Derek from the team? Well, he's here...in the guest room."

Jazmin rolled over to face him, a puzzled expression on her face. She shielded her squinting eyes from the light.

"I'm sorry for waking you, but we need to pray for him. I think he's hit rock bottom. He was so drunk—so sick—that I brought him home with me. And I think God is up to something big because I keep feeling the need to pray for him."

Taking Jazmin's hand, a peaceful assurance washed over him. Prayer was certainly a powerful weapon. Especially when two or more were gathered in Christ's name. His poor wife looked like a zombie, but she nodded her head in affirmation, interlacing her fingers with his.

Timothy cleared his throat. "Let us pray."

CHAPTER THIRTY-ONE

What else would he expect to be on TV at Timothy's house other than TCT—Total Christian Television? Derek placed his finger on the *channel up* button, but something unexpectedly captured his attention. Beneath a dark-headed man who was being interviewed read a caption: "Science led a former atheist biochemist to God."

This Dr. Anthony Crowell was full of enthusiasm. Derek couldn't help but be intrigued by his apparent knowledge as he discussed several supposed flaws with the theory of evolution. He would have to *Google* what the guy called the "Cambrian explosion." He was also going to see if Jesus really did fulfill more than 300 prophesies.

Using exuberant hand gestures, the scientist continued on, talking about the impossible odds of one protein molecule coming together in a Petri dish, even if all the necessary amino acid-building blocks were purposely placed there. It had been a long time since freshman biology class, but the terms the man used sounded legit.

"If there's anyone out there listening who's an atheist, I beg you to investigate the evidence for yourself. Believe me, I get you…I know where you're coming from because I was once there myself." The guy continued trying to persuade his viewers to allow science to prove the existence, rather than the nonexistence, of intelligent design. And after the TV host did an advertising spiel for the scientist's new book, Dr. Crowell urged skeptics to follow along with him in prayer. A prayer for God to reveal Himself in a mighty way.

Something unfamiliar sprang to life in Derek's mind, something which hadn't crossed it in years: the idea that God was a possibility. A small possibility, but, considering the scientist's rather persuasive points, a big enough possibility that he couldn't completely dismiss it.

What the heck? What could it hurt to follow along with the prayer? He certainly had nothing to lose.

Derek pushed through the awkwardness and began repeating the man's words in his head. Closing his eyes, he even continued with his own silent plea after the "Amen." *God, if you're real, you best be giving me a sign. Or else—*

A few tears leaked out of his closed eyes and trickled down his cheeks. He had tinkered with the idea of suicide a couple of times in the past few months, but now, disgraced by this current predicament, that option was more appealing than ever. More necessary. He could actually empathize with his mom if she had purposefully overdosed, even though it would've been wrong in her case because she had a child depending on her. But, since his own wife didn't want or need him anymore, suicide wouldn't be selfish in his case. In fact, it would be just the opposite, considering what a burden he was becoming to everyone. Aunt Diana was going to have to put her life in Atlanta on hold for two weeks to care for him after surgery. Derek had ruined his life, and now he was ruining everyone else's.

He was like an old dog who needed to be put out of its misery. What use was there in fighting? Why go under the knife and suffer through physical therapy just to get back to his baseline of a lonely existence? To win another Super Bowl?

In his mind, Derek laughed sarcastically.

The Super Bowl. He had been there and done that, checked it off his to-do list. Accomplishing his greatest goal and wearing the gigantic ring he had to show for it hadn't done much for him, though. Yeah, it proved his father wrong. But it didn't take away his knee pain or the fact that he needed surgery...didn't fix his broken heart.

Fame and fortune were highly overrated. Having Abby back was the only way his life would be worthwhile again, but she had made it clear at the park there was no chance of that ever happening. It was just a matter of time before she found someone new. And he would much rather be dead than to see her with another man.

With his head still bowed, Derek was 99 percent sure the words he was about to say would run past his ears only, but everything in him clung to the one percent chance of hope he had managed to dig up from somewhere deep inside. With every fiber of his being, he longed for there to be Someone out there, Someone able to pull him out of this dark, lonely pit. "God, if You're real, please show me. Please help me."

⇒⟊ ⟊⇐

"No matter what your relationship is with your earthly father, I assure you that you've got a Heavenly Father Who loves you. He loves you so much He gave up His life for you."

What in the—? A woman's voice, plus something jabbing him in the back, startled Derek from a deep sleep. He must have rolled over on the remote control. Yep. He pulled it from the sticky skin on his back.

One mystery solved. Now, where was he?

His eyes met a cross-shaped picture frame on the wall beside the television, displaying a photo of a smiling African American family of five. He now knew where he was: in Timothy's guest bedroom.

Vague memories of the evening before began to dance around in his head. A vivid one now surfaced, one which caused his heart to flipflop. Could this be a sign? Him rolling over on the remote, turning the TV on to a sermon? About a loving, Heavenly Father?

Not necessarily. This wasn't the first time he had ever rolled onto a remote control and inadvertently turned the TV on. *But wait.* Goosebumps popped up on Derek's forearms as he distinctly remembered turning the channel to Sports Center before falling asleep. He had watched the atheist-turned-Christian scientist for a while, long enough to shoot up a prayer—if it could even be considered that—but then he had watched a segment on Sports Center. A documentary about Tyler McCrae, the arrogant 49ers quarterback he couldn't stand. And he was 100 percent sure he had turned the TV off immediately after watching that.

So, how could it be on the Christian channel?

Derek's heartbeat reverberated in his ear, beating like a drum against the pillow. Maybe this was the sign he had asked for. How unlikely was it for him to roll over on the remote control and turn on the TV, much less for it to be on a different channel than when he had turned it off?

His inner skeptic instantly overruled the voice telling him this was a supernatural sign. It's not like it would've been impossible for him to have rolled onto the *previous channel* button right after the TV turned on, which would explain why it reverted back to the station he had been watching before Sports Center.

"The enemy is a liar. Actually, the father of lies. John 10:10 says he does nothing but kill, steal, and destroy. He will do whatever he can to keep you from discovering the Truth, to keep you from the abundant life God has planned for you." The blonde female preacher on television practically shouted the words…words which seemed as focused as a laser beam on him.

More goosebumps.

He hadn't been this spooked since he was a kid, back when he and his childhood friend, Will, told ghost stories in the dark. Not only because of the lady's words, but because a strange presence seemed to have just entered the room. Derek pulled the sheet up, shivering.

Although he couldn't see anything, something—or some*one*, rather—was in the room with him. This wasn't just a feeling or a figment of his imagination.

It was tangible. More concrete than any fact his skeptical-self had ever known.

CHAPTER THIRTY-TWO

"Derek—"

John? After doing a double take, Derek was sure the person standing in front of him was, in fact, his father-in-law. Something was different about him, though. He wasn't wearing his glasses: that was it. Wow, he looked so much younger without them.

"What are you—"

"Shhh." John shushed him, pressing his index finger to his lips. A tingly sensation instantly spread from Derek's lips to his toes. "Call Abby," his father-in-law commanded. There was an urgency in his voice, but his presence was soothing. Calming.

John was suddenly radiant, all aglow in white clothes so bright they nearly blinded him. "Call Abby right now!"

Derek opened his eyes, his heart racing. His skin was damp with sweat. What was going on? He surveyed his surroundings. He was still in bed in Timothy's guest room. Had he fallen back to sleep? He must have. Because he had just had the most bizarre dream. Shivers ran down his spine as he recapped the vivid encounter. What did it mean? John had been so adamant.

"Call Abby right now" kept running through his mind, refusing to let up. His heart jumped to his throat. Something must be wrong with Abby. He fumbled around for his phone. Wait, what was he doing? It was only 4:23 a.m. Calling her at this hour was absurd.

With John's image and voice continuing to play over and over again in his head, logic wouldn't stop him.

Pick up, Ab! A dizzy spell came over him on the third ring. Derek willed himself to calm down and take some deep breaths. But when his call went to voicemail, his anxiety kicked into high gear. "Hey, it's me. Please call me! I'm sorry if I'm waking you, but I'm worried. I can't explain right now. Just call me!"

The desperation in his voice would surely convince her to call him back...if she could, that is. A wave of panic hit as he pictured Abby hurt or stranded on the highway somewhere. He was probably being irrational, but he couldn't help it. He redialed her, holding his breath.

Straight to voicemail.

Derek slung his phone down on the bed. No more than two seconds later, it dinged. He dove for the red-encased object as if it were a loose football. "Abby." He exhaled. At the very least, she was alive. He read her text message as fast as he could.

Derek's jaw dropped. He read Abby's text again, sure he had misread it the first time.

But he hadn't.

Suddenly, he was woozy.

Completely frozen in place, all he could do was stare at the unbelievable sentence on the screen of his phone: "Can't talk. Daddy just went to Heaven."

⟫⟪

The room started spinning as the full implication of Abby's words hit him head-on. He was fading, being sucked into a tunnel. A time warp. A place where everything stood still.

Derek's chin fell to his chest, his head simply too heavy to hold up. The floodgates of his soul were bursting wide open. "Oh my God! You're real!" He simultaneously laughed and cried the words, his jaw quivering. How could he be so excited and devastated at the same time?

John was dead. This realization sent a spear through his chest. But joy bubbled up from some foreign place inside, somehow overriding the pain.

"No," he exclaimed, shaking his head. John wasn't dead. Not really...not in the way he had always assumed a person died. Actually, he was more alive than ever. Derek had seen this firsthand. Whether in reality or a dream, it didn't matter. He had seen his father-in-law—a different *version* of him, but him nonetheless—at the exact moment he died. Evidently, right as he was passing from this world to the next.

No question, this was a sign from God.

"I can't believe it. You're really real!" The elation in his voice sparked even more excitement from that unfamiliar place inside, setting off a cascade of tears. Tears of...of what?

Awe? Gratitude? Humility?

All of the above.

How could God be so big and so *small*? So gigantic that He created the universe, yet *small* enough to hear one person's cynical prayer? Derek shook beneath violent sobs, layers of guilt threatening to bury him alive. He had refused to acknowledge God, mocking and bashing Christians practically his entire adult life. So, why would—?

Grace. The word wasn't audible, but it didn't originate in his mind. It was like a whisper *and* a shout, the way it resonated through him so silently, yet with such force. A force powerful enough to penetrate every cell of his body. *God, I'm sorry. Thank you!* "Thank you!" Saying it aloud still wasn't sufficient. What could he possibly say or do to express his gratitude? His amazement? Any- and everything would fall pathetically short.

Amazing grace. There it was again: that *loud* whisper.

An image of Gram instantly came to mind. She was standing in the church pew beside him in a long blue dress, her hair in a bun, singing "Amazing Grace" at the top of her lungs. Her face glowed with an unearthly joy. Maybe it was the same kind of joy which was flooding over him now.

"You were right all along, Gram...and John." They could hear him, right? If God could hear him, and Gram and John were with God, that meant they could hear him too, didn't it?

Thousands of questions bombarded him, toggling around in his head. But, even though his mind was tangled in a web of confusion, his world was right in a way it had never been before. Because his heart and soul were no longer confused.

God was real, and He cared about him.

Somewhere deep down, he had always known there was a Creator. When studying the stars through his telescope, logic said there had to be. Derek had never let that logic impact him, though, being certain there couldn't be a God like the Christians believed in. Not with all the evil in the world. And with all the world's religions, how could Jesus be the only *right* way? But now he knew the God his Gram had taught him about was the One true God. Questions or not, there was no denying that Jesus loved him, just like the simple song he'd learned in Sunday School proclaimed. Because the warmth of His presence was just as real as if Abby were sitting beside him.

Thinking of Abby, excitement swelled in his chest; she would be so happy when he told her about this. Derek's excitement quickly faded when he remembered the reason he found himself in this moment. How was she doing? Her dad meant the world to her.

John now meant the world to him too.

He squeezed the bridge of his stinging nose. If only he could talk to his father-in-law again. Even if only one more time, to apologize for bashing his faith all these years. He was thankful for the last conversation he and John had shared. Surprisingly, John hadn't seemed angry with him for breaking his daughter's heart. He said he had forgiven him and that he loved him and was praying for him. And, after just being informed of John's grim prognosis, Derek had expressed his feelings of love and appreciation toward him as well. It's almost as if they had known they were saying their goodbyes.

He tried to swallow his sorrow. He shouldn't be grieving over John; he should be happy for the amazing man who was now in Heaven, free of pain. He would see John—and Gram—in Heaven one day if he believed in Jesus, right? If he followed Him? Derek's heart skipped a beat at the thought of seeing Gram again, imagining himself wrapped in her arms. Come to think of it, though, Gram would be wrapped in *his* arms, since he had grown to nearly twice her size. But that would be just fine.

A tear slid down his cheek. The emotions overtaking his soul were so foreign, so overwhelming. Pieces of himself were fitting together like pieces of a puzzle…pieces of himself he hadn't even known before now.

Derek was about to burst. He couldn't keep all this to himself for another minute. He needed to tell someone how God had answered him and miraculously proved Himself, how He was pulling him out of a dark pit into the light of day.

He could tell Timothy. He was in the guy's house, after all, and if not for that, none of this would've happened. Suddenly, more than his next breath, he needed to thank the compassionate man who had continuously reached out to him. And to apologize for his arrogance and standoffishness. He also needed answers to the dozens of questions still running through his head, and there was no better person to provide them than Timothy.

Derek picked up his phone, trembling. It would surely be better to call him than to knock at his—and his wife's—bedroom door. The wind left his sails when he realized he didn't have Timothy's phone number. Thankfully, he quickly found it on the team's private network. He hit the *call* button, feeling like a kid on Christmas morning.

Wait! Calling and waking Timothy, and probably his wife, before dawn was certainly no way to thank him. Derek held his breath, his finger darting to the *end call* button. He couldn't do it, though—couldn't terminate the call. Because something inside him pleaded for him not to.

Something assuring him that his new friend would be more than okay with being awakened by the miraculously changed man down his hall.

CHAPTER THIRTY-THREE

"'It Is Well With My Soul'—the song we just sang—was John's favorite." Pastor Sam's voice broke, and he paused to gather himself. Abby was sure this funeral was the most difficult one the man had ever preached. Because, not only was her dad a devoted member of Pastor Sam's congregation, he was also one of his closest friends.

"And I believe that says a lot about him," the preacher continued. "I think the song sums up the basic philosophy of John's life: that no matter what his circumstances, his soul could be at peace, resting in his Lord's sovereignty, love, and grace."

Abby glanced at Sarah and her mom through tear-filled eyes. How was she going to get through this service without breaking down?

Her mom blotted her eyes, and Sarah leaned into Zack, whose arm embraced her and squeezed her close. Would the hole in Abby's heart be any smaller if someone's arms were around her? No, probably not. If she and Derek were still together, he would help comfort and console her, but this hole would be just as vast and deep. Because there was a special place in her heart which belonged to her Daddy, and now that he was gone, a vacancy would remain there forever.

Tears slid down her cheeks as she stared at the burnished wooden coffin at the front of the church. It was covered with an impressive array of flowers, most of which were lilies and white roses. A cold draft of air whisked by, carrying with it the scent of the flowers...a scent reminding her of the torturous evening at the funeral home the prior evening. Abby shivered.

"'Whatever my lot, thou hast taught me to say it is well, it is well with my soul.' What powerful lyrics. For a man to be able to say and truly mean those words, he has to be solid in his faith. Deeply rooted in Christ." Pastor Sam's eyes momentarily locked with hers before he continued. "I can honestly say that John Gibbs was one of the most faithful men I've ever had the privilege of knowing. His faith never wavered, no matter what struggles came his way. Sure, the cancer caused him pain, and it robbed him of many things. But it never robbed him of his faith. Or of the joy and hope he found in his Heavenly Father. As a matter of fact, John's bout with this terrible disease actually strengthened his faith."

Her mom sniffled, and Abby grabbed her hand. Worry instantly seized her. How was her mom going to survive without her *other half*, her best friend?

"I went to visit John in the hospital a few weeks ago, right before the decision was made to bring in hospice care,"

Pastor Sam said. "And when I arrived, he was wincing in pain. He said the nurse had just given him some medicine, but it obviously hadn't taken effect yet. And do you know what he told me? While he was lying there in the midst of excruciating pa—"

Abby looked away, squirming. Seeing a grown man cry would definitely push her over the edge. Thank God, the preacher quickly regained his composure. But, just to be safe, she would listen without looking; she would keep her eyes fixed on the burgundy carpet beneath her feet.

"John told me not to worry about him because—and I'm quoting—'this suffering isn't even worthy to be compared to the glory I'll see soon. So please don't pity me. Rejoice for me!'"

The sermon became background sound as she recalled the visit she shared with her Daddy that day. He had quoted the same Scripture to her: Romans 8:18. Not by coincidence, it was the same verse she had written down and memorized at Wanda's request while at the beach. But in this case, her Daddy had referenced it for her sake, not his. He had wanted to uplift her, to encourage her to persevere and remain steadfast in her faith, even in the midst of painful circumstances.

The corners of Abby's mouth lifted as she imagined the glorious day when she and her Daddy would meet in "Glory Land." A day when they could celebrate their pains and heartaches being distant remnants of the past. A day when happiness, love, and joy would far outweigh the troubles of this life.

"No, it may not *feel* well," Pastor Sam said, his voice rising an octave. "But it *is* well. Because our God promises to work *all* things out for our good…in His timing, of course. Our hope may be deferred, but praise God, our rewards are coming. Hallelujah! You can take that one to the bank," he exclaimed, raising one hand in the air and wiping the sweat from his brow with the other.

"Amen!" Papaw Gibbs held his hand high, tears pouring down his cheeks. Another wave of grief engulfed her as she thought of the grief he and Nana were experiencing. How unnatural and terrible it must be to lose a child, even when that child was a 57-year-old man.

Sarah sniffled. She grabbed her sister's hand, more tears flooding her own eyes. Wouldn't there come a point when, physically, she couldn't cry anymore? Wouldn't her well of tears eventually run dry?

The preacher quoted another section from her dad's favorite hymn, saying something about a trumpet…and the clouds rolling back. Goosebumps pricked Abby's arms, an image of that scene playing across her mind. *Please God, sound that trumpet now. Rapture us from all this.*

"Whosoever believes upon Christ and makes Him Lord and Savior of his life will rise to everlasting life. In a new, perfect place which the Bible says is beyond anything we've ever seen, heard, or imagined. So let's praise His holy name. Even on this day of heartache, let's give God praise for John's life and his glorious homecoming, for his wonderful—" Pastor Sam's jaw suddenly dropped. He looked like a deer in the headlights.

The closing of the narthex door interrupted an awkward silence, its reverberation startling the entire congregation. What in the world?

Abby turned to find out and gasped loud enough for everyone to hear. She would've been less shocked to see a ghost...or perhaps even Jesus. She squinted to get a better look. Sure enough, it was him, scanning the crowd until his eyes found hers: Derek.

⇒⟨⟩⇐

How much faster could her heart accelerate without flying through her chest? Ever since Derek walked through the door, Abby had been a prisoner to her adrenaline-saturated body. Confined to a place and time where there was no way to get the answers she needed.

Hadn't she made it clear in the text she sent him that he was not to come to the funeral? Did he need to repeat the first grade and learn to read? She told Derek he could come to the funeral home...if he absolutely had to, for the sake of closure. But *not* the funeral.

This day was about her dad; how dare he turn it into a celebrity-sighting spectacle.

Abby turned back to catch a glimpse of him, and their eyes met and held. *Why did you come here and ruin the last moment I have with my Daddy?* She tried to kill him with a look, but the loving look in his eyes nearly killed her instead.

Guilt suddenly blanketed her. Even though Derek and her dad had never been particularly close, she knew he loved him. He was probably having a difficult time with all this, and it had been pretty selfish of her not to return his phone calls. It's not like she planned on never talking to him again, though; she just needed to get past the funeral first.

Abby had truly forgiven him—until now, at least—but that didn't mean she could be in his presence and hold onto her sanity, especially at a time like this. She still had to try to protect herself...to minimize the amount of trauma to her heart.

She turned to find Sarah with her face buried in her hands. A dagger pierced Abby's chest, leaving behind a burning, lingering ache. Maybe being distracted by Derek wasn't such a bad thing, after all. She looked at her watch. How much longer could this service drag on?

Her mother's gentle pat to her knee refocused her attention, enabling her to tune back in to Pastor Sam's words. "If you knew John, then you know how passionate he was about sharing the Gospel. So, it's no surprise his wish was to have an altar call at his memorial service. 'Make sure it's more about the Lord than me,' is what he said. So typical of our brother," the preacher said, his eyes filling with tears.

"So, in John's memory and honor, I'm asking that if you've never accepted Christ as Lord and Savior, do it today. Folks, we're not guaranteed another breath. Oh, how the devil has blinded so many people in this world today," he exclaimed, looking in Derek's direction.

Yep, he certainly had him pegged.

"We're *all* guilty, though. We *all* deserve sin's penalty of death and Hell...which, by the way, was originally created just for Satan and the fallen angels who rebelled against God."

Abby looked away and swallowed hard. Here she was thinking of Derek's faults when she, too, had definitely made her share of mistakes. *Lord, forgive me. Thank You for Your grace.*

"But God loves us too much to give us the judgement we deserve," Pastor Sam continued. "He wants to spend eternity with you and me so badly that He built a bridge of reconciliation between us and Him. Notice how I said *a* bridge," he said, pausing to make sure he had everyone's attention. "The one and only *bridge* is His one and only Son, Jesus Christ. Only *He* lived a sinless life. Only *He* took our punishment by dying a criminal's death on the cross. Only *He* rose from the dead."

Pastor Sam stopped talking and scratched his head. "You know, the world today tells people to look inside themselves to find happiness. Christianity seems to be the laughing stock of our culture. But you know, the Bible says it will be this way. 1 Corinthians 1:18 says, 'For the message of the cross is foolishness to those who are perishing, but to us who are being saved it is the power of God.' Wow, isn't that the truth! The Gospel has changed my life and the lives of many, many people I've come to know through my role as a pastor. You see, we don't have to have all the intellectual answers...for ourselves or for the skeptics. God's ways aren't our ways, and there's lots of things we'll never understand this side of Heaven. But there's this amazing little thing called faith."

Pastor Sam coughed and cleared his throat. "Excuse me," he said, taking a sip of water. "Believe it or not, if you do your research and discover all the facts supporting Christianity, you'll find it takes more faith *not* to believe in the Lord Jesus Christ than to believe in Him. But child-like faith is what pleases God. And you know something? You need only to ask Him for faith, and He will honor that prayer. If you're in doubt, ask the Lord to give you spiritual eyes to see and spiritual ears to hear, and I guarantee you'll hear from Him. He doesn't want a single person to perish, and He will go to great measures to help you find Him if you'll truly seek Him. Because our God is a God of love, mercy, and grace. Amen?"

The passion in the preacher's glistening eyes was undeniable. He truly loved to tell the story. Abby noticed him looking toward Derek again, his eyes soft and compassionate. "If you've never invited Jesus into your heart, will you come on up here and do it today? Come receive that love, mercy, and grace?"

Pastor Sam extended his arm, pointing toward the petite, gray-haired lady who had served the Lord and His people at Forest Hill Church with her musical talent since Abby was a child. The organ began to play "Just As I Am," and God's presence filled the church. It was almost as tangible as her mother's hand, which she now clasped in hers.

"Come on, choose life today," the preacher pleaded, motioning toward the altar. "Choose love today. You know, 1 John 4:19 tells us that we love God because He first loved us. If you don't know Jesus, come on up here and receive His love...the unconditional love that will forever change your life."

Pastor Sam motioned toward the altar again. "If you've never asked Jesus to be your Lord and Savior, please come. I want to pray with you. I want you to discover what it truly means to live...here and now on this earth, then for all eternity."

A red-headed woman whom Abby didn't recognize was making her way down the aisle of the church, blotting her eyes. Joy began to crowd out the sorrow in Abby's heart. Her

Daddy was probably rejoicing with God this very moment over the lost sheep who was coming into the fold—as he would say.

Pastor Sam continued with fervor. "Come on up here. Make the decision which will ensure that when you take your final breath, you'll be in Heaven with God, along with Brother John and all the Lord's children."

Suddenly, Abby thought she may have, in fact, just taken her last breath…because the scene playing out in front of her was breathtakingly unbelievable. Pastor Sam's face was glowing. Sarah turned toward her, her dropped jaw transforming into a mile-wide smile. Abby would've reciprocated the smile if she could have. But she couldn't.

She was as frozen as a statue, the impossible taking place before her very eyes: the prodigal son was coming home.

CHAPTER THIRTY-FOUR

Derek had won some big games, including *the* big game, but no victory had ever tasted so sweet. On his knees in front of the church where he and Abby were married, he was finally free.

Free from his self-centeredness and self-reliance. Free from the need to perform and score enough touchdowns to stay on top. Free from the guilt and shame of his past. Free from the need to drink himself to oblivion. God had even freed him from his knee pain.

Feeling not even a twinge of pain since that miraculous night, Derek couldn't help but wonder if God had healed him. Maybe he wouldn't need surgery, after all.

Preacher Sam was still speaking, but he couldn't soak in the man's words; his emotions were too overwhelming. He didn't really need to hear anything else, though. He was a forgiven child of God, and that's all that mattered right now.

As soon as Timothy led him through the *sinner's prayer*—when he confessed his sins and invited Jesus into his heart—he had become a new man. Derek had been eager for this moment, though...for this chance to publicly acknowledge Jesus as his Lord and Savior. It was the least he could do to express his gratitude to God for saving a wretch like him.

Now, before this congregation at his beloved father-in-law's funeral, he was filled with even more freedom than he had experienced over the last few days. It was so unnatural, the way he felt no need to prove himself to anyone. Not even Dave Holder.

"Derek—" An angelic voice from behind startled him. He wiped his eyes and turned to find Abby, her mom and Sarah only a few feet behind.

"Hey," he exclaimed with outstretched arms. He didn't think about whether or not it was appropriate to sweep Abby off her feet and twirl her around; he just did it. And her arms were now around him, right where they belonged. But she suddenly stiffened.

Releasing her was painful, but not half as painful as the stab to his chest when he caught Abby making eyes at some dark-haired guy a few feet away. Derek was about to ask her who the dude was when someone embraced him from behind.

"I know John is smiling down right now." The voice was barely above a whisper. The preacher's face was beaming, his eyes glistening with tears.

"Why don't you two go to the conference room?" Pastor Sam pointed toward a door to their right. "I'm going to have everyone start making their way to the cemetery now, but I'm sure you two need some time alone."

"Thanks." He hugged the kind man whom he hadn't seen since his wedding, then walked toward the indicated door. Derek glanced over his shoulder, and sure enough, Mr. Preppy was still staring in their direction. He flashed the guy a warning glare.

Abby closed the door once they entered the conference room, and his heart kicked into high gear. What was going through her mind right now? He couldn't read her, her eyelids too swollen to even see the green of her eyes. But she was bound to be thrilled he had come to faith in Christ, right? Or, maybe she resented him for coming to the funeral against her wishes...especially since he had made a grand entrance thirty minutes after it started.

Derek couldn't help that, though. He had been stuck in traffic for 45 minutes due to a wreck, and he wasn't about to let that stop him. Since Abby refused to talk to him, claiming she couldn't handle any additional emotional strain, he thought coming to the service was his best option...He had been right in suspecting there would be an altar call at his devout father-in-law's funeral, and what better time would there be to let Abby know about his life-altering decision than at the service honoring her dad—the man who led him to God?

"I hope you're not upset with me for being here." He finally broke the silence. "It's just that I have some major things to tell you, things I wasn't about to send in a text message."

Abby scrunched her brows together. "So you came to tell me some things, and you ended up—"

"Let me explain." He interrupted her, aching for her to know the miraculous story. How could he explain it, though? Especially when he didn't have time to include all the details?

"Your dad saved me, Ab. I mean, *God* saved me, but it was through your dad." Abby's eyes widened. The flicker of hope he saw there made him even more eager to continue. "Do you remember how I called you in a panic the night he died?"

She nodded.

"Well, there's a long story leading up to this, but I had a dream about your dad. Or maybe it was a vision. Whatever it was, it was super-real. And your dad told me to call you." Derek sucked in a breath of air. Having so much to say with so little time, it's like he was doing a running drill at practice. "It was weird because he was younger-looking, and he had on a white robe or something. Anyway, he was adamant that I call you right away. And based on the timing of the text you sent me, this all happened at the exact moment he di...passed away."

Abby's lips curled into a faint smile as tears escaped her question-filled eyes. She was so beautiful, even in her darkest hour. Captive beneath her spell, Derek had the overwhelming urge to touch her. He tentatively placed his hand on Abby's shoulder, and when she didn't pull away, he rubbed her back. A tingly sensation started in his fingertips and work its way to his soul.

"So, you believe in God now?"

"Absolutely. How could I not? Especially considering the rest of the story, which I doubt I have time to tell you." He looked at his watch. "When do you think we should go? To the...the cemetery?" Derek cringed, wishing there was a less-depressing word to use. But *graveyard* definitely seemed worse.

Abby's face contorted. "I miss him so m—"

The creaking of the conference room door startled both of them. The preacher poked his head in, alarm flashing through his eyes when he glanced toward Abby. Derek looked at her and became alarmed himself. Was she about to faint? "Ab?" He extended his arms just as she fell into them.

"I miss him so much!" Her body shook. She pressed her face against his chest, saturating his starched white shirt with tears. "I don't think...I can go...to the...cemetery," she said, punctuating every few syllables with a sharp gasp for air, each one hammering a nail deeper into Derek's chest.

He held her, stroking her hair. He and Pastor Sam exchanged a *knowing* look, a nonverbal declaration saying they had to do all they could to get Abby to the graveside service. Because she would probably always regret it if she didn't go.

"I know. I miss him too. You can do it, though." Derek kissed the top of her head. Breathing in her nearness, he grew dizzy. Tears began trickling down his cheeks: some shed for Abby, some for John, and now, with a memory playing through his mind, some for Gram. Attending Gram's graveside service had been the most difficult experience of his life. Up until he lost Abby. "We'll see him again." Those reassuring words flooded his soul with peace, a peace he prayed would wash over Abby and give her the strength to carry on. Suddenly, Gram's favorite Bible verse echoed through his spirit, begging to be spoken. Etched on her tombstone, Derek had read Psalm 30:5 hundreds of times, but not until now had it rung true: "'Weeping may stay for the night, but rejoicing comes in the morning.'"

Abby pulled away, looking up at him as if she had seen a ghost. And he totally understood why. If those words sounded foreign to his own ears, he could only imagine how strange they sounded to her. He cupped her face in his hands and looked into her puzzled eyes, willing her to believe the words he was about to say...and more importantly, for her to believe in the new man he'd become. "You. Can. Do. This. With God, you're stronger than you think," he proclaimed, nodding his head for added emphasis.

Preacher Sam eyeballed him before exiting the room, quietly shutting the door behind him. It was time to head to the cemetery. He looked into Abby's eyes, praying he could convince her to go. "Come on. I'll be right here beside you, every step of the way." Derek had barely gotten the words out before a grueling reminder taunted him: he couldn't just assume Abby would let him back into her life now that he'd become a Christian.

That's definitely how things *should* play out, though, and he silently reminded God of this.

Derek's pulse throbbed in his neck. *God, I know I don't deserve it, but please!* "That is, I'll be here if...if"—he swallowed, then cleared his throat—"if you want me to be."

CHAPTER THIRTY-FIVE

"Here, let me get it." Derek took the key from Abby's hand as she unsuccessfully attempted to unlock the door of her parents' house.

Between the crippling sadness over burying her dad, the surprise and confusion regarding Derek's coming-to-Jesus moment, and the fact that she had barely eaten in two days, Abby was too jittery to hold the key steady.

"Thanks." She pushed the door open after Derek unlocked it, the woodsy scent of his cologne putting her on edge...even more so than she already was. And guilty too. It just didn't seem right to be the least bit excited on the day her Daddy had been buried.

She dropped her purse on the laminate kitchen countertop, wondering what to do...how to act...what to say. The clanking of her heels against the hardwood floor only exaggerated the looming silence. But this was all her doing.

Knowing Derek would offer to drive her home, she had told everyone she was too exhausted to remain at the reception in the church fellowship hall following the graveside service.

Abby really was physically and emotionally spent. And one more minute with her patronizing great-aunt Melba or her nosy cousin Taylor may have done her in. But she couldn't lie to her own self, couldn't deny the reason she wanted to leave early was to be alone with Derek. Well, she had gotten her wish. Now what?

"Go get comfortable," Derek said, his deep voice startling her. "I'm going to find you something to eat. I watched you take only two bites of mashed potatoes at the church."

Abby shuddered, the mere thought of food turning her stomach. "Ugh. I can't eat right now. But you can pour me a glass of tea and bring it to my room. I'll be finished changing in a few minutes."

"Okay, but you've got to eat something soon, Ab. You're worrying me."

The warmth and concern in Derek's voice drowned out her nausea and sent her floating down the hall to her bedroom, her feet never touching the floor. Never in a million years had she seen this one coming. Derek, a Christian? Because of a supernatural encounter with her Daddy?

Happy tears stung her eyes. Joy and hope enveloped her heart and overshadowed the grief that had suffocated her for days.

Abby slipped out of her black dress and searched the closet for something to wear. Something comfortable, yet flattering. And maybe a little playful and fun. *Really?* Yes, really. Her Daddy would be fine with that. Actually, her Daddy would want her to jump up and down and celebrate, she decided, grabbing some white leggings and a favorite fuchsia blouse.

The irony was uncanny. Here she was shedding her black dress and putting on something white and bright, like her time of mourning the loss of her husband was through… like she was finally free to shed the biblical *sackcloth* and put on garments of praise. Now that Derek was a believer, he was a new man. A Christian man like God had called her to seek. A man she could trust with her heart. Unless—

She could barely finish the thought, her bubble of happiness bursting the instant it flashed across her mind. What if Derek was lying? What if all this was a facade, a last ditch-effort to win her back?

Abby exhaled in exasperation. She was definitely in a vulnerable position right now, desperate for hope after losing her Daddy. Naive emotions could easily drown out sound judgement. Even though she needed to believe all this was true—almost more than she needed her next breath—she couldn't. Not yet, anyway. *God, please help me. Give me discernment and wisdom to uncover the truth.*

Her heart literally ached after ending the silent prayer. Did she really mean it? Did she really want to know the truth, if the truth was that this whole thing was a lie?

No, she didn't. But, unfortunately, like so many things in life, what she needed and what she wanted may be two entirely different things.

Abby sat cross-legged on her bed with a pillow in her lap when Derek knocked at the door. "Come in."

The door creaked open slowly, but her pulse skyrocketed. Her head began to spin when Derek's eyes locked on hers. There was definitely something different about him.

"Here," he said, handing her a glass of iced tea. "Drink all of it, okay? You've got to stay hydrated."

She took it from his hands and began chugging it, despite the feeling of fullness in her throat. Whatever it took to speed up this process and have answers to the billions of questions darting through her mind.

Derek took his shoes off and sat down on the bed beside her. Somehow, he was both humble and exceptionally confident. He placed her empty glass on the nightstand, then pulled her toward him with urgency, pressing her head against his chest and kissing the top of her forehead. His breath swept over her skin. Completely caught off guard, Abby defaulted to instinct and stayed in his arms. For a few seconds, she allowed Derek's love to flow through her, to revive her...as if it were electricity. Then she willed herself to pull away.

"I want you to know this isn't just an act, Abby. I've truly changed and given my heart to God."

Obviously, he had picked up on her doubt. The truth would be found in his eyes, though, so Abby gathered the courage to search them again. His baby blues captured her breath. They were full of *real* joy, along with an undeniable sincerity.

"That night was amazing, Ab. The way God spoke to me, the way your dad came to me."

Derek's eyes glistened with tears which provoked her own. Her sweet Daddy had always been passionate about reaching him, somehow remaining confident he would one day—that *God* would. But, truth be told, she never believed it would happen. Derek was just too bullheaded, completely close-minded to matters of faith. But, sure enough, her

Daddy had been right. He had accomplished what he had set out to do; nonetheless, on his deathbed. Through a genuine miracle of God.

"Will you tell me the story again?"

A smile lit up Derek's face. As he told her everything about the night at Timothy's house, she was in awe. God was so amazing, the way He could orchestrate so many tiny details. Her heart leapt when Derek mentioned the phone call he had made to her right after her Daddy died. God had even provided tangible evidence to validate her husband's account, proof which erased every last ounce of doubt she had regarding his conversion. *Thank you, God.*

And thank you, Daddy. Whether it was actually him or a messenger of God, her dad had played the ultimate part in opening the door for the Holy Spirit to draw Derek in. A bittersweet tear slid down Abby's cheek. How she longed to see her Daddy in all his glory, the way Derek said he had looked that night.

"Baby, nothing matters to me now except you and God." The reference to her as *baby* snapped her back to the present. She found herself lost in the sincerity of Derek's eyes as he spoke life-giving words to her soul. "I'm so thankful and excited because I feel like God has given me a second chance...a *replay* like I got in the Super Bowl," he said, tracing his thumb along her wet cheek.

She felt a grin playing on her lips. It was just like her sports-crazed husband to bring football into any discussion, even one about God.

"Please forgive me. Please give me another chance." The intense desperation in Derek's eyes seared a path to her soul, melting away all her defenses.

Abby leaned into his hand, the one caressing her cheek, then she took it and interlaced her fingers with his. But Derek's hand instantly became a hot coal, the way it repelled her when an uninvited image flashed across her mind. An image of him with Cassidy—the way she envisioned her, anyway—in bed together, curled up in each other's arms. Abby pulled her hand away, pangs of jealousy and hurt ripping through her like shrapnel. She stared at a purple flower on her bedspread, unable to look at the man who had nearly killed her. The man who could destroy her again if she gave him the opportunity to.

There were no guarantees. Christians certainly made mistakes, especially when faced with powerful temptations like the ones Derek would be up against. Could she take that risk? Could she survive going through everything all over again?

"Look at me, please," Derek pleaded, his sincere voice subduing her frantic thoughts. "If you give me another chance—a chance to replay all this—you'll never be sorry. Please let me prove it to you. Let me win back your trust. I'll be the godly man you need and deserve, Ab. I promise." His soul was shining through his eyes, and that soul was definitely pure. And God-filled.

Something quickened in Abby's spirit, bringing to mind God's grace. That amazing grace, how sweet the sound.

How many second chances had Jesus given her, even though she had been unfaithful to Him time and time again? And why? Because of His love. His perfect, *real* love. The 1 Corinthians 13-kind of love…love that is patient, kind, forgiving, trusting, and perseverant.

The kind of love that never fails.

Abby unlatched the chains around her heart. It was time to *let go and let God*, as her Daddy would say. Her heart was safe in her Heavenly Father's hands, even if Derek ended up betraying her again. God would never leave or forsake her, so she could step out in faith and take some risks in life. This was certainly a risk worth taking.

Her mind was made up. Abby could barely breathe, her heart swelling, taking up her entire chest. No words would come. None that could come close to describing the feelings erupting inside of her...feelings which couldn't stay bottled in another second. She did the only thing she knew to do, something she had never stopped longing to do. She drew in a shaky breath and inched closer to Derek's face, her gaze shifting from his anxious eyes to his quivering lips.

The moment their lips touched, a wave of dizziness swept over her. Time stood still. The warmth of their kiss began to thaw her frigid world. Suddenly, everything was warm. Perfect. Complete. She was floating somewhere in the clouds when Derek placed his hand on the back of her neck, his fingers working through her hair. Passion grew as he pulled her closer, pressing his lips harder against hers, his stubble pricking her cheek. Abby could feel the wetness of his tears. Tears mingling with her own.

Derek finally pulled back, only to begin placing delicate, butterfly kisses on the tip of her nose...her forehead... her closed eyelids.

Falling into his embrace, a wonderful, unfamiliar feeling enfolded her like a fleece blanket on a winter's night. Security: that's what it was. For the first time ever, she was totally safe and secure in her husband's love. *Wait,* was this a dream?

Abby's stomach dropped. She was probably dreaming, just as she had done a hundred times before.

No, this was real life. A wisp of Derek's minty breath across her face assured her of that. She exhaled in sweet relief. Soaking it all in, every lingering trace of doubt and fear began to vanish. Her husband—the man of her dreams—now knew God, and he was here to stay. Sure, they would have hard times, just like every other couple in this fallen world. But somehow, Abby now knew with every fiber of her being that Derek would remain true to her, that he would love and cherish her for the rest of her life.

"I love you so much, Ab. I've always loved you, but now... I don't know, there's no way to describe it." Derek leaned in for another kiss before she could declare her feelings for him. Feelings which made her heart spread wings and fly.

How was it possible to experience the worst pain *and* the most fulfillment she had ever known, all in the same day?

Only with God, that's how.

She rested her head on Derek's muscular chest. With each beat of his heart, her passion flared. "I love you too... so much." Abby nuzzled into him, kissing her way up from his delicious-smelling neck to his lips.

"Thank You, God! Thank You, thank You, thank You!" Derek startled her, practically shouting the words as he looked and pointed upward. Then he squeezed her close, laughing as if in disbelief. "I've never been so happy in all my life. Aside from missing your dad, of course. But, even with that, I'm glad—for him, I mean. It's like we're all getting new starts...new and better lives."

Abby pulled away from his embrace to look into his eyes. They were as blue as ever, glistening with happy tears. Overwhelmed by emotions, all she could do was nod in agreement.

Yes, God had worked things out for their good, just as His Word promised. Her Heavenly Father was sovereign, even in the valley of the shadow of death. He was right beside her, holding her hand along this journey of grief. And along every journey she would ever take in life, including this delightful one she was beginning with her new husband.

Never in a million years would she have chosen for her husband to betray her or for her Daddy to die, but if it weren't for these tragedies, where would she be today? Where would Derek be?

If it weren't for all the pain and hopelessness, she may have never truly surrendered her life to Christ. And Abby was almost certain if it weren't for the heartache she and Derek had been through—along with her Daddy's passing—her husband would have never found the Lord.

Warm liquid joy began trickling down her cheeks. God had certainly traced the storm clouds they had weathered with a shiny silver lining. Her dad's foremost prayer had been answered in the most miraculous way possible. And now, one glorious day they would all be reunited...her Daddy's whole family, each one of them whole.

Forever and ever.

EPILOGUE

Abby took hold of her brother-in-law's hand, stepping down from a pristine stagecoach pulled by four white stallions. With Cinderella's castle set against the backdrop of a cloudless sky, the moment couldn't have been any more magical...unless her Daddy were here.

She adjusted her headpiece, then placed her hand over her chest. Her Daddy *was* here. He was always and forever in her heart, and his spirit and legacy lived on. Abby looked up at the baby blue sky, hoping God had given him a front row seat from Heaven.

"Ready?" Zack winked.

"Yep!" Excitement swelled as she locked arms with her brother-in-law, her beloved escort.

What had she done to deserve all this? A second wedding in "The Happiest Place on Earth," a place which held many cherished memories from her childhood. Derek had surprised her a few days ago with the news that they, along with several special friends and family members, were flying to Disney World for a vow renewal service. And now, here she was practically floating down the walkway toward her handsome prince.

In her periphery were the smiling faces of her closest loved ones, but Abby's eyes were fixed on her husband. He was a total knockout in that white tux.

Once she reached the makeshift altar near the entrance of the storybook castle, she took Derek's hand. His watery eyes were breathtaking...blue mirrors reflecting the beauty of his soul. His *new* soul.

"I love you." He mouthed the words.

Abby smiled and whispered the words back to him, meaning them more than ever before.

Derek had not ceased to amaze her over the past three months as he matured in his newfound faith. The day they were baptized together in Lake Norman was one of the happiest days of her life. And she was so proud of him for tracking down and calling his father to make peace with his past. They may never have a great relationship, but anger and resentment no longer resided in her husband's heart. He was definitely a changed man. A man on fire for the Lord, determined to reach as many lost souls as he could through the expansive platform of the NFL.

Derek had also encouraged her to chase her dream of becoming a physical therapist. It was so exciting to think that she may be in grad school next year this time.

Abby nodded at Timothy as he patted Derek's back and took a seat on the front row. The amazing man who had helped lead her husband to Christ was now his best friend, his best man for today's ceremony.

Derek turned around and fist-bumped the cute little guy Timothy sat down beside of...Aidan was a nine-year-old boy with leukemia whose dream was to hang out with his superstar idol: the one and only Timothy Whitaker. A great role model indeed. Thanks to the wonderful organization, Dream On 3, this kid's lifelong wish was becoming a reality this very second. Aidan's smile was as wide as Texas.

Zack gave Abby a quick hug, and Sarah took the bouquet of white roses and peonies from her hand, kissing her cheek. Then they rounded up her two precious flower girls, with all their ruffles and curls, and took their seats on the front row—right beside of her lovely, resilient Mama. Abby winked at them and smiled, the sight of her sister's baby bump prompting tears.

God's timing was perfect. Sarah found out she was pregnant exactly one week after their Daddy died, and after her ultrasound three days ago, she and Zack announced that a little boy was on the way. Baby John was due to arrive in mid-January.

A tear slid down Abby's cheek. *Thank you, Father.*

The only reason she was standing here was because of her Heavenly Father's love and grace. She was under no illusion that life would be a fairytale; pain and trials were always just around the corner in this fallen world. But, come what may, she and Derek would persevere and live in victory. Because they were now clothed in white—literally, in this moment, and forever in the righteousness of Christ.

Disney World and fairytales aside, Derek was a prince and she was a princess, both of them beloved children of the King of kings.

NOTE TO READER

Dear Reader,

Thank you so much for taking this journey with Derek and Abby. I'm honored you chose to take time out of your life to read this story, and I hope you were blessed by it.

I pray that you know you are loved by God, more so than you can possibly imagine. The Author of life envisioned and created you to be a unique and important character in His never-ending love story. The blood of Jesus has paid for your sins in full, and His death and resurrection have made a way for you to be made brand new and whole…a way for you to write new, exciting chapters in your life by having a relationship with God. I pray you have taken—or will take—this amazing opportunity by inviting Jesus to be your personal Lord and Savior. Only through Him will you discover your true self, love yourself, and successfully carry out your God-ordained role in this world.

Speaking of roles, do not underestimate the impact of yours. Wanda and Timothy didn't take up many pages in this book, but weren't their parts crucial to the outcome of the story? No matter what titles we hold—or do *not* hold—all of us have key roles to play in and for God's kingdom—His overall story.

Thankfully, God has redeemed me and given me many *replays* in life. I still struggle with issues, and I will until the day He calls me home; but, praise God, His mercies are new each morning (Lamentations 3:22-23). He Who lives in me is greater than he who is in this fallen world (John 4:4), so I'll eventually reach the goal line. So can you, my friend! Never give up! Through Christ Who loves us, we are more than conquerors (Romans 8:37).

Again, thanks for reading *Replay*. If you enjoyed this story, please consider leaving a book review on Amazon (and any other book review website). You have no idea how much it blesses me to hear how people have been touched by the words God has inspired me to write. And *your* words may encourage someone else to read this story and be blessed by it.

I may not know you, but I hope and pray to celebrate with you in Heaven one day. I also hope we will meet a few Dereks, Abbys, Johns, Sarahs, and other *Replay* characters there!

Blessings,
Mandy

ACKNOWLEDGEMENTS

I would like to give a very special thanks to my husband **Shane**. Thank you for faithfully loving and supporting me over the past 13 years. You have been my number one fan, always encouraging me and cheering me on to become the woman God wants me to be. Your hard work has made it possible for me to complete this book.

I also want to thank you for your patience. You're probably as relieved as I am that this book is finally finished! Thanks for hanging in there with me. I am so blessed to have your support and unconditional love. I love you!

Thank you to all the **family and friends** who have faithfully loved and encouraged me. You each hold a very special place in my heart. I love you all!

Glenda Cook and **Carrie B. McWhorter**, thank you so much for helping me with edits. Your assistance and literary expertise have been greatly appreciated. **Jodie Bailey,** thank you for taking time out of your busy life to read and endorse this book.

Your advice and guidance have meant more than you know. **Peggy Conrad, Lori Frank Cecil, Krista Boles,** and **Mama (Amy Horn),** thank you all for reading the manuscript and giving me feedback and encouragement. May God bless you all.

Last, but certainly not least, I want to thank **God.** Thanks for Your many blessings—the people and things I too often take for granted. Thanks for planting this story in my heart and helping me bring it to completion...*finally!!* Most importantly, thank You for the sacrifices You made to save me.

Jesus, You are my Savior, my Lord, and my Best Friend. I'm so grateful for Your unconditional love and forgiveness. There's no way I can ever praise or glorify You enough. I love You!

"LEGACY OF LOVE"
Carl Felton Conrad
March 20, 1929—September 14, 2017

Papaw,
There are no words to express what you mean to me
Or the ways you have shaped my life.
You were a constant source of love and stability
In this chaotic world of evil and strife.

You were a simple man,
But oh how your soul ran deep.
Always eager to lend a helping hand,
It's obvious your greatest joy was to give, not keep.

How I loved your stories of good ole days gone by
And all your funny lines and tales;
Also, the way you weren't ashamed to cry
When the fierce winds of life assailed.

You worked hard,
You played hard.

You were determined to give life your all,
Remaining "as stubborn as a mule" even when you
began to fall.

You tilled the land;
You planted and reaped.
And the Good Lord's commands
You did your best to keep.

I love the way you loved Granny with all your heart,
Carrying her to South Carolina to be wed
So that no one could keep the two of you apart—
Or, probably so she wouldn't change her mind
instead!

You two started out with nothing but love,
With barely enough money to go around;
Yet it was just like you to take out a loan for a coon
hound!

You planted everything under the sun
And generously shared your harvest,
Even though no one contributed to your "bucket" fund.

You grew the best corn, squash, cucumbers, beans
and *taters;*
Okra, melons, muscadines, apples, greens, and *maters.*
Above all, you planted seeds of love into the hearts
of all you knew
And instilled Christian values and faith in the family
you grew.

You laughed and loved,
And boy, did you eat!
But, as do we all, you sinned and experienced defeat.

You knew you needed mercy and grace,
So you put your trust in God's one and only Son,
Clinging to Him until you finished your race;
And now you're hearing, "My good and faithful servant, well done."

Your trials and sorrows are finally through—
Never again will you grieve or feel pain.
Though it's hard to let you go, I'm so happy for you.
Our family's great loss is certainly Heaven's gain.

Although you would say I'm one day older than you,
You managed to beat me to those Pearly Gates;
And the flood of tears that now cloud my view
Are because your love leaves me longing for the glory that awaits.

Papaw, fly high in the sky—
Rejoice with your Lord and many loved ones above,
Knowing your legacy here will never die
Because it was paved by Christ's never-ending love.

I know your humble heart wouldn't want all this praise,
But you deserve it...and so much more.
So, it's with hands raised
That our family prays:

Thank you, God, for the blessing of this man who's
greater than words can explain,
For giving us a treasure trove of memories that will
forever remain.
Lord, please comfort us and give us peace,
And help us live and love like Papaw more
Until that glorious day we're forever reunited on
Heaven's beautiful shore.

I'll love you forever, Papaw!
Love, Mandy